SNOWBOUND WITH THE SCOUNDREL

THE WEATHERBY WALLFLOWERS

BOOK TWO

COURTNEY MCCASKILL

HAZEL GROVE BOOKS

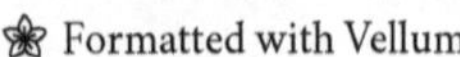 Formatted with Vellum

ALSO BY COURTNEY MCCASKILL

The Weatherby Wallflowers

Book 1: A Wallflower Never Surrenders

Book 2: Snowbound with the Scoundrel

Book 3: One Bed for the Bluestocking (Coming Soon)

Book 4: How He Won His Wallflower (Coming Soon)

The Astley Chronicles

Book 1: How to Train Your Viscount

Book 2: What's an Earl Gotta Do?

Book 3: The Sea Siren of Broadwater Bottom

Book 4: The Duke's Dark Secret

Book 5: Let Me Be Your Hero

Book 6: Romancing the Rifleman

Book 7: A Laird for Lady Lucy (Coming Soon)

My Favorite Mistake: An Astley Chronicles Novella

The Wicked Widows' League

Book 1: Scoundrel for Sale

Book 2: A Very Roguish Boxing Day

Other Books:

One Fine May (The Rake Review)

For more information, visit www.courtneymccaskill.com.

CHAPTER 1

December 1823
York, England

The wind yanked at Clarissa Weatherby's cloak as she hurried across the River Foss. She grabbed it with her free hand to keep it from blowing away, but she did not slow her stride. The mail coach would leave the Black Swan Inn at a quarter past six, and she had to be on it.

It was already six o'clock—full dark this time of year, but there was light enough coming from the shops and taverns that lined the street to prevent her from tripping over the cobblestones. It was still warm enough that the scattered snowflakes being blown about were melting as soon as they hit the ground, but it was colder than Clarissa had expected. The temperature had probably dropped five degrees since she had stepped outside, and she found herself wishing she'd worn her thicker cloak.

She lifted her chin. It did not matter. She still had to get on that coach regardless of the worsening weather. She would just have to hope for the best.

The road widened into Peasholme Green, and Clarissa spotted the old inn, its dark timber frame stark against its whitewashed plaster. She hurried through the door beneath one of its twin gables and approached the bar. "I need passage to Helmsley," she said, pushing her hood back.

The barman had a friendly look about him, with a balding head and a few grey hairs in his thick mustache. "Helmsley?" he asked, pausing in the act of polishing a pint glass. "Oh, no, miss. You don't want to be going to Helmsley tonight. Not with the storm that's brewing."

Clarissa pulled a handful of coins from her pocket and began counting them out. "I don't much want to go. But I have no choice in the matter."

"Oh?" the barman asked. "And what is of such great urgency?"

Clarissa paused. The truth was, she did not know, and she would not know until she had the chance to read the letter her employer, Lady Winnifred FitzSimon, had pressed into her hand as she hurried her out the door.

But her ladyship had communicated that the errand, whatever it was, was of the utmost urgency. It was so crucial, in fact, that Lady Winnifred—who had been laid up in bed for the past three days, trembling with fever—had insisted upon sending Clarissa to Helmsley Castle alone, even though her training as an agent for the Home Office was nowhere near complete.

The barman was waiting for an answer. "It's my mother," Clarissa lied. "She has been unwell these past few years. I had a letter from my sister, and she fears it is her time."

"Ah. I can see why you would chance it, then." He accepted the handful of coins Clarissa passed him. "It happens that there's one other soul crazy enough to try it in this weather."

"Oh?" Clarissa asked, hoisting her valise.

"A gentleman, by the looks of him," the barman confirmed. "Now, if you're wanting a hot brick for your feet, that will be an extra penny."

Clarissa did want the hot brick. Hopefully, that would be enough to get her to the next coaching inn without freezing. Having finalized her arrangements, she returned to the inn yard, where the red and black mail coach was waiting.

As there were so few passengers, the coachman allowed her to keep her valise with her. Clarissa climbed in, curious to see who her traveling companion for the next twenty hours would be.

The only greeting she received upon entering the coach was a soft snore. Her fellow passenger was slumped in a corner of the front-facing seat, head tipped back at an angle that seemed destined to leave him with a crick in his neck. Before surrendering to Hypnos's spell, he had spread his black, mink-lined cloak over himself like a blanket, meaning that Clarissa could only see his face. He looked to be around Clarissa's own age, which was to say, young for a man, and hopelessly on the shelf for a woman. She could not tell if he was handsome, with his head lolling back and his mouth hanging open, but she saw that he had blond hair and a bump on his nose.

Settling into the opposite corner of the rear-facing seat, Clarissa debated the merits of pulling out the letter Lady Winnifred had given her detailing her mission. On the one hand, she was dreadfully curious about what it might say. It also seemed like a good idea to know what task she was to undertake before she went strolling into the lion's den. Besides, her companion gave every indication of being out cold.

On the other hand, Clarissa knew from personal experience that appearances could be deceiving. Pretending to snooze in a chair next to the fire was the preferred method Lady Winnifred employed when there was eavesdropping to be done.

Clarissa was ostensibly serving as Lady Winnifred's companion. When the world looked at Lady Winnifred, they saw the seventy-two-year-old aunt of the current Duke of Wroxley.

But Winnifred FitzSimon was more than that.

She was a *spy*.

Clarissa had been introduced to Lady Winnifred by her great-niece, Lady Francesca FitzSimon. Guests at the same house party, Clarissa and Francesca had struck up a friendship while rehearsing a scene from Shakespeare to entertain their fellow guests on a rainy day. It had been something of an unlikely pairing. Lady Francesca was the daughter of a duke, while Clarissa was the penniless daughter of an unsuccessful naturalist. Lady Francesca was beautiful and demure, and Clarissa was a tart-tongued spinster.

But the thing they had in common was that they both chafed at the roles society had laid out for them. Lady Francesca had no desire to marry, but her parents were determined to see her wed to a lord within a year. Clarissa had no taste for marriage, either. Years ago, she had been betrothed to a man named Rupert Dupree, who was the younger son of the Earl of Rottenbury. It had been a match arranged by one of her dearly departed mother's distant cousins, the Countess of Milthorpe, meaning that Clarissa had never clapped eyes upon her intended.

This had not prevented Rotten Rupert, as Clarissa now thought of him, from penning a scathing letter forcefully rejecting his proposed union with Clarissa. Even worse, instead of having the letter delivered to Clarissa privately, he had sent it to every newspaper from Shetland to Cornwall. This had set off a brief but furious frenzy in which not only Clarissa but also her three sisters, Eleanor, Kate, and Pippa, had been derided in the scandal sheets. The gossip rags had even given them a nickname—the Weatherby Wallflowers.

Fortunately for him, Rupert Dupree had decamped for the Continent by the time those newspapers reached Boroughbridge, the tiny village in Yorkshire where Clarissa had grown up. She might be slight in build and without training in fencing, fisticuffs, and the like, but nonetheless, it would not go well for Rotten Rupert were he to encounter her in a dark alley.

After that, the blush was off the rose as far as marriage was concerned. Not that Clarissa was the type of girl who had been planning their wedding since the age of six. The thing that Clarissa wanted most was the chance to make use of her wits. Were she a man, she fancied she would have been a Member of Parliament, ferociously debating the issues of the day and crafting legislation that would make the world a better place. She wanted to leave her mark, to do something important, not waste away in a tiny village, embroidering handkerchiefs and never getting the chance to use the six languages she had taught herself from books borrowed from the circulating library.

That also happened to be the reason Lady Francesca had thought to introduce Clarissa to her great-aunt. After her jilting, Clarissa had taken to wearing gowns in dull colors, which her sisters referred to as "Clarissa's dirt-colored dresses."

"Why would I want to draw the notice of a man?" Clarissa had asked Lady Francesca, who understood. "I *prefer* to blend into the wallpaper. Although perhaps my drab dresses are a little too effective in this regard. You would be astonished at the things I overhear sometimes. People don't even realize that I'm standing beside them."

Clarissa would never forget the way her friend's spine had gone ramrod straight. Glancing about to make sure they were alone, Lady Francesca had asked, "Have I ever told you about my Great-Aunt Winnifred?"

What Lady Francesca had proceeded to explain was that spies did not look the way they were portrayed in novels. A dashing young army officer in a red coat would draw every eye in the room and arouse every suspicion as well.

The seventy-two-year-old woman snoozing by the fire, on the other hand? According to Lady Winnifred, old women were all but invisible to begin with. Close your eyes and throw in a fake snore and every villain from here to Thurso would discuss their most dastardly plans right in front of you, not even bothering to lower their voices.

And so, spies were usually the last person you suspected. The old lady. The scullery maid.

The wallflower in the dirt-colored dress.

Lady Francesca had offered to make introductions, an offer Clarissa had accepted with alacrity. Sure enough, Lady Winnifred thought Clarissa had great potential, an assessment echoed by her contact at the Home Office, Sir Henry Kenchington. Sir Henry had spent a half hour peppering Clarissa with rapid-fire questions. He had seemed pleased with her command of French, Spanish, High German, Low German, Dutch, and even Russian.

Once the interview concluded, Sir Henry removed his spectacles, rubbing his nose. "I have a theory, Miss Weatherby, that behind every weakness, there lies a strength, if you have the wit to see it. You have described yourself as a wallflower. Society derides wallflowers, of course, as spinsters in the making. They are unadmired and, most importantly, unnoticed." He had fixed her with his pale blue gaze. "Congratulations, Miss Weatherby. Your weakness is now your strength. I hope this is the start of a mutually beneficial arrangement."

It had been the best thing to ever happen to Clarissa. No longer would she be stuck frittering her days away embroidering handkerchiefs. She would be able to make use of her natural abilities. She was going to do something important!

She was assigned to train under Lady Winnifred. The two of them had just completed their first assignment, a simple mission to gather information about a gentleman smuggling French wine in Whitby. They had been heading back to London to await their next mission when Lady Winnifred fell ill in York. Her ladyship had sent a letter to Sir Henry to let him know that they would stay there so she could convalesce.

Sir Henry's reply was presently burning a hole in Clarissa's pocket.

With a cry from the driver, the mail coach set forth. The man on the opposite bench seat lurched forward, then backward, his head thumping against the thin grey padding that lined the wall of the coach. But he did not awaken.

Clarissa peered at him. He really did seem to be asleep. And what were the chances he could read the contents of her letter from the facing seat? She would be hard-pressed to make out the words by the carriage lamps as it was.

Were he to awaken, all he would see was a woman reading a letter. There was nothing inherently suspicious about that!

Thus resolved, Clarissa removed the letter from her pocket and unfolded it eagerly.

CHAPTER 2

*L*ady Winnifred,

    I am sorry to hear that you find yourself unwell, especially in light of the grim news I have received today. It concerns Mr. Oliver Baxter, a prominent member of the House of Commons with whom you are no doubt familiar.

There have been a number of unusual occurrences in Mr. Baxter's household this past month. A stray bullet that came through the window of his morning room, missing him by inches. A wheel that broke on his curricle in such a way that it was a miracle he was not thrown from the vehicle. And a scullery maid who became sickened after tasting the crawfish soup to see if it had enough salt.

Mr. Baxter's wife grew concerned and insisted that her husband contact Bow Street. Upon investigation, the soup was found to be tainted with arsenic, and the curricle showed signs of intentional tampering.

When the Runner went to notify Mr. Baxter of his findings, he learned that the entire household, consisting of Mr. Baxter, Mrs. Baxter, and one of her spinster cousins, had recently departed for

Yorkshire to attend a house party being hosted by the Earl and Countess of Helmsley.

The Runner formed the impression that Mr. Baxter believed his wife had overreacted to this sequence of events, which he dismissed as mere coincidences. He therefore departed London unaware that someone is trying to kill him. You are the only agent within a hundred miles of the house party's location. I therefore implore you, if you are remotely well enough to undertake the journey, to go to Helmsley Castle with all possible haste. I believe you are acquainted with Lord and Lady Helmsley, but I have provided a letter of introduction explaining your presence at the house party, as well as a letter for Mr. Baxter.

Hopefully, the would-be killer has remained behind in London, but we must take no chances. You are, therefore, to remain at the house party, watching for any signs of another attack. I have also enclosed an analysis of Mr. Baxter's political positions, and which of the house party's known guests would face significant losses were he to succeed in enacting legislation in accordance with those positions.

Given the urgency of the situation, I will send as many additional assets to the Helmsley estate as can be made available. In particular, one of my best men will return any day from a lengthy assignment on the Continent. I will have him on the first carriage north.

I remain yours &c.,

H.K.

Clarissa swallowed. Just her second assignment, and she was already facing a life-and-death situation! A part of her was thrilled to have been given the chance to do something so important. But she was inexperienced, and she knew it. What if she was not up to the task?

She shivered, partly out of nervousness but also because the brick at her feet had already lost most of its heat. She was now certain that the temperature was dropping, and she was shivering beneath her cloak. How she wished she had thought to don a couple of flannel petticoats and bring a thick woolen carriage blanket! Well, there was nothing for it now. There hadn't been time to pack properly, so she had hastily shoved a few things in her valise with the understanding that Lady Winnifred would send her trunk after her the following day.

Clarissa wedged herself into the corner, trying to find a little warmth amongst the sparsely padded squabs. It would be an uncomfortable journey, but it wasn't far to Helmsley. She could endure it.

She read through the letter a second time. As an avid reader of the papers, she knew of Oliver Baxter. Young and charismatic, his name was often mentioned as a potential candidate for Prime Minister should the Whigs regain power. He advocated for a number of reformist initiatives that Clarissa supported strongly, including eradicating slavery from the British Empire. He also argued in favor of parliamentary reform, including an expansion of voting rights to include the working and middle classes and the elimination of so-called "pocket boroughs" whose populations had shrunk over the years, leaving a scant handful of voters whose support could easily be bought and sold.

Many a family fortune depended on these hotly debated issues, so it was easy to imagine that Mr. Baxter might have enemies.

Unfolding the second sheet of paper enclosed, she saw that Sir Henry's thoughts had gone in a similar direction:

Possible Suspects:

(1) Mr. Ulysses F. Humphrey—Mr. Humphrey's fortune is derived from a large sugar cane plantation on the island of Antigua employing slave labor. He faces significant losses should the emancipation proposals Mr. Baxter supports succeed.

(2) Mr. Richard Garroway—MP representing the pocket borough of Dunwich. Most of the town has fallen into the sea, leaving only thirty-two voters in the entire constituency. If Mr. Baxter succeeds in passing parliamentary reform, Mr. Garroway will surely lose his seat.

A different hand, one Clarissa recognized as that of Lady Winnifred, had scrawled an additional name in the lower margin:

(3) Arabella Anstruther, Dowager Duchess of Kimbolton—a good friend of Lord and Lady Helmsley and likely to be in attendance. Mother of fourteen children including eleven boys. Mr. Baxter has advocated for church livings and political appointments to be granted based on merit, rather than connections. He has been vocal in shaming those who bequeath positions in their gift to unqualified family members or who sell them outright. This has made it impossible for a number of the duchess's shiftless sons to secure a living, and I have heard her complain bitterly about the expense of maintaining them out of the family coffers. She will become increasingly desperate as more of her sons reach the age of majority.

Clarissa sat back. How like Lady Winnifred to consider not only the male guests, but also the ladies. It was a good reminder that Clarissa must scrutinize every possible suspect.

She noted her letters of introduction to Lord and Lady Helmsley and to Mr. Baxter, still folded and sealed. Tucking everything back together, she returned the letter to her valise and settled against the thin grey squabs.

Just as the brick at her feet lost the last of its heat, the coach hit a bump, jolting her slumbering companion awake.

He blinked groggily, then did a double take as he saw that he was not alone in the coach. "Blimey! I do beg your pardon, miss. Wouldn't have nodded off had I realized I wasn't alone." He gave a great, seemingly involuntary yawn. "I've come up straight from London, you see, so I'm just about fagged to death."

Clarissa did not see, not precisely, but she took it that this meant he was tired. "That's quite all right, sir."

He rubbed his eye with the heel of his hand. "Won't be much longer now, though. I'm only going through to Helmsley."

"Helmsley!" Clarissa exclaimed. At his curious look, she explained, "That is my destination as well. I don't suppose you are bound for Helmsley Castle?"

"Happens that I am. I'm en route to the earl and countess's house party."

"As am I," Clarissa said.

He smiled at her, and something inside Clarissa shifted. He wasn't what you would call classically handsome. In addition to the bump on his nose, his smile was lopsided, and his fair hair a bit too shaggy. But in spite of these flaws, his features somehow came together in a way that was tremendously appealing.

She decided it was because he looked so affable, as if he were utterly delighted to find himself with her in that carriage, in spite of the fact that he was *fagged to death*, whatever that meant. And the impression that someone was genuinely pleased to be in your company held a strong allure.

He shook his head, rueful. "But look at me—I've gone and put the cart before the horse! I pray you won't tell Lady H. how I prattled on without remembering to make introductions." He smiled again, holding out a hand. "I'm Rupert. Rupert Dupree."

The carriage veered off the road and tumbled over a cliff, falling end-over-end until it finally smashed into pieces on the rocks below.

Not really. But that was how receiving this news felt to Clarissa. It was impossible to understate how discombobulating it was to learn that the amiable fellow sitting not three feet away was *Rupert Dupree*, the very cad who had jilted her in the most humiliating manner possible and made a very creditable attempt at ruining her life!

His smile faltered. "I say, is everything all right?"

Was everything all right? Of course, everything was not all right! She was stuck in a carriage with Rotten Rupert, and if she somehow managed to survive that, she would find herself confined to the same remote, snowbound castle for weeks on end!

Clarissa gripped the seat cushion as hard as she could, as she thought it a good idea to give her hands something to do other than reaching across the carriage to strangle him.

He studied her, concern creasing his brow. "Say, you're not about to flash the hash, are you?"

This nonsensical medley of words managed to penetrate her angry red haze. "Am I about to *what*?"

"You know—shoot the cat. Flay the fox. Cast the craw."

"Cast the—" Clarissa peered at him, perplexed. "Are you asking me if I'm about to cast my accounts?"

He held both hands out in front of him. "It's nothing to be

embarrassed about. I know carriage travel affects some people in that—"

"Mr. Dupree!" Clarissa snapped. "You have misunderstood. I am not feeling remotely queasy. I was merely startled when you said your name because"—she drew herself up, lifting her chin—"I am Clarissa Weatherby."

She had expected him to turn pale, for horror to come into his eyes as he was forced to face the woman he had so grievously wronged.

Instead, his genial grin returned, bigger than ever.

"Are you really?" He laughed, looking delighted. "Well, this is a bit of a chance, isn't it?"

Clarissa stared at him, dumbfounded. What was going on?

It was as if he did not understand that he was the most repulsive person she knew.

Of course, there were precisely two things she knew about Rupert Dupree, and one of them was that he was remarkably dimwitted. Two years ago, whenever she had told someone about her betrothal, the conversations always went roughly the same way:

First, there would be some variation of, *"Rupert Dupree? You lucky thing!"* which was followed by a strangely inevitable fit of giggling.

Next, the qualifier: "To be sure, the man is as dumb as a door-hinge. But *still!*"

Clarissa had found this baffling. If her intended was indeed very stupid, why was she so universally regarded as fortunate?

She had attempted to ascertain the answer through discreet questioning. She had learned that, although Mr. Dupree had inherited an estate from a childless aunt that produced a respectable income of two thousand a year, he was not what you would call absurdly rich. Nor was he regarded as particularly handsome. His elder brother, Viscount Riddington, had already produced three sons, so there was no appreciable chance that he would one day inherit his father's earldom. The source of his appeal remained elusive.

Finally, a similar conversation had taken place with someone Clarissa knew well enough to ask. She and her sisters were taking tea with Jane Crowley, the married daughter of their more prosperous neighbors, the Ramsays. Clarissa mentioned her recent engagement, and Jane promptly said, "Lucky girl!" then broke into the requisite fit of giggles.

"Why does everyone keep saying that?" Clarissa moaned. "Because in the next breath, I know you're going to tell me that he's—"

"As dull as an anvil," Jane supplied.

"Precisely!" Clarissa peevishly snatched a ginger biscuit from the tray. "What, I should like to know, is fortunate about *that*?"

Jane's eyes went wide. "Do you truly not know?"

"Know what?"

Jane glanced about as if to make sure her parents were not within hearing range. Instinctively, the four Weatherby sisters leaned forward.

Jane waggled her eyebrows. "Mr. Dupree is exceptionally talented in the bedchamber."

Clarissa, who had never in her life been stunned speechless, found herself stunned speechless. She could feel her cheeks burning as she exchanged astonished looks with her sisters.

She set her biscuit on the saucer of her teacup with trembling fingers. "How do you know this?" she finally managed to blurt.

Jane laughed. "Rumors! Only by rumors, I swear." She

arched an eyebrow. "Although the rumors are remarkably consistent. So, cheer up, Clarissa—you may find yourself happier in this marriage than you think."

The conversation moved on, even if Clarissa hadn't been able to attend to a word of it. She had fumbled through the rest of the visit and was lucky not to have broken her teacup.

And now, here she was, face to face with the man who had humiliated her. Who was reportedly the most bacon-brained man in all of Britain.

Who was *exceptionally talented* in the bedchamber.

"How have you been?" he asked, voice brimming with affection, as if he were an old friend rather than her archnemesis.

"Not so well, Mr. Dupree," she replied in a clipped voice. "Not so well at all."

His face fell. "Oh, no. It's not something to do with one of your sisters, is it? You have three of them, if I recall correctly."

Clarissa lifted her chin. "You recall perfectly, and my sisters are thriving. In fact, my eldest sister, Eleanor, is recently wed to the Duke of Norwood."

He leaned forward, abruptly cheerful again. "I heard about that! I was only in London for less time than it takes to milk an aardvark—"

Clarissa squinted at him. "Less time than it takes to *what*?"

"—but it was on everybody's lips. I was at school with Norwood, you know." He shook his head, smiling softly. "Capital fellow. Absolutely capital. I daresay your sister is going to be well-pleased with him."

"Thank you. I'm sure she—*ugh*." Clarissa rubbed her temple. What was she *doing*? This was not a normal conversation, and Rupert Dupree was the most despicable man she knew.

Why did she have to keep reminding herself of that fact?

Clenching her jaw, Clarissa began again. "I mentioned that I have not been doing so well. My troubles began around two years ago when I received a great blow to my reputation."

His face fell. "How awful. I suppose that explains why I hadn't heard anything about it. You see, two years ago is right around the time I left for the Continent."

Did he truly think he could play dumb? That she would let him off so easily? Not a chance! "Indeed, the incident which proved so damaging occurred on the eve of your departure."

"Did it?" Confusion was a natural expression on Mr. Dupree's face, one Clarissa took it that he wore with some frequency. "That's quite the coincidence."

Clarissa glared across the carriage. "No coincidence at all, Mr. Dupree, considering the catalyst to my downfall was you jilting me!"

CHAPTER 3

Rupert blinked at Clarissa Weatherby in the cold, shadowy carriage.

He knew he wasn't a clever sort of fellow.

But he really thought he would have remembered doing something like that.

"Come again?" he asked, tilting his head to the side and shaking it in hopes it might jar the memory loose in his brain.

"Don't pretend you don't remember!" Miss Weatherby snapped, her brown eyes full of poison. "Not only did you jilt me, but you also sent copies of your letter to every major newspaper in Britain!"

Rupert *really* did not remember doing that. He did remember sending Clarissa a letter releasing her from the betrothal she clearly had not wanted.

Or, to put a finer point on it, the betrothal she had been railing against, at considerable volume, in the middle of Boroughbridge's Crown Hotel.

"I don't understand," he began. "I did write you a note. But I didn't send it to any papers."

She was still glaring at him as if he'd just kicked a puppy. "Well, the papers somehow got a hold of it."

He rubbed his temple, still struggling to wrap his brain around whatever was going on. "But I don't see why that would ruin your reputation. I didn't say a word against you."

She huffed. "Not a word against me?" She reached for her valise and began unlatching the leather straps. "It happens that I keep a copy with me." She leafed through the pages of a journal, pulling out a newspaper clipping. "Let's see if this refreshes your memory."

Grimacing, Rupert accepted the slip of paper. *Perfect.* Just when he thought things couldn't get any worse, here he was, out of the frying pan and straight into the old fire.

The truth was, Rupert could read, but he was deuced slow at it. His brain was, how you say, skimble-skamble, and had this way of turning b's into d's, and p's into q's. Some people were all at sixes and sevens, but old Rupert? He was at sixes and nines, because he literally could not tell them apart. And don't ask him *who* or *how*, at least, not in writing. Because he somehow managed to swap one for the other without any sort of warning.

At the ripe old age of eight and twenty, he knew what his most common bear traps were well enough that he could manage to pick his way—*slowly*—through a letter. Under the best of circumstances, that was.

With his heart hammering out a military tattoo and Clarissa Weatherby giving him the sort of look that had been known to turn a man to stone, this was not what you would call the best of circumstances.

Stay calm, Rupert. This wasn't the first time he'd had to brazen his way through this situation, and it wouldn't be the last.

Deep breath. You know what to do.

He made a show of squinting at the clipping in the dim carriage light, as if struggling to make out the tiny print.

After a moment, he glanced up. "I packed my spectacles in my trunk, which is up top. Could you read it to me?"

Clarissa's gaze remained as frosty as the Yorkshire night. But she nodded, took the article from him, and began to read.

To the Editor:

I write to you today to make you aware of a situation that will be of the most material interest to your readers. You see, I have narrowly escaped a terrible predicament, and I know it to be a circumstance your faithful subscribers will be most keen to avoid:

Betrothal to one of the Weatherby sisters.

Who, one might reasonably ask, are the Weatherby sisters? To be sure, they do not possess the notoriety of a Beau Brummell or an Emma Hamilton.

But these four young women do have something in common with those two stalwarts of society: They have the finances of Brummell, and the morals of Mrs. Hamilton.

Would that the Weatherby sisters possessed the looks of either of these figures, but I can assure you—they do not.

As I mentioned, I recently found myself in the unfortunate circumstance of being betrothed by my father to the second oldest Weatherby sister, Clarissa. She is arguably the worst of the bunch (although please do not mistake me; they are all extremely bad.) Miss Clarissa Weatherby is a bluestocking and not the sort of bluestocking one admires for her intellect and high-minded thinking. She is as strident as she is shrill, the type who thinks herself smarter than every man in the room. She has nothing in the form of physical charms to recommend her. Such an undesirable creature should at least have the decency to bring to her prospective union a sizeable fortune, but, like her sisters, Miss Clarissa is destitute.

I am fortunate to have discovered the truth about these Weatherby Wallflowers before it was too late, and the parson had done his work. I now implore your readers toward vigilance, so that they might have the perspicacity to avoid these avaricious vituperators.

Your loyal servant,
Rupert Dupree

She looked up as if daring him to defend himself. Rupert's mouth was hanging open. She'd said it was horrid, but it had somehow managed to be ten times worse than he'd imagined. "They didn't actually print that?"

She glared at him down her nose. "Oh, but they did. In just about every paper in England. As I'm sure you intended!"

Panic fluttered in his stomach; maybe *he* would be the one to flash the hash. "I didn't write that!"

She gave him a scowl that could've curdled milk. "You expect me to believe that?"

"I didn't! It doesn't even sound like me." He raked a hand through his hair. "*So that they might have the perspicacity to avoid these avaricious vituperators?* I don't even know what half those words mean!"

She paused, narrowing her eyes, and for a second, he thought he'd convinced her.

It was a good argument, after all, seeing as it happened to be the truth.

But then, she shook herself, and the poisonous glare snapped back into place. "A likely story, Mr. Dupree."

He cast his eyes toward the carriage's ceiling in despair. "Look, I can see why you hate me if you think I wrote *that.*

But I didn't know a blessed thing about it. Did you not receive my letter?"

Her lips tightened. "What letter? What are you talking about?"

Rupert leaned forward. "You should have received it with your mail around the same time I was to come to Boroughbridge."

"I received nothing from you, Mr. Dupree," she said, her voice cold.

He groaned. "I have no idea who wrote that letter or how it came to be in the papers. Although…"

The words died on his lips as he remembered. Because, as usual, he'd known what he wanted to say, but he'd needed help penning his letter. And the person who'd been on hand, the one he had turned to for help, had been *William Ellison.*

He should have known better than to trust one of his brother's friends.

Rupert ran a hand over his face. "Actually, that's not true. I've a fair idea who sabotaged me."

Clarissa rolled her eyes. "Sabotaged you? Is that the best tale you can come up with?"

He ignored her barb. It wasn't difficult to understand why she was furious, and what was she to think other than that he had been the one behind it? "I promise you this—I am going to make this right."

Clarissa crossed her arms. It suddenly struck Rupert that she was trembling. Probably with rage, although now that he thought on it, she looked deuced cold. Her cloak was what you would call an autumn weight…

She glowered at him. "Just how do you propose to do that?"

He was still working that bit out, but he had a few ideas. "For starters, I'm going to—*ugh!*"

The words died on Rupert's lips as the carriage jolted, jerked to a halt, and tilted precariously.

The sudden change in momentum sent Clarissa flying forward into Rupert's seat.

He caught her by the shoulder before her face smashed into the thinly cushioned seatback. "Whoa, there. Are you all right?"

She did *not* need Rotten Rupert's help. Flushing, Clarissa extricated herself and returned to her seat. "I'm fine. What's happening?"

Outside the carriage, she could hear the driver and guard conferring. After a moment, the door opened, ushering in a blast of even colder air. "Apologies, miss, sir," the driver said, touching the brim of his hat. "But one of the wheels has broken. Must've hit a rock or some such."

Clarissa bit down a trace of panic. She was already freezing, already longing to reach the next waypoint where she could exchange her cold brick for a hot one. The last thing she needed was to be stuck out here in the cold. "What will you do?" she asked, pleased that her voice was steady in spite of the fear welling in her chest.

"We'll ride ahead to the next village and fetch the wheelwright. It's only about an hour on."

An hour. That meant it would be another hour back, plus whatever time it took for the wheelwright to rouse himself, collect his tools, and repair the wheel.

Now, Clarissa was feeling more than a trace of panic. "Is there a farmhouse nearby where we could seek shelter?"

The coachman looked apologetic. "I'm afraid not. There's nothing for miles." He turned to Rupert. "We're unhitching the horses now. You could go on with us, sir, if you don't mind riding bareback." He turned to Clarissa. "Apologies, miss, but we don't have anything like a sidesaddle."

The words that emerged from Clarissa's mouth were, "That's quite all right." Because she prided herself on being stalwart and undaunted. She was self-reliant to a fault and didn't have it in her to succumb to hysteria, even when she was honestly terrified that she was about to succumb to the cold.

"Kind of you to offer," Rupert told the coachman, "but I don't like the thought of Miss Weatherby being out here all alone. I'll stay with her while we await your return."

The coachman bowed. "As you like, sir. I'd best be getting on, then. Sooner we start, the sooner we finish and all that."

"Of course," Rupert answered. "Godspeed to you both."

The coachman shut the door, and Clarissa once again found herself alone with Rupert Dupree.

She wanted to ask him about what he had said before they hit that rock—about his plan to make things right. But after the blast of cold air that had entered the carriage when the coachman opened the door, her lips weren't working as well as they ought to have been.

Her brain wasn't functioning very well, either. Her thoughts felt sluggish, which was the most alarming thing of all. Because she was Clarissa Weatherby. Her thoughts were *never* sluggish.

Wrapping her cloak more tightly about her shoulders, she uttered a silent prayer that she would make it through the night.

CHAPTER 4

*R*upert peered at Clarissa across the dim carriage. Her eyes looked a bit muzzy, and her color wasn't very good unless your favorite color happened to be blue, in which case, her color was excellent.

"I say, Miss Weatherby, are you all right?"

"Fine," she gasped. "Just fine. Why do you ask?"

"Because you're looking like one of those Pictish fellows."

"Oh?" Clarissa looked like she was nodding off. "H-how so?"

"Mostly that you're blue." He patted the bench beside him. "Why don't you come and sit over here? My cloak is big enough to spread over both of us."

"That's probably wise," Clarissa muttered, but instead of coming over to join him, her eyes drifted closed and she slumped down in the corner of her own seat.

Rupert had the feeling this was not a good idea. It was like they'd told him when he visited Switzerland—if you were hiking in the Alps, no matter how tired you thought you were, the one thing you didn't want to do was lie down in the snow for "just a minute." People who lay down in the snow for "just a minute" didn't get back up.

Gad, but this was improper. But she looked to be pretty far along the path toward freezing to death, so *improper* was somewhat low on his list of concerns.

"Here," he said, taking her by the shoulders. She was a little thing, but she was pretty well insensible, and it was deuced awkward maneuvering her dead weight across the cramped space.

But after a minute of giving it the old heave-ho, he managed to settle Clarissa on the bench seat next to him. Only then did it occur to him that he could've just gone and sat next to her. Ah well, wasn't that the way it always happened with him?

He spread his cloak—mink-lined and warm enough for the winter he'd spent in Oslo—over both of them, then wrapped an arm around Clarissa's shoulders. It was a mark of how cold she was that instead of trying to strangle him, she made a little whimpering sound, then wrapped her arms around his chest and buried her face in his shoulder.

It felt good to have her in his arms. It felt strangely right, as if she was supposed to be there. And, of course, she wasn't. That was an echo of another life, one he'd been on the brink of, but ultimately, wasn't supposed to have. The one where she was Clarissa Dupree, and she was glad to have Rupert in her life.

Ah, well. At least he could be useful to her for body heat, if nothing else. That was something Rupert liked—feeling useful. He'd managed to do it for the past two years, and it was deuced addicting.

As he drifted off to sleep, images of a world in which Clarissa actually wanted him flitted through his head.

~

Clarissa was having the most pleasant dream.

She was inside a confectionary shop, perusing a display case full of bonbons, marzipan, and delicate biscuits dusted with sugar. It was warm inside—probably because of the oven in back—and everything smelled delicious. The only thing marring the experience was the incessant pounding. Were they kneading some dough in the back room? Chopping almonds, perhaps? Shouldn't they have finished that before they opened to customers?

Blinking herself awake, Clarissa found herself in the dim carriage. The pounding was someone knocking at the door. Other elements of her dream proved correct as well—she *was* warm, through some miracle, and the sweet smell?

That was Rupert Dupree, who was yawning and stretching beside her. Clarissa saw that he had brought her over to sit beside him, covering both of them with his cloak and even holding her close for good measure. She flushed as she disentangled her arms, one of which had slipped *inside* his coat, from his person. It was probably necessary that they had huddled together, as she was fairly certain she had been on the brink of freezing to death.

But it was difficult to square the fact that this gallant gesture had come from the most repulsive man she knew.

The button on her sleeve snagged on something, preventing her from scooting away as quickly as she would have liked. She drew in a lungful of air, getting another whiff of his cologne, as her nose was mere inches from his jawline. He smelled just like an almond biscuit. She would've expected a dandy like Rupert Dupree to slather himself in Bay Rum. Thank God he hadn't; she couldn't stand the pungent scent.

Sitting up, Clarissa saw that she was snagged on some sort of necklace. As she struggled to disentangle herself, the pendant popped open, proving to be a locket. A painting of a pale blue eye stared back at her within the silver frame.

Noticing her predicament, Rupert clucked. "How did that get loose? Let's see here." He peeled one of his black leather gloves off and went to work unwinding the chain from around her button. Clarissa was wearing gloves, too, but his fingertips brushed the bare skin on her wrist, causing her to shiver, this time not from the cold.

He managed to free her sleeve, and she scooted to the far side of the bench seat, not leaving the warmth of his cloak. She studied him out of the corner of her eye as he closed the locket and tucked it back inside his shirt. Who *was* this strange man? He seemed a bundle of contradictions.

Straightening his coat, Rupert leaned forward and opened the carriage door. The person knocking proved to be the coachman. "Begging your pardon, sir, but the wheelwright's here. He had a wheel sized to fit, but he needs to put it on. You'll both have to get out."

"Ah. Jolly good," Rupert said, rolling his shoulders. He slid out from beneath his cloak, ducking his head as he climbed out the door.

"You forgot your cloak," Clarissa said, holding it out to him. The rush of cold air that swept under it made her immediately regret the gesture, but pride demanded that she surrender it.

"You take it," Rupert said, holding out a hand to help her from the carriage.

"Oh, I couldn't possibly. I have my own cloak, after all, and—"

"I insist." Rupert took the cloak from her but only to wrap it around her shoulders. *Lud* but that felt good—the warmth of the cloak around her, and the brush of his hands on her shoulders.

She peered at him in the dim light of the carriage lamps.

A scattering of snowflakes swirled around his head, one occasionally settling in his golden hair. She saw that the temperature had dropped sufficiently that the snow was now piling up in drifts.

"But what about you?" she asked.

He waved this off. "Don't worry about old Rupert. I just came from Switzerland, and this time last year, I was in Norway. I'll be fine."

"I see. Thank you," she added hastily.

She was spared from having to make further conversation by the coachman, who called Rupert over to help lift the carriage so the wheelwright could do his work. Clarissa watched from a discreet distance. Rupert made no complaint about being asked to grasp the underside of the muddy carriage and lift. As if to prove that he was used to the cold, he peeled off his tailcoat with a good-natured remark about keeping it clean, tossed it into the carriage, and took up his position at the back corner of the carriage. He performed the task cheerfully and solicitously asked the guard if he was all right when his foot slipped in the mud.

Clarissa had to own that Rupert Dupree wasn't what she had expected. He had somehow managed to make a good impression in spite of the fact that, in line with the rumors about him, he did not appear to be of the greatest intelligence.

An hour ago, Clarissa would have said that intelligence was the most important quality she looked for in any friend. Yet Rupert Dupree had her questioning her own judgment in this regard. In fact, were it not for the fact that she already hated him, Clarissa rather thought she would have liked him.

This was not Clarissa's only alarming revelation about Rupert Dupree. The sun was just starting to rise, giving her an unimpeded view as he strained to lift the mail coach. The mortifying thought that her nemesis filled out his buckskin breeches rather splendidly drifted unbidden across her mind —a result, no doubt, of some combination of exhaustion and hypothermia. She knew she should avert her eyes but found the prospect strangely difficult. His posterior was not what you would call large, but nor was it scrawny. The word *taut* came to mind. An unbearable urge to reach out and squeeze it came over her, and she grasped a handful of his cloak to contain the strange urges welling inside of her.

The carriage suddenly shifted. Grunting, Rupert bent his knees, straining to hold it aloft as his muscles shifted and flexed beneath the buckskin. A warbling sound emerged unbidden from her lips, and she made a hasty attempt to disguise it as coughing.

It took around fifteen minutes to swap out the wheel. Rupert rubbed snow on his hands to rinse off the mud before he handed Clarissa into the carriage.

He frowned as he settled into his seat. "I say, I hope you weren't overheated in my cloak."

"Not at all," she said, her voice emerging slightly breathless. "Why do you ask?"

He made a circular gesture toward his own face. "You're a bit flushed is all."

"Oh." She could hardly say, *it's because I've been staring at your arse for the last quarter of an hour.* She cleared her throat, blushing even harder. "Er, speaking of your cloak..." She tried to hand it back, but he held up a palm in refusal. "It's all right," she insisted. "We're inside now, and we'll be getting underway soon."

He shook his head as he pulled on his jacket. "It's not going to get any warmer in here just because the carriage is moving."

Clarissa bit her lip. He was right. Still, she hated the fact that she'd been unprepared almost as much as she hated being beholden to someone, much less to Rupert Dupree. "I cannot in good conscience deprive you of your cloak for such a long duration."

He shook his head. "I'd a thousand times rather I go without it than you. Did you know that you turned blue earlier?"

She started. "Did I?"

"You did. So, let's have no more talk of you going without that cloak. Old Rupert will be all right."

Clarissa swallowed back the bile rising in her throat. She could not *believe* what she was about to suggest. "Perhaps we could… sit next to one another."

He twisted his lips to the side. "I wouldn't want to make you uncomfortable."

"You wouldn't," Clarissa hastened to reassure him.

"Because what I did earlier… That was just desperate measures and all that. As I mentioned, you were turning blue—"

"And I appreciate what you did. I must confess that, although I was too proud to ask for assistance, I was not doing well and was beginning to grow concerned." She cleared her throat, then forced herself to say, "Thank you, Mr. Dupree. This time, as I am already warm, I feel confident that it would be sufficient to sit next to each other in a more… customary manner."

He frowned, studying her for a beat. "If you're sure…"

"I am."

He slowly moved from the rear-facing seat to the forward-facing one where Clarissa sat. The seat wasn't wide, but he was careful to leave a good six inches between them, which was all that the carriage allowed. Clarissa handed him the edge of his cloak, and they settled it across themselves like a blanket.

They were both wide awake and staring at each other awkwardly. "So…" Clarissa began, casting about for a topic.

"So," Rupert replied cheerfully.

"I noticed your locket earlier," she hedged. "The one with the eye miniature. My sister, Kate, is a good artist. She paints those sometimes, for people who want a memento of their sweetheart."

She looked away. *Brilliant, Clarissa.* That sounded like she was digging, trying to find out if he had a sweetheart. Not that she cared in the least!

Genial as always, Rupert fished the locket out from between the buttons on his shirt. "I remember Lady Milthorpe singing your sister's praises two years ago. I'm sure her miniatures must be very popular." He flipped the locket open, showing her. "Mine was a gift from my Aunt Imogen. That's her eye you see there. She said this way, she could always watch over me."

Clarissa exhaled, relieved that the conversation was back in safer territory. "It sounds as though you two are close."

The lopsided grin returned, although it didn't quite reach his eyes. "We were. She died two years ago. A malignancy, the doctors said."

"I'm so sorry."

Rupert nodded. "As am I. Auntie Im was my mother's sister. My mother died when I was eight—"

"Mine died when I was five," Clarissa noted.

"Ah." Rupert inclined his head graciously. "Then you understand."

Clarissa nodded sadly.

"After my mother died, Auntie Im was the one who looked out for me."

"Not your father?" Clarissa asked.

Rupert shrugged. "My father wasn't horrible to me or anything like that. But I've always known I was a disappointment to him. He prefers my older brother, Francis."

Clarissa decided it would not be tactful to ask why he was such a tremendous disappointment to his father. "I see. If it makes you feel any better, my father is utterly horrible. He sold our house so he could take an around-the-world voyage. He's a naturalist, you see. Not a very good one."

Rupert frowned. "He sold your house? Where were the four of you supposed to live, then?"

Clarissa laughed bitterly. "That was left to us to figure out. Fortunately, Lady Milthorpe invited us to a house party, where Eleanor met the Duke of Norwood. Had they not wound up marrying, we would have been in a world of trouble."

Rupert's lips were bunched up in a pout. "I say, that's bad form on your father's part. Tremendously bad form, leaving you unprotected and whatnot."

"I won't argue with you there." He had shut his locket and was starting to tuck it away. The metal had an unusual gleam under the dim carriage lights. "Say, what kind of metal is that? It doesn't look quite like silver."

"It's not. It's actually steel." Rupert gave a rueful chuckle. "The first one she gave me was silver, but I managed to destroy it during my school days. I probably should've taken it off for the wall game, but you can't leave anything valuable lying about at Eton. It'll get nicked, sure as eggs are eggs. So, Auntie Im had a replacement made out of steel, and it's held up much better."

"Practical as well as kind." Clarissa tried—and failed—to stifle a yawn. "I have a feeling I would have liked her."

"I'm sure you would have done. But look at me, yammering on when you're tired. I'll let you get some rest."

Clarissa didn't deny it. She slumped back into the corner and pulled the cloak up to her chin.

But there was one thing she wanted to do before she drifted off. "Mr. Dupree?"

"Hmm?" he said, suppressing a yawn of his own.

She could not believe she was about to utter these words. "Thank you. For everything."

"You're most welcome, Miss Weatherby."

Those were the last words Clarissa heard before she drifted off to sleep.

CHAPTER 5

They arrived in Helmsley mid-morning.

Rupert yawned and stretched as he climbed out of the carriage in the yard of the New Inn. The earl's estate was only about two miles from town, and Clarissa tried to insist that she would walk the rest of the way. Rupert would have none of it. He might've been tempted to try it had he been on his own. He had his cloak, after all, and having spent the better part of a week stuffed in a mail coach, God knew he could use a chance to stretch his legs.

But it was well below freezing, and Miss Weatherby was a bit under-attired for the conditions. So, he insisted upon renting a post-chaise for them to share.

They settled into an awkward silence in their new conveyance. Although they'd forged an unlikely alliance after being trapped together overnight, Rupert knew she was still upset with him over the rumpus in the press while he'd been abroad. He was going to make that right. He already had a couple of ideas as to where he should start.

But the sad truth was, too much water had passed under that particular bridge, and Clarissa Weatherby was probably never going to like him. Which was a shame. He quite liked her. When they'd been talking last night about his aunt and their mothers and their fathers… he'd felt as if she'd heard him. That they'd made a real connection, that she hadn't been smiling out of politeness while thinking the whole while, *how long until I can get out of talking to this idiot?*

He surreptitiously watched her peeking out the carriage window, hoping to get a glimpse of Helmsley Castle, her face bathed in soft morning light.

She really was quite pretty in spite of the dull dress she wore. Brown was probably the most practical color for carriage travel. All the dust of the road and whatnot. But even in her sensible gown, Clarissa was pretty and clever, and she knew what it meant to lose your mother much too soon. It was a shame their betrothal hadn't worked out. He had the feeling they would've done just fine.

Ah, well. You didn't always get what you hoped for.

Rupert knew the truth of that old chestnut all too well.

He resolved to give Clarissa a wide berth during the house party. That was clearly what she wanted, after all. He could still work behind the scenes to make what repairs he could to her reputation.

The carriage pulled up to Helmsley Castle. It was the home of his old school chum, Lawrence, and a familiar sight. When it came to school holidays, if Rupert hadn't been visiting Auntie Imogen, he had typically come here, rarely opting to go to the old family pile in Devon.

According to Laurie, there had been a castle on this site for nine hundred years, but most of the present structure had been built by Laurie's grandfather. Rupert thought the previous Lord Helmsley had done a bang-up job of it. The castle had been built in what you might call a Tudor style, with a pair of octagonal towers flanking the front door and matching towers on each of the four corners. It had all the features you wanted out of a castle—crenellations, arched windows, a roaring fire in the great-hall-cum-dining-room, and every modern convenience a fellow could possibly wish for.

Best of all, it was home to the de Roos family—Lord and Lady Helmsley, Laurie, and his three brothers and two sisters. They were wonderful people, all of them, and Rupert was quite looking forward to spending Christmas here.

Inside, Rupert greeted the butler, Toddington, who had been with the family since Rupert's first visit at the age of twelve.

Toddington clasped his hand. "Master Lawrence will be beside himself that you're back in England. James," he said, turning to a footman, "go and fetch Master Lawrence. Tell him Mr. Rupert Dupree is here."

Rupert was so busy catching up with Toddy that he didn't notice that Clarissa was skulking in the corner until Laurie came striding into the entry hall. "Crikey, Rupe—it really is you! Come here, you old dog," he said, grabbing Rupert by the shoulders.

"Laurie!" Rupert exclaimed, thumping his friend on the back. "Hope you don't mind me besieging the castle uninvited."

"You're always invited, and you know it," Laurie said firmly. "Mama will tell you the same thing—here she is."

Sure enough, the Countess of Helmsley had appeared at the top of the landing. She was peering down the stairs. She'd never much liked wearing her spectacles. Thought they made her look old. But Rupert thought she was an exceptionally handsome woman with or without her spectacles, and the sight of her warmed his heart.

"Lawrence, is that you?" Lady Helmsley asked, squinting. "Tell me, is it true? Has Rupert returned to us at last?"

"It's true, Mama." Laurie grinned. "How's that for a Christmas present?"

Lady H. picked her way down the stairs. "It is the best present, the best one we could possibly receive." Reaching Rupert, she framed his face. "Oh, dear boy—you have been away from us for far too long!"

Rupert kissed her on the cheek. "Hope you don't mind my imposing myself upon you."

"Imposing!" She swatted his wrist. "You are never an imposition. Now, Rupert, I must insist that you stay with us through the Christmas holidays. You must not even consider abandoning us to go be with those horrible people."

Rupert laughed, taking no offense that the horrible people she was referring to were his father and brother. "I should like nothing better."

Lady Helmsley noticed Clarissa lurking beside a suit of armor. "Is this a friend of yours?" she asked, looking at Rupert.

"A recent friend," Rupert said, gesturing for Clarissa to come forward. "We met on the mail coach. May I present Miss Clarissa Weatherby?"

Lady Helmsley's mouth fell open, and Laurie's eyes all but bugged out of his head, suggesting that the rumors Clarissa had mentioned had been every bit as bad as she implied.

Clarissa stepped forward, clutching her valise with white knuckles. "Lady Helmsley, I apologize for the intrusion. Is there any way we could have a private word?"

Lady H. glanced at Rupert. He nodded reassuringly.

"Of course, dear. Of course. Have you broken your fast?" Clarissa shook her head, and the countess turned to Toddington. "Have a tea tray sent to the morning room with some morsels for Miss Weatherby. Come, child." She placed her hand on Clarissa's back and led her down the hall.

Rupert turned to Laurie. "Say, I was wondering if—"

"Did you truly meet *Clarissa Weatherby* in the carriage?" Laurie hissed.

Rupert laughed. "I did."

Laurie was studying him. "And do you know about…?"

"The scandal? I do now. She told me all about it. Come on." Rupert put a hand on his friend's shoulder, steering him toward the library. "That's actually what I need your help with."

Laurie asked Toddington to send them one of those tea trays as well, and the next thing you knew, they were settling into the pair of leather wingchairs before the fire.

"I can't imagine Miss Weatherby was too pleased to make your acquaintance," Laurie said.

"She was not," Rupert confirmed. "The thing is, Laurie, I didn't write that letter. Didn't even know about it until a few hours ago."

Laurie snorted. "You think I don't know that? They ran it the day after you sailed for France. I tried to write to you so you'd know what was going on, but I take it my letters never reached you. The timing was wretched."

It warmed Rupert's heart that his friend had believed the best of him. "I appreciate that, Laurie. I really do. I was moving around quite a bit. But now that I do know, I want to set things right. And that's where I need your help."

It had occurred to Rupert in the carriage. Laurie was the third son of the earl and countess and a very bright fellow. He had set himself up as a solicitor.

Rupert explained what he had in mind. "I want to make it clear that I never wrote that letter, that I never insulted Miss Weatherby. That every word they printed is a bunch of rot."

Laurie frowned. "The strange thing is that it wasn't just one paper that ran it. Almost every paper from here to Portsmouth somehow had a copy. I know it wasn't you. But who could it have been?"

Rupert made a bleak sound. "I've a fair idea. It was two years ago, and I'd gone up to Boroughbridge to meet Miss Weatherby. I'd just arrived at the Crown Hotel after traveling all day, so I figured I'd go to bed early in hopes that I might look a little more the thing the following morning. I was sitting in the common room, waiting for my supper, when who should walk in but Miss Clarissa."

Laurie tilted his head. "You met her, then?"

"I did not. She was there to collect her family's post. I happened to be seated just behind her. She had her back to me, so I never saw her face, but I couldn't help but overhear her conversation with the barmaid."

Laurie was studying him, no doubt noticing that Rupert's typical happy-go-lucky expression had taken a leave of absence. "What happened, Rupe?" he asked softly.

Rupert sighed. "The barmaid, Becky, asked when I was to arrive. And…"

"And?" Laurie asked gently.

What made it so particularly painful to recall was that he'd gone and got his hopes up. Lady Milthorpe had assured him that he and Clarissa would suit each other to perfection.

Rupert was not unaware of his own flaws. Indeed, it would've been hard to remain oblivious, as glaring as they were. That he'd made it through school was a mark of how much Eton and Oxford had wanted his school fees, because there wasn't a drop of academic merit involved.

But according to Lady M., Clarissa Weatherby was every bit as clever as Rupert was duncical, which sounded *perfect*. He needed someone like her who could help him run Drayford House, the small estate left to him by his aunt, to say nothing of the portfolio of investments. He stood about as good a chance of managing those by himself as a rhinoceros did of learning to dance the *pas de deux*. Some men took umbrage at the notion that a woman might be more intelligent than him. Not old Rupert. He wanted the cleverest gel who would have him.

But then, Lady Milthorpe had gone and done it. It wasn't just that Miss Clarissa would be good for Rupert.

According to the countess, he would be good for her, too.

"The world has not been overly kind to the Weatherby sisters," Lady Milthorpe had explained. "And Clarissa in particular has a chip on her shoulder. She needs a kind man, a patient man, and someone who will appreciate her intellect, not take it as a threat." He could still picture the way Lady M. had smiled as she patted his hand. "And that's you, Rupert."

He'd been so *hopeful* about Clarissa Weatherby. He'd spent most of his life as the butt of everyone's joke—poor old Rupert, dumb as a box of rocks. It had been nice to think, for once, that he had some positive personal qualities beyond his talents in the bedchamber and the usual stuff about being in possession of enough money to save a woman from destitution.

But Lady Milthorpe had been wrong. Miss Clarissa had not been enthusiastic about the match.

Quite the opposite, as she'd made inescapably clear.

He could still hear Clarissa's crisp response to Becky's question. "He's due to arrive in three days. And he's not *my* Mr. Dupree."

He'd tried not to take that personally. After all, they still needed to meet and make sure they would suit one another and whatnot.

Behind him, Becky had laughed. "Oh, but he will be! And I'll warrant you won't have that sour look on your face after the wedding." She'd dropped her voice low, but not so low that Rupert couldn't hear. "I hear your future husband knows *just* how to put a smile on a woman's face."

Good lord—how had those rumors reached this little

village in Yorkshire? Normally, Rupert didn't mind people alluding to his eagerness to please in the bedchamber overly much. It was nice for people to have something to say about him other than what an idiot he was.

But it was one thing for a pair of widows to whisper such a *bon mot* to each other behind their fans, or for Rupert's friends to joke about it over drinks at their club.

He felt a lot less pleased to hear it being discussed at full volume in the middle of a busy inn, in front of his future bride and a considerable portion of her acquaintance.

Speaking of his future bride, Clarissa had summoned the wherewithal to answer. "He is not my future husband, not if I have any say in the matter. How I wish Lady Milthorpe had never involved me in this ridiculous scheme!"

Rupert's heart had sunken down to about the level of his spleen. Not that he knew where his spleen was or what it did, but the point was, he was starting to feel *deuced* disappointed.

Becky's tone turned somber. "You don't mean that, Miss Clarissa. Why, he's the son of an earl, and a right good match, from everything I hear."

Thank you, Becky, Rupert had thought to himself. He could remember sitting there, shoulders stiff, holding his breath, hoping to God that Clarissa would say, *You're right. I'm just nervous about marrying a man I've never met. I should at least give him a chance.*

Instead, she had said, "He's supposed to be a blithering idiot, from everything I hear. What could Lady Milthorpe have been thinking? I would never consider such a man for my husband, not if he were the last man on earth!"

She took her leave shortly thereafter. He did turn his head as she swept out of the room, but the only glimpse he got was of the back of her bonnet.

Ah, well. Rupert should have known it was all too good to be true.

As disappointed as he'd been, he could never find it in himself to be mad at Clarissa Weatherby about it.

After all, who would want to marry a stupid fellow like him?

"Rupert? Are you all right?"

Rupert shook his head, recalling himself to the present. Laurie. Helmsley Castle. Right, right. "Sorry about that. Suffice it to say, Miss Weatherby made it clear that she didn't share my enthusiasm about the match."

Laurie's eyes were sympathetic. "I'm sorry."

Rupert shrugged. "As was I. In any case, I was worried her father would force her into it. From what I'd heard, the man didn't have a sixpence to scratch with. I therefore determined that I should be the one to release her from any sense of obligation. I figured there was no use making things more awkward than they already were, so I would send her a note."

Laurie's shoulders stiffened. They'd been friends a long time. He knew where this was going. "A note?"

"That was my downfall, all right."

The thing was, whatever the rumors said, Rupert could write. He was just deuced slow at it, and his handwriting was atrocious. Given his exhaustion from three days of travel and the crushing disappointment he'd just had, he'd known there wasn't much hope of him scratching out a coherent sentence, much less a proper missive.

That's when he'd spotted a familiar face—William Ellison, a friend of Rupert's brother, Francis. Not that this was a point in his favor. Francis held no affection for his younger brother and had been horrible to Rupert growing up, both at school and outside of it.

But Ellison had never done anything to Rupert personally. To be sure, he had stood there and laughed while his brother pushed him down the stairs.

But that had been years ago. Surely, he had matured since then!

And Rupert had been desperate.

So, he'd crossed the room and greeted Ellison as if they were old friends. Ignoring his glare, Rupert had pulled out a chair. He'd explained the situation in hushed tones, giving the excuse he always used, even though Ellison knew him well enough that he probably didn't believe it—that he'd misplaced his spectacles. Would Ellison write out the note for him?

Suddenly, Ellison had been delighted to help. Rupert had told him just what to say. It had been a self-effacing note about how it wouldn't do for a bright young thing like Clarissa to shackle herself to a dull fellow like Rupert, and he was, therefore, releasing her from any obligation she might have felt toward him while wishing her all the best.

He'd left the note with Becky to be added to the Weatherby family's stack of mail and left for London the following morning. The situation was resolved.

Or so he had thought.

Laurie was still waiting for an answer. "I needed some help writing out the note. And it happened that someone I knew was there in the common room of the inn. You'll remember him from school—William Ellison."

Laurie slumped down in his chair. "Tell me you didn't ask William *bloody* Ellison."

"I didn't think he was that bad!" Rupert protested.

Laurie gave him a look. "He's friends with your *brother*," he said as if that explained everything, and honestly, it more or less did.

Rupert leaned forward, steepling his fingers. "Is there anything we can do?"

Laurie went and perched on the corner of the desk with one hip. Pulling out a sheet of paper, he began scribbling down some notes. "Damn straight, there's something we can do. We'll demand a retraction and threaten to sue for defamation of both you and Miss Weatherby."

Rupert perked up. "Defamation—that's the theme. Yes, to all of that."

"We should write to the Duke of Norwood," Laurie mused, rubbing his jaw. "The papers insulted not only Miss Clarissa, but also his new duchess. I expect he'll want to join you should it come down to filing suit. If we can mention his name, that will really put the fear of God in them. He's got deep pockets and loads of influence."

"That's a brilliant suggestion." Norwood would help him. Rupert knew he would. Capital fellow, absolutely capital, and not the type to brook any insult to his wife.

A footman appeared, bearing a well-laden tea tray. Laurie abandoned his perch on the desk, and they tucked in.

"I appreciate you helping me out of this mess," Rupert said between bites of scone. "In retrospect, asking Ellison for help was a stupid decision. Possibly the stupidest decision I've ever made, in a long line of—"

"Hey!" Laurie punctuated this exclamation by throwing a scrap of crumpet at him. "None of that, now."

Rupert couldn't help but smile. Laurie had never tolerated anyone calling him an idiot, and that included himself.

He really did have the best friends.

"So," Rupert said, "do you really think we can nail Ellison?"

"I do." Laurie sipped his coffee, considering. "But we must proceed carefully. His father made enough money selling guns to the army over the past two decades to set the family up for life. We'll need solid proof he was the one who fed those lies to the papers. What we have right now is circumstantial."

"Right." Rupert set down his cup, sloshing tea onto the saucer. Suddenly, he felt like he was twelve years old all over again, getting shoved into the wall by one of the older boys looking to curry favor with his brother.

"Don't look so glum," Laurie said. "I'm not saying we won't go after him. We just have to take it one step at a time. As part of my letter, I'll demand to know how the papers came into possession of the letter they printed. They'll be eager to give him up, to shift the blame away from themselves."

"If they even know who sent the letter," Rupert mused. "They'll have to maintain that they thought I'd really written it. It's their only excuse, isn't it?"

"True. But they may be able to provide us with some details that will help. Was it delivered by a footman? In what livery? If it was posted, where was it posted from? Do they still have the original letter? Is it in his hand? That sort of thing."

Rupert nodded. It was a damn sight better than sitting around doing nothing. "Good thoughts, all of them."

"And if we can get Norwood on our side, we can go toe-to-toe with them financially. Then we'll see what shakes out."

"Good. Good." Rupert gave an involuntary yawn. "I appreciate your help."

"You said you came in on the mail coach?"

Rupert nodded. "Straight through from London."

Laurie gave a low whistle. "You must be exhausted. James!" he called to the footman standing at attention in the hallway. "Find Mr. Dupree a bedroom, will you?"

James appeared in the doorway. "His usual room has already been made up, sir."

"Perfect." Laurie shooed him out the door. "I'll get to work on those letters. You go get some rest."

"Thanks, mate."

Laurie squeezed his shoulder. "It's good to have you back."

Rupert smiled sleepily over his shoulder as he followed James down the hall. "It's good to be back."

And it was. He might have been sent here on business rather than pleasure.

But spending Christmas at Helmsley Castle, surrounded by people who were truly his friends, would be a pleasure, nonetheless.

CHAPTER 6

larissa settled gingerly on a cerulean-striped Chippendale chair in Lady Helmsley's morning room. "I apologize for arriving at your home uninvited," she said as she opened the buckles on her valise. "I assure you, I have only come due to the greatest necessity. This letter will explain more." She passed Sir Henry's missive to the countess.

Lady Helmsley pulled a pair of spectacles out of her pocket and began to read. Her eyes went wide almost immediately.

"Gracious me," she said when she was finished, peeling off her glasses and rubbing her eyes. "Surely the assassin cannot think to murder him at Christmastime!"

Clarissa thought that someone so deranged as to want to murder someone at all would probably pay little heed to the festive season, but she nodded sympathetically. "It is my hope that the threat has remained in London, and there will be no incidents to mar your house party. But we must take every precaution."

"You're right, of course." A footman appeared with the tea

tray the countess had requested. "Bring that over here, Richard," she instructed.

Once the tea tray was arrayed on a side table, Lady Helmsley gestured for Clarissa to help herself. "Go on, child. You must be famished."

Clarissa was, and she helped herself to a pastry dripping with peach preserves. It was so good, and she was so hungry, she had to force herself to nibble it daintily instead of devouring the whole thing in three bites.

Once Lady Helmsley had prepared them each a cup of tea, she leaned back in her seat. "I'm still trying to wrap my head around the notion of such a delicate young lady working for the Home Office!"

Clarissa chuckled. "I fear I am not so young and not at all delicate."

The countess waved this off. "You seem young to me. Wait until you're my age. You'll understand."

"As to my employment with the Home Office, I must ask you to keep that confidential. I would not ask you to keep a secret from your husband. But if you could not tell anyone else, and if you could impress upon his lordship the importance of keeping this information to himself, I would appreciate it most sincerely."

"Of course, dear. Of course."

"There is one more thing. Sir Henry told me he would be sending at least one additional agent to watch over Mr. Baxter. This person is unknown to me. Should someone approach you with a similar letter of introduction, I would appreciate it if you could point them out to me so we can coordinate."

"I most certainly will. And I will tell Toddington to make up a bedchamber for you. Has your trunk been brought in?"

Clarissa cringed. "I fear I departed in such haste, I had to leave my trunk behind. The plan was that my associate would send it on the following day. But with the sudden turn the weather took, I worry it might not arrive for some time."

"Don't fret, child. You're of a size with my Emily. Believe me, she has enough gowns for both of you. I will tell her you were separated from your luggage, and we are working to get it back."

Clarissa felt tears pricking at the back of her eyes. The countess was being so kind.

After years of being made to feel like a pariah, despised by all good society and mocked behind her back at every turn, she had almost forgotten that there were still good people in the world.

The countess was peering at her with concern. "Is everything all right, child?"

"Yes, I—" Clarissa drew in a shaky breath, rubbing at her eye. "You're being so tremendously kind about all of this. I appreciate it more than I can say."

Lady Helmsley was studying her. "The world has not been overly kind to you these past few years."

Clarissa gave a weak smile. "That is something of an understatement."

The countess tilted her head, seeming to weigh her words. "I know that the papers printed all manner of awful things about you two years ago. But many people did not believe those articles, dear."

"Everyone I've met in the intervening years seems to have believed them," Clarissa said, unable to keep the woefulness from her voice.

"I will not ply you with false reassurances by claiming no one listened to those lies. But everyone who knows Rupert understood at once that the letter was a fabrication. I have been saying for years that those rumors were a bunch of rot. I know that Lord Helmsley has been doing the same. I can see why you might have believed yourself to be friendless. But you aren't, and the truth is, you never were."

Clarissa nodded tightly, suddenly having trouble forming words.

"Rupert will also be staying through the holidays," Lady Helmsley noted. "But that will be all right, won't it? Now that you know he didn't write that letter, things will not be awkward between the two of you, I hope."

Clarissa paused. The truth was, she was still struggling to untangle her confused feelings about Rupert Dupree. He insisted that he was innocent, and Lady Helmsley seemed sincere in her conviction that he was telling the truth.

But Clarissa found it difficult to sweep two years of cursing his name aside in one day. Rupert Dupree was the man who had ruined her life and the man who had most probably saved it last night when he prevented her from freezing to death. He was the village idiot, and one of the kindest, most agreeable people she had ever met.

He claimed he was innocent, and part of her wanted to believe him. But was that just a convenient excuse?

Clarissa didn't know what to think anymore. She was confused—an uncomfortable state for someone who prided herself on being incisive.

Lady Helmsley was awaiting a response. "It is hard for me," Clarissa finally said. "If you could only know what the last two years have been like…" Her voice cracked, and she trailed off.

Lady Helmsley leaned forward, pressing her hands. "My dear child!"

Clarissa surprised herself by saying, "The worst part was not that my own reputation had been ruined. But they dragged my sisters' names through the mud as well."

Lady Helmsley was stroking the back of her hands with

her thumbs. "I am sure it must have been terribly distressing."

Clarissa swallowed. "But I can admit that Mr. Dupree is not the monster I was expecting. I am... open to the possibility that he is innocent in all of this, something I could never imagine saying before today. And I promise that I will not be the cause of any unpleasantness to mar your house party."

Lady Helmsley squeezed her hands again before sitting back. "Considering all you have been through I think that is more than reasonable. Come," she said, rising from her seat, "I'm sure you are weary from your journey. I'll have a footman show you to your room."

After thanking Lady Helmsley again, Clarissa followed a footman up the stairs. She felt relieved to have made it inside the house party.

But now the real challenge—protecting Oliver Baxter from his would-be assassin—would commence.

As Clarissa shut the door to her rooms behind her, she wondered if she would prove equal to it.

The soft light of a winter afternoon streamed through the windows when Clarissa awoke several hours later. Someone had set out a wrapper and a pair of slippers for her, and she hurried to put them on. Even with a fire roaring in the grate, the room was chilled—unsurprising for December in Yorkshire.

She started as she caught sight of herself in the mirror. The wrapper was a soft pink, the same shade as peonies. After two years of wearing nothing but brown, taupe, and walnut, she was unaccustomed to seeing herself in such a bright color.

Clarissa had started wearing her signature dirt-colored dresses, as her sisters called them, in the aftermath of her jilting. She'd been receiving quite enough attention, thank you very much, and anything that made her stand out was something she desired to avoid.

But now, her brown wardrobe was a key to her success as a spy. She literally blended into the castle's wood-paneled walls! It was amazing how little attention people paid to a woman thought of as dowdy, and Clarissa had overheard all variety of secrets over the years.

She was counting on doing it again this week.

There was a soft knock at the door. "Come in," Clarissa called, assuming it might be a maid.

It proved to be three maids, along with a smiling young lady with dark hair and dimples. "You must be Miss Weatherby! Did I awaken you? I hope I didn't awaken you. But it will be time to dress for dinner soon, so I thought I ought to bring over a few gowns. I'm Emily, by the by."

Clarissa curtseyed. "Lady Emily, it is a pleasure. I cannot thank you enough for lending me a few gowns until my wardrobe catches up with me."

Lady Emily seized her hand. "It is the least I could do! I cannot imagine your distress, for your wardrobe to be goodness knows where. It is a tragedy of the first order!"

Clarissa hadn't given the matter much thought. To be sure, now that she was sister-in-law to a duke, she had a wardrobe of new dresses cut in the most fashionable styles, if not the most fashionable colors.

But Clarissa had never been one to pay much mind to her wardrobe. Still, she didn't want to be disagreeable, so she replied, "Oh, er… Yes. Yes, indeed."

Lady Emily gestured for the maids, who each bore a heavy armful of dresses, to lay their burdens out on the bed.

That was when Clarissa noticed the problem.

There were gowns of pink and yellow and blue. Celadon green and orange sorbet. Vivid reds and brilliant purples.

But there wasn't a trace of brown to be seen.

"What do you think about this one?" Lady Emily asked, pulling out a gown of bright fuchsia silk adorned with *crystals*. It was all Clarissa could do not to gasp in horror.

"Oh! It's lovely," Clarissa said. And it was. Her youngest sister, Pippa, would have looked wonderful in it. "But I don't usually wear such bright colors."

Lady Emily took this in stride. "Oh. All right, then." She sifted through one of the piles. "I have just the thing—this one is a bit more demure."

The gown she held out was of emerald-green velvet with a daring neckline. While the color was an improvement over the pink, Clarissa had a feeling it would draw even more stares.

Peering at the stack of dresses, Clarissa asked, "You wouldn't have anything in a nice shade of brown?"

"Brown? Gracious, no!" Lady Emily shook her head so hard, you would have thought Clarissa had asked if she had a burlap sack she could borrow. "I don't have anything like *that*! Brown is for spinsters and dowagers."

Clarissa chuckled awkwardly. "Which is why I wear it. I am five and twenty. Very firmly on the shelf."

Lady Emily gifted her with a glowing smile. "Not after I'm through with you! We're going to make you the belle of the ball. Just you wait, Miss Clarissa!"

The belle of the ball? Clarissa felt slightly ill. She had to blend into the wallpaper! "Oh, that's all right. I honestly don't want to be the belle of the ball."

"Don't be so modest." Putting her hands on Clarissa's shoulders, Lady Emily propelled her with surprising force to the cheval mirror. "Leave everything to me!"

Clarissa's sputtering protests were bowled over by a tidal

wave of benevolence. Lady Emily was determined to show her that she could be beautiful, but how to explain that she did not *want* to be beautiful?

As bright dress after bright dress was held up to her in the mirror, Clarissa began to panic. "If not brown, do you have something in black or grey? Perhaps a nice olive—"

"*I have it!*" Lady Emily cried, digging through one of the piles of gowns on the bed. When she spun around, she clutched a gown of bright, cherry-red silk.

Clarissa took an involuntary step back—the way most people did when confronted by a large, hairy spider.

"I daresay that this one will flatter you *to perfection*," Lady Emily said, bearing down on her with a look of absolute assurance.

"I don't... I couldn't possibly..." Clarissa spluttered.

Lady Emily held the horrific garment up before her. All three maids *oohed* in appreciation.

"That's the one, all right," the petite maid with brown curls said.

"Red really is your color, if you don't mind my saying so, miss," the plump one with blonde hair agreed.

It happened that Clarissa *did* mind her saying so. *Brown* was her color. *Brown!* But her stammered protests were summarily ignored. In the space of three minutes, Clarissa found herself stuffed into a fresh shift, stays, and petticoat, then thrust into the red silk gown.

She stared in horror at the sight that greeted her in the mirror. Not only did the color make her stand out like one of Mr. Newsham's fire engines, but the neckline was a good three inches lower than what Clarissa typically wore. Worst of all, the red silk hugged her every curve.

She looked... *pretty.* Dear God, this would not do, this would not do at all! She looked like Cinderella after the fairy godmother had done her work, when she needed to look like the before version.

"I have a wonderful idea!" Lady Emily exclaimed. Clarissa could see herself in the mirror, and her eyes had taken on a wild quality, like a fox cornered by a pack of dogs.

Lady Emily did not seem to have noticed, for she was happily sweeping Clarissa's hair back into a chignon. "What if we do something like this, with a few pieces to frame her face, and then pin a little cluster of holly just behind her ear?"

The three maids squealed in delight. "That will look right smart."

"It will be perfect for Christmas!"

The third maid seized a brush from the dressing table. "Here," she said, pushing Clarissa down onto the padded stool, "If one of you will fetch some holly, I'll get started on it."

Clarissa blinked at herself in the mirror, dazed and horrified, and wondered what on earth she was going to do now.

CHAPTER 7

*R*upert felt much more the thing as he headed down to dinner. Six hours of sleep in a proper bed had worked wonders on his back and neck, to say nothing of his disposition. Add in some good nosh, and he would be back to his cheerful self in no time flat.

As he reached the bottom of the staircase, he heard a thump from behind the curtain of a little alcove in the entryway. Rupert frowned. It was probably nothing, but considering the reason he was here, it probably behooved him to make sure there wasn't an assassin lurking in there with a gun.

Creeping up to the alcove, he whipped the tapestried curtain open…

… and Clarissa Weatherby gasped as she wheeled around, one hand flying to her heart.

Just like that, Rupert's head went all muddly… well, more muddly than it usually was. *Blimey.* Clarissa Weatherby was *gorgeous.* Suddenly, the notion that he might have married this woman seemed even more ridiculous. What on earth would this stunning creature want with the likes of *him*?

It occurred to Rupert that he should say something rather than stand there gaping at her. "Sorry, I thought I heard something. You look beautiful, by the by."

For some reason, her face fell upon hearing this compliment. "Thank you," she muttered.

Rupert cleared his throat. "May I escort you in to dinner?"

She considered it for a beat. "That's probably a good idea." At his confused look, she added, "There's bound to be some gossip with the two of us in attendance. If we are seen behaving civilly toward one another from the start, hopefully, that will set the tone."

"Just so." Rupert offered his arm. "Shall we, then?"

Rupert led her toward the blue and white parlor where the de Roos family usually gathered before dinner.

"You seem to know your way around the castle," Clarissa noted. "I take it you are good friends with the de Roos family?"

"Oh, yes. I was at school with Lawrence, who's the third son. Used to spend some of my school holidays here. Lovely people, absolutely lovely."

"I met Lady Helmsley and Lady Emily today, and they do, indeed, seem very kind."

Rupert glanced down at Clarissa. Her lips were set in a tight, thin line. "Do you not know many people here, then?"

"I do not," she confirmed.

"I'll introduce you around if you like," Rupert offered.

She drew in a breath. "That would be very much appreciated."

They attracted more than a few stares when they entered the room together. Which wasn't surprising. But Clarissa kept her chin up, and as for Rupert, he was used to that sort of thing.

Rupert had a few people he was hoping to speak with

tonight, but that could wait. He introduced Clarissa to the rest of the de Rooses, then to the Duchess of Kimbolton. He presented her to a couple of young ladies local to Helmsley—Miss Eliza Swanton and Miss Marianne Pickering.

Then, as luck would have it, he spied Oliver Baxter, the very reason he was here, standing nearby! Rupert knew him a little bit. They'd been at Oxford at the same time, but at different colleges.

Catching his eye, Rupert strode up. "Baxter, it's deuced good to see you again. May I present Miss Clarissa Weatherby? Miss Weatherby, this is Mr. Oliver Baxter."

Baxter bowed neatly over her hand. "How do you do, Miss Weatherby? Please allow me to introduce my wife, Rosalind, and my wife's cousin, Miss Phyllis Cuthbert."

While he made his bows, Rupert surreptitiously studied the trio. Baxter had always been a good-looking fellow in a bookish sort of way—brown hair, pale skin from spending all day in the library, sensitive poetical expression, soft hands, tweed waistcoats, that sort of thing. One thing was for certain, he looked remarkably calm, considering someone was trying to kill him. Of course, he hadn't yet been informed that someone was *definitely* trying to kill him, so maybe that explained it.

His wife, on the other hand, looked drawn. Which might've been exhaustion from the carriage ride north, but Rupert rather thought it was worry creasing her brow, not fatigue. She had that shade of hair somewhere between brown and blonde and green eyes. Rupert was surprised, because he'd always heard that she was a great sportswoman, so he hadn't expected her to be as thin and wan as she appeared. He supposed that went to show that you never knew.

As for Miss Cuthbert, she struck Rupert as the nervous sort and was wringing her gloved hands in a way that looked habitual. Rupert had heard she was a spinster, and she certainly dressed like one, with a grey dress that buttoned all the way up to her chin. But Rupert thought if someone would put her in a more flattering gown and do something with her dark brown hair other than twist it into a tight knot, she would've been as pretty as any woman in the room.

Well… he found his eyes straying to Clarissa Weatherby. Maybe not quite as pretty as *every* woman in the room. But downright handsome.

Rupert was about to see if he could worm anything useful out of them when Toddington announced that dinner was served.

Inside the great hall, Rupert surrendered Clarissa, who was seated on the opposite end of the table. He was seated between Lady Helmsley and Lady Emily.

He wouldn't learn much of use there, but Rupert didn't mind. He handed both ladies into their chairs and prepared to pass the meal in the company of two of his favorite people.

CHAPTER 8

Much to Clarissa's delight, the place card to her left indicated that she would be sitting next to Richard Garroway. Mr. Garroway was one of the three suspects Sir Henry had mentioned in his letter, the one who had been elected to the House of Commons representing the rotten pocket borough of Dunwich. Dinner promised to be an excellent opportunity to assess how highly Mr. Garroway ranked on her list of suspects.

As the guests found their seats, Clarissa glanced around the Great Hall. It was a gorgeous room with carved wooden beams visible beneath the high ceiling and a ten-foot-wide stone fireplace, complete with a roaring Yule log. A long table ran the length of the room with shield-back chairs lining either side. The wood-paneled walls were painted vermilion red and lined with real tapestries between the arched windows.

A lady settled into the seat to Clarissa's right, introducing herself as the Marchioness of Ashington. She mentioned that she had made her debut with Clarissa's mother, and had fond memories of her, which caused Clarissa to warm to her at once.

After a few minutes of reminiscing, Lady Ashington dropped her voice low. "I must confess, I was a bit surprised to learn who you were, especially after seeing you enter on the arm of Rupert Dupree. Do you truly not harbor any ill feelings toward him?"

Clarissa sipped from her wineglass as she considered her answer. "Mr. Dupree has assured me that he was not the author of the letter that went around the papers two years ago. In fact, he told me that he knew nothing of it, as he has been traveling on the Continent."

Lady Ashington regarded her steadily. "And you believe him?"

"I don't know what to believe," Clarissa admitted. "But the de Roos family seems to regard him very highly. I certainly don't want to be the cause of any unpleasantness at their gathering. So, I am trying to give Mr. Dupree the benefit of the doubt."

The marchioness nodded, a look of approval settling over her face. "Do you want to know what I think?"

"I would." Clarissa was honestly curious. She had known Lady Ashington for all of two minutes, but she seemed sensible. Clarissa had no idea how she felt about the whole business, and she rather thought she could do with a little guidance.

Lady Ashington leaned forward, dropping her voice low. "It's obvious he didn't write that letter. Weatherby Wallflower, my shoe. Just look at you! Some wallflower."

Clarissa suspected her cheeks had turned as red as her dress. "Oh, er…"

"And your sister is now a *duchess*. The Duke of Norwood could have had his pick of any woman in England. I am yet to meet your sister, but she could not possibly be the hag described in the papers."

Clarissa's heart squeezed. "She's not. Eleanor is lovely, inside and out."

"So, it is obvious that column was nothing but rubbish. And there is no possibility that Rupert Dupree was its author."

"What makes you say that?" Clarissa asked.

"Why, just look at him, child—he can't take his eyes off you!"

Clarissa blanched. That couldn't possibly be right. The legendary Lothario Rupert Dupree could not possibly be staring at the likes of her.

Don't look, she ordered herself. *Don't look, don't look, don't—*

Of course, she looked.

Rupert's head swiveled to face the far end of the table with suspicious alacrity.

Clarissa glanced at Lady Ashington and found the marchioness regarding her with a smug smile. "What did I tell you?"

Clarissa was still having difficulty believing that any man, much less Rupert Dupree, might find her attractive. "I don't know. The letter came out long before I ever met Mr. Dupree."

"And what would be his motive in writing such a letter about a woman he's never met?" The marchioness shook her head. "Mark my words, Miss Weatherby—figure out who had something to gain by slandering you. Because that person is the author of the letter."

Clarissa was stunned that Lady Ashington was treating her so civilly. She had expected the other guests to wonder at the fact that Lord and Lady Helmsley had invited her, a Weatherby Wallflower, to their gathering. But when Lady

Ashington introduced her to the guests seated in their vicinity, Clarissa did not receive one snide look.

Maybe it was the fact that Lady Ashington was able to introduce her as "sister-in-law to the Duke of Norwood." By marrying Jasper St. James, Eleanor had saved her, which was a very Eleanor-like thing to do. Perhaps it was the fact that thanks to Lady Emily, Clarissa didn't look like a wallflower. It had never occurred to her that she could silence her critics by looking ravishingly beautiful, but to be fair, looking ravishingly beautiful had been a much more daunting prospect when her family had been so poor that even her nicest gowns had been years out of date and fraying at the hem.

Or maybe Lady Helmsley's guests wanted to return to London with the latest *on dit*—that they had beheld Clarissa Weatherby, wallflower amongst wallflowers, with their own eyes, and she hadn't been at all what you would expect. Not only that, but they had even watched her interact with *Rupert Dupree* and could provide a full report. Everyone present would be able to dine out on that gossip for at least a week or two.

Clarissa found that she did not mind this unlooked for sea change—*Clarissa Weatherby, a wallflower? Oh, dear, haven't you heard?*—on a personal level. She had always thought of herself as a bookish sort of girl. Her youngest sister, Pippa, was the pretty one. It had never occurred to her that she could be pretty, too. She still couldn't quite wrap her head around it. But one thing was for certain, it was a thousand times better than being known as a Weatherby Wallflower!

But in terms of her work for the Home Office, it was a disaster. She had been selected for being the girl no one noticed. Now, she was drawing every eye in the room, not merely for being pretty but for her newfound notoriety.

How on earth was she supposed to overhear her fellow guests' secrets if they were fascinated by her every move?

Clarissa was pondering this debacle when Mr. Garroway turned to her with a smile. He was a handsome man, perhaps in his early thirties, with brown hair, blue eyes, and a jaded air. "I don't believe we've been introduced. I'm Richard Garroway."

"Mr. Garroway, a pleasure," she said, inclining her head. "I am Clarissa Weatherby."

He laughed, but in a startled way, not a cruel one. "Are you really?"

Clarissa's lips twisted into a wry smile. "I see that my reputation has preceded me."

His gaze swept slowly down her frame, lingering for a beat on her bosom. "Your entirely inaccurate reputation, you mean."

Clarissa's sense of disbelief grew. Was Richard Garroway *flirting* with her? She had never had a man flirt with her, not once in her twenty-five years.

Of course... that might not be entirely down to her threadbare wardrobe. Clarissa had always been unafraid to speak her mind and to do so about topics most ladies would not touch with a ten-foot pole—current events, politics, and the like. It was a quality that many men found unappealing.

But Clarissa had to own that there was more to it than that. Ever since that cursed letter appeared in all the papers, rendering her a laughingstock, she had assumed any man who approached her did so intending malice. She had adopted a policy of preemptively lashing out, of humiliating them before they could humiliate her.

But the de Roos family was so kind, it was perhaps unsurprising that their friends were kind, too. For the first time in two years, there was no need for Clarissa to strike first. It wasn't as if she was going to become a shrinking violet overnight. But in a single day, she had been stripped of so many of her sharp edges. She simply did not need them anymore.

It was startling to realize that something Clarissa had thought of as an intrinsic part of her personality was actually a product of the environment in which she had found herself. That, while she might be confident and opinionated, she wasn't actually caustic, as she had come to believe.

Still, she wasn't confident enough to flirt back at Richard Garroway, so Clarissa replied, "I've heard of you, too. You are a Member of Parliament, are you not?"

"Right you are. I'm surprised you know that."

Clarissa shrugged. "I'm one of those tiresome people who read the paper every day. Tell me, Mr. Garroway, what positions do you support?"

She had expected a man who had bought his seat in the House of Commons to have a limited knowledge of the issues. Goodness knew there were enough men like that, who held the title M.P., but who could rarely be bothered to show up to vote, much less attend parliamentary debate.

But Richard Garroway surprised her. To be sure, he was no William Wilberforce, galvanized by a great passion to change the world for the better. He was both sardonic and flippant, but Clarissa had to admit that he knew the issues. He had carefully considered the best interests of his constituents, and most of his positions were ones she agreed with.

When he mentioned that he represented Dunwich, Clarissa saw her opening. Dunwich was well-known as a rotten borough with so few voters that it was easily bought and sold.

She gave him a teasing look. "Dunwich? Really?"

He laughed, taking her comment in stride. "I know what you're thinking. Yes, I'm that horrible fellow."

Clarissa lowered her voice and tried to make her expression wry, even though her heart was pounding. "Is it not awkward for you to be in the same room with Mr. Baxter, the great champion of parliamentary reform?"

He took a sip of his wine. "It was my father's idea, buying me the Dunwich seat. I hadn't thought to stand for Parliament, but that was the career he set out for me. I've taken to it more than I thought, and I've tried to do a decent job. But privately, I agree with Baxter, and if he manages to get his bill up for a vote, I plan on supporting it."

Clarissa gave him an incredulous look. "You would vote yourself out of office?"

He inclined his head, seeming unperturbed. "Quite possibly. My father would be furious. Although, who knows —I think I've acquitted myself better than a lot of the men in Parliament. Perhaps I could win an election on my own merits. And if I can't"—he shrugged—"then I suppose I don't deserve to be there after all."

"My gracious, Mr. Garroway—what a noble sentiment! Not at all what I was expecting from the representative from *Dunwich*."

He leaned in close. "I pray you won't tell anyone. It would quite ruin my reputation."

The conversation moved on. By the end of the evening, Clarissa had not struck Mr. Garroway from her list of suspects entirely. There was always the possibility that he was lying.

But her instincts told her that he was sincere. She would still keep an eye on him.

But it was time to shift her focus to the next name on her list.

CHAPTER 9

The following morning, Rosalind Baxter exited the breakfast room just as Clarissa was about to enter it.

"Mrs. Baxter," Clarissa said, stepping into her path, "I apologize for the imposition, but could I speak with you and your husband privately? The situation is urgent."

Comprehension flared in Mrs. Baxter's eyes. "My husband was just finishing his coffee. I will bring him to you. Where shall we meet?"

"The orangery," Clarissa said quickly. "I doubt anyone will be in there this time of the morning."

Mrs. Baxter nodded tightly, and Clarissa headed for the back gardens.

The orangery was a lovely building set on a picturesque rise on the far side of the garden. Its architectural style echoed that of the castle, with faux towers on the corners and crenellations on the roof. A covered walkway connected it to the main castle, and Clarissa was grateful that it did, as eight inches of snow had fallen overnight, and she was wearing a pair of slippers borrowed from Lady Emily rather than her own sturdy half boots.

Even after so short a walk, stepping into the warmth of the orangery was a relief. A quick lap around the building confirmed it was deserted. She was just admiring the sweet scent of a lemon tree in bloom when she heard the glass door swing open.

Clarissa hurried over. "Mrs. Baxter, Mr. Baxter, thank you for taking the time to speak with me. I have news for you from Bow Street and the Home Office."

She led them to a cluster of chairs beneath the glass dome at the center of the orangery's ceiling. Once everyone was settled, she handed Mr. Baxter the letter from Sir Henry. Mrs. Baxter leaned in, reading over her husband's shoulder.

"I knew it!" Mrs. Baxter exclaimed. "Did I not tell you that—"

"*Hush*, Rosalind," he said, holding his hand palm out. "Let me read."

Mrs. Baxter quieted but shifted anxiously in her seat as they finished reading the letter.

"Well," Mr. Baxter said once he was done, "that certainly is concerning. Arsenic in the soup! That suggests that whoever is behind this managed to infiltrate our household."

Mrs. Baxter wrung her gloved hands. "All of the servants have been with us for years. I can't believe it would be any of them. Do you think it could be someone at the butcher's shop, or perhaps the greengrocer—"

"That is one point of comfort," Mr. Baxter said, bowling over his wife. "That whoever is behind this, they remained in London."

"But how can we be sure?" Mrs. Baxter asked.

"Well, the only servants we brought up with us are your maid and my valet. Surely you don't think it was Lydia or Pritchard?"

"Gracious, no!" Mrs. Baxter cried. "They are the last two I would ever suspect. But—"

He held out a palm. "No buts, darling. You've been so anxious about this situation, and I must now admit that there seems to be something to your concerns. But we're safe here. I want you to rest and enjoy the Christmas season."

Mrs. Baxter fell silent, but she did not look comforted.

Mr. Baxter was studying Clarissa. "Say, how did a young lady such as yourself come to be the bearer of such a missive?"

"The Home Office employs me to perform certain sensitive tasks. I trust that you will both keep that in absolute confidence. I will also be endeavoring to keep you safe, Mr. Baxter, for the duration of the house party."

Mr. Baxter smirked, seeming to find her offer more amusing than anything else, but before he could say anything, his wife leaned forward. "Are you truly an agent for the Home Office?"

"I am," Clarissa said firmly. There was no need to mention what a short duration she had been employed in this capacity. Not when Mrs. Baxter was so clearly nervous.

"That is such a relief," Mrs. Baxter breathed. "There are a few things I've thought of since I spoke with Bow Street. Details that did not strike me as being important until after the fact. Firstly—"

"Darling," Mr. Baxter said, "let's not trouble Miss Weatherby with your ruminations."

"No, truly, I would like to hear them," Clarissa said. "You never know which detail might turn out to be significant."

Mr. Baxter laughed. "Trust me when I say, not these details."

Mrs. Baxter flushed. "But—"

"Run along to the house, darling," Mr. Baxter said. When his wife opened her mouth to protest, he added, *"Now."*

Mrs. Baxter's eyes were fixed on the floor as she rose from her seat and headed for the orangery's exit.

Her husband stood as well. "I apologize for my wife, Miss Weatherby. She is hysterical."

She had not struck Clarissa as hysterical. And, even if she were, some degree of nerves seemed natural, given the circumstances.

But she did not wish to alienate the man she was charged with guarding. "That is quite all right. I will speak with Mrs. Baxter privately and—"

"There's no need," he said crisply. "As I said, the threat remains in London. We will have a nice respite here in Yorkshire, and when we return home, I'm sure the Home Office will be able to assign an officer who is a little bit more"—his lips twisted upward, but not in a nice way—"seasoned."

Clarissa knew well enough what that meant. The truth was, she wasn't seasoned. She'd only had time for a month of training before necessity had thrust her onto the road alone.

But Oliver Baxter did not know that, and she would have bet her favorite brown ballgown that what he really meant was that she was a woman.

A month ago, Clarissa would have told him off. She'd spent the past two years feeling bitter, convinced the whole world was pitted against her, and it had made her temper short.

But now, Oliver Baxter was one irksome man, not one of the legions she believed to be arrayed against her.

That made it easier to exercise some patience for once in her life.

"As you prefer, Mr. Baxter. I will remain vigilant and inform you of any new developments. It would be better if we were not seen returning together." She gestured toward the door. "Please, go ahead, and I will follow in a few minutes."

She waited for five minutes, then hugged her arms to her chest as she stepped outside. As she walked along the covered gallery, she admired the lovely scene of the snowy garden with the castle in the background. A hedge maze occupied the central part of the garden, and the recent snowfall made it look like a frosted confection.

Mrs. Baxter had gone down into the garden and was pacing back and forth along the graveled path closest to the castle. Her posture was stiff and her head angled down. She looked nervous, even from this distance.

A cluster of snow falling from the roof above Mrs. Baxter caught Clarissa's eye. Looking up, she could just make out a black-clad figure moving around behind the crenellated wall —a servant, perhaps, checking to see how the roof was holding up after the heavy snowfall?

Mr. Baxter suddenly burst into this scene, jogging down the six steps that led from the covered walkway down into the gardens. He strode briskly down the path, looking intent upon retrieving his wife.

That was when Clarissa heard it—a scraping sound of stone upon stone. Her eyes flew to the roof. A large stone disrupted the crenellations' even spacing, the same type used to construct the castle. Someone had hefted it up onto the battlement wall. She could just make out the black-clad figure standing behind it.

Clarissa realized what was about to happen an instant before there came a second creak of stone upon stone. The black-clad figure had positioned themselves just above the spot where Mrs. Baxter was pacing.

Where her husband would be standing in mere seconds.

"Look out!" Clarissa cried, her voice stark in the empty

garden. She broke into a run. "Above you! Move back, move back!"

Her heart in her throat, Clarissa sprinted along the covered gallery, wondering if she was too late.

CHAPTER 10

Considering the volume of brandy he had drunk the night before, Rupert was feeling remarkably sprightly. But, of course, that was why Sir Henry had recruited him—because he could imbibe incredible amounts of alcohol without becoming foxed and because he remembered deuced near every word someone told him.

His target had been Mr. Ulysses F. Humphrey, one of the suspects Sir Henry had asked him to keep an eye on. Chap owned a big sugar cane plantation on Antigua run by slaves —not the sort of fellow Rupert would normally choose to chum around with, but this wouldn't be the first time he'd had to feign a liking for a rotten egg. All part of the job and whatnot.

After dinner, some of the men had retreated to Lord Helmsley's study. Rupert had put on his usual show— draining his glass, matching everyone at the table drink for drink, slurring his words and acting a lot more groggified than he actually was. After about an hour of this performance, he had collapsed into the chair next to Humphrey and poured them both a double.

"So, Humpy," he began, then frowned, staring across the room. "That's not right. It's Humpo… Humplee… Say, you don't mind if I call you Humpy, do you?"

Humphrey, who was already several cups into it, had laughed. "Not at all, Dupree. Not at all."

This was Sir Henry's number one rule for success as a spy: you had to be the last person anyone would ever suspect. And the dumber and drunker Rupert acted, the less likely it was to occur to anyone that maybe they shouldn't go spilling their deepest, darkest secrets.

Rupert and his new mate "Humpy" had drunk another half a bottle, by which time Humphrey had related his whole life story. By the time he got around to his decision to buy the plantation in Antigua, Rupert had the opening he needed.

"I say!" he exclaimed, trying to look alarmed on Humphrey's behalf. "It's not awkward for you, being here with"—he dropped his voice low and cut his eyes to Baxter, who was sitting across the room—"*you know.*"

"Who, Baxter?" Humphrey slurred. "What makes you s-say that?"

"Well, isn't he what you call one of those abominable… No, not abominable… aboriginal…" Rupert shook his head. "That's not it either. Ab… Ab… abracadabra?" He peered at Humphrey, crossing his eyes ever so slightly. "What's the term again?"

"Abolitionists," Humphrey supplied.

"Abolitionists!" Rupert said, pumping his fist so hard he lilted to the side. "That's the one. I mean, if Baxter has his way, he'd cleave you from your living with one fell stroke." He shook his head as if in sympathy. "*Deuced* unsporting of him."

Humphrey laughed. "I don't waste one minute worrying about that. It'll never happen."

"You don't think?" Rupert asked, refilling their glasses.

"Not a chance." At this point, Humphrey launched into a bunch of drivel about white people being 'the superior race' and black people being 'brutes' with 'inferior minds.'

Bollocks. Rupert had friends who were black, and they were a darn sight more intelligent than he was.

But even if Humphrey were right, it wouldn't matter. There were more important things than being clever, and just because you weren't clever didn't mean you deserved to be treated like rubbish.

Rupert should know. He wasn't clever, after all. But at least he wasn't a terrible person, like Ulysses F. Humphrey.

Not that Rupert said any of this. He had a job to do. So, he made surprised noises as if Humphrey were enlightening him to something other than the fact that he was a toad, and when it was clear Humphrey wasn't going to say anything new, Rupert made a great show of yawning and sliding halfway off his chair. Humphrey called for a pair of footmen to carry him up to his rooms, and Rupert was rid of him at last.

Now, as he jogged down the stairs to get some breakfast, he reviewed everything Humphrey had said last night. Not that Rupert ever cleared someone from suspicion unless the evidence was ironclad.

But he very much doubted that Humphrey was the assassin. He didn't seem to consider Baxter a threat. Of course, Humphrey might have been lying about that.

But Rupert had got him as drunk as a wheelbarrow. And when a fellow was that drunk, he tended to say what he really meant, whether it was good, bad, or ugly.

The next order of business was to look in on the Baxters. Rupert hadn't bothered to inform them that he was an agent. He'd learned the hard way that no one ever believed him. And really, why would they? Rupert Dupree, one of the stupidest fellows in all of England, a special operative for the

Home Office? The very notion was preposterous. More than one person had suggested he was having delusions of grandeur.

Still, he needed to identify the other agent for the Home Office. In extreme circumstances, Rupert would scratch out a note for Sir Henry himself. But given the abysmal state of his handwriting, he usually worked with a partner who would take care of reporting back to headquarters. Much better all-around that way, and Sir Henry had said he would be sending someone.

Now, Rupert just needed to find them.

Peeking inside the breakfast room, Rupert saw that the Baxters weren't there. He cheerfully asked the footman posted in the hall if they'd been down to breakfast yet and was informed that both Mr. and Mrs. Baxter had stepped outside for a turn about the gardens.

Rupert headed for a parlor with a nice view out the back of the castle. He spotted Mrs. Baxter easily enough, as she was pacing back and forth just outside his window. She was wringing her hands, and her face was a portrait of misery, which made Rupert wonder if something of a distressing nature had occurred.

Just then, Mr. Baxter came jogging into the scene. Unlike his wife, who looked distraught, Mr. Baxter merely looked annoyed. Rupert watched him grab his wife's arm and try to drag her inside the house.

From across the garden, a woman's voice shouted, "Look out! Above you! Move back, move back!"

Rupert sprinted for the door. As he flung it open, there was a heavy thump, and a spray of snow flew into the air. Rupert saw that it was a large carved stone of the same sort from which the castle was built. From the look of things, it had fallen from above, and it had only missed the Baxters by about two feet.

Clarissa Weatherby came sprinting down the stairs from the covered walkway that led to the orangery. She seized Mrs. Baxter's elbow. "Get inside. Hurry!"

That got Rupert's attention. He would've expected her to say, "Good heavens, what was that?" and perhaps fly into a panic, as Mrs. Baxter was doing.

But, unless Rupert was very much mistaken, the assassination attempt had not come as a surprise.

Clarissa Weatherby had been expecting it.

Rupert wondered if *she* was the agent Sir Henry had dispatched.

It made a certain amount of sense. Rupert had never worked with a female agent before. But Clarissa was terribly clever, and she had an undaunted quality about her. Rupert could only imagine that she was fantastic at her job.

Speaking of the job at hand, Rupert hurried over. "I say, did that stone just fall?"

"It did!" Mrs. Baxter cried. "Someone is trying to kill us!"

"Now, darling," her husband said, sounding annoyed, "don't be irrational. It was probably just a bit of loose masonry."

Rupert didn't know if Baxter really believed that, or if he was just making an excuse because he didn't realize that Rupert worked for the Home Office.

Clarissa took charge. "Mr. Baxter, please escort your wife inside. I will check the roof and see what might have occurred."

Now Rupert was sure Clarissa was his partner on this mission. Because there was no earthly reason for a guest at a house party to go up on the castle's roof to evaluate its structural integrity. A guest would have alerted Lord Helmsley, who would have sent a servant up to have a look.

"I'll go with you," Rupert offered. She was his partner,

even if she didn't know it yet, and he obviously couldn't let her go up on the roof to confront the murderer alone.

"Thank you, Mr. Dupree, but that will not be necessary," she said crisply, already striding toward the back door.

"I insist," he said, dogging her steps.

"There is no reason for you to go up on the roof."

He snorted. "I have about as much reason to inspect the roof as you do."

She peered over her shoulder at him, eyes narrow and flinty.

"Listen, Clarissa—"

She jerked to a halt. "What did you just call me?"

"Sorry. Miss Weatherby."

"Now, Mr. Dupree, *if* you will excuse me—"

Rupert grabbed her elbow. "You're heading the wrong way, you know."

She glanced about, startled. "I'm… what?"

He steered her toward the northwest corner of the house, as the servants' stairs back there were the only ones that went all the way to the roof. "See? You need me. I've been coming here for years, after all."

She bristled but didn't protest, although he could tell that it irked her.

He opened the door to the correct stairway and held it for her. "Thank you, Mr. Dupree." She stepped in front of him, blocking his way. "I can handle things from here."

"Not a chance," he said cheerfully, slipping under her arm and taking the stairs two at a time. He wanted to be in front. The murderer might still be up there and, in the event that they had a gun, he didn't like the idea of Clarissa being the first one through the door.

Clarissa ran after him, staying right on his heels. "Why are you so determined to accompany me, anyway?"

He slowed. He probably ought to tell her that he was

working for Sir Henry, too. The operation would be easier if they could coordinate. "Because I'm—"

"Oh!" A startled cry came from the landing above them. Rupert glanced up and saw a maid bearing an armful of clean sheets. "I'm sorry, sir, miss. I didn't realize, er…"

Naturally, the maid would be surprised to find two invited guests using the servants' stairs. "Don't mind us," he said to the maid, stepping to the side. "We'll be out of your way in a trice."

Once the maid had passed, Rupert resumed his progress up the stairs. He took the steps two at a time, but Clarissa ran so she could keep up. "What were you going to say? About why you're bound and determined to go with me to the roof?"

"Because I'm also—"

"Mr. Dupree?" Rupert glanced over to see James, one of the de Roos family's footmen, silhouetted in the doorway to the second-floor corridor.

Son of a biscuit, these stairs weren't nearly as private as Rupert had hoped. Probably not the best place to have a conversation about his top-secret mission for the Home Office and whatnot.

James's expression was solicitous. "Did you get turned around, sir?"

Rupert decided it was best not to answer that question. "James, I'm glad you're here. Rosalind Baxter just had a tremendous fright. Go and fetch Lady Helmsley and bring her to the back gardens post-haste."

James snapped to attention. "Right away, sir!"

While he was busy with James, Clarissa managed to slip around him. Rupert ran to catch up.

Once she noticed him on her heels, she cast him a ferocious scowl. "Why do you not head to the back gardens as well? I'm sure you would be a great comfort to Lady Helmsley."

"Because I am"—Rupert cut himself off as another startled maid came down the stairs—"a gentleman," he improvised, "and a gentleman would not allow you to walk into a dangerous situation alone."

She tossed her head. "It's just a roof, Mr. Dupree. Not particularly dangerous."

"Not under normal circumstances, no. But it's bound to be icy up there, and it appears it might be a bit crumbly, too. I'm afraid you'll just have to tolerate my company."

She huffed but did not argue.

They had reached the top of the corner tower that concealed the door to the roof. Putting on a burst of speed, Rupert passed Clarissa on the outside, ignoring her cries of protest.

As he pulled open the door, he made a point of squaring off his shoulders so she couldn't slip around him, but there was no need. The roof, which was wide and flat, was deserted.

But there were footprints in the snow, quite a lot of them. And wouldn't you know it, they led to the stretch of wall just above where the Baxters had been standing when that rock came down.

He let down his guard as soon as he saw the murderer wasn't about, and Clarissa seized the opportunity to slip under his arm. She followed the path of the footprints to the stretch of wall from which the rock had fallen, trampling much of the evidence in the process.

Rupert managed to find a few of the original footprints a little way off to the side. He bent over to inspect them. They were smaller than he'd been expecting. He pressed his own booted foot into the snow next to one, then removed it. The assassin's footprints were a good inch shorter than his own, and narrower as well. He would guess they belonged to a small man or perhaps a woman.

Shaking himself, he hurried over to the crenelated wall Clarissa was inspecting. "Find anything over here?"

Her eyes shot to him, wary. "Nothing much. I don't see any missing stones. Do you?"

Rupert did not. He did, however, notice a nice, thick stripe on top of the battlements where the snow had been scraped clear. It was obviously the spot where someone had pushed the stone over the edge. Leaning forward, he saw that, sure enough, the stone had settled just below.

"It looks like someone pushed it from here."

"Pushed it?" Clarissa gave a forced laugh. "Good heavens, why would someone do that?"

Oh, right—he hadn't told her yet. "There's no need to pretend. You see, I'm—"

"Miss Weatherby?"

Rupert turned and saw Lord Helmsley standing in the doorway to the servants' stairs, blinking at the bright sunlight reflecting off the snow.

"I happened upon Mr. and Mrs. Baxter," the earl explained. His eyes widened as he noticed Rupert's presence. "They said there had been an, uh… an accident."

"An accident," Clarissa said. "Precisely. It looks like you have some repairs planned, my lord?" She gestured to a stack of cut grey stones neatly stacked in the corner.

"Ah—yes. Yes, we do."

Clarissa hugged her arms across her chest. "It would appear that the mason left one of the stones stacked perilously close to the edge."

Between the fresh set of footprints leading from the stack of stones to the wall and the fact that all the stones were covered in a thick layer of snow save for one spot on top, where a stone had clearly been removed, even Rupert wasn't dim enough to fall for that story.

But he hadn't told Lord Helmsley the real reason he was attending his house party, nor was he prepared to. Rupert therefore shook his head. "That was deuced careless of him, wasn't it?"

"It certainly was!" Clarissa agreed a little too ardently. "But I do not see any more stones stacked in a similar fashion, so I think we can conclude that the danger has passed."

"Good to know." Lord Helmsley peered at Rupert as if wanting to make sure he had fallen for this whopper.

Rupert made a point of smiling vacantly across the roof.

The earl nodded. "Come, Miss Weatherby, let us go and reassure Mr. and Mrs. Baxter on that account."

"I'm sure they'll appreciate that," Rupert said. "Well, I suppose I'll go and have some breakfast."

"An excellent idea!" Clarissa cried. "Please, don't let us delay your meal."

Rupert let them make their escape. He would find a chance to have a little chat with Clarissa at the first opportunity, and they could coordinate their activities.

On the one hand, it would be nice to have a partner, especially a clever thing like Clarissa.

On the other hand, it appeared that danger had followed the Baxters to Helmsley Castle, making their task significantly more challenging.

His thoughts aswirl, Rupert trotted down the stairs.

CHAPTER 11

Clarissa gathered with the Baxters and Lord and Lady Helmsley in the sitting room of Mr. and Mrs. Baxter's suite.

After Clarissa related what she had observed from her vantage point at the orangery, as well as what she had found on the roof, she said, "I think it is reasonable to conclude that whatever threat you faced in London, it has followed you here. We must take precautions."

"I think we should leave," Mrs. Baxter said.

"To what end?" her husband replied, pushing up from the sofa in frustration. He stalked across the room and leaned a hand on the mantelpiece. "If they've followed us here, what's to stop them from following us again?"

"Perhaps if you were to depart in the dead of night—" Lady Helmsley began.

"In this weather, we'll be just as likely to slide off the road to our death." Mr. Baxter curled his hand into a fist. "Where will we be safer than inside a castle?"

Clarissa considered. There were risks to both approaches,

but the castle did have certain advantages. "Perhaps if you were to feign being sick and confine yourselves to your rooms. We could have the room guarded under the guise of a footman posted in the corridor to wait on you and make sure that only the most trusted servants have access to your food—"

Mr. Baxter wheeled around. "And if we do, the threat will simply follow us when we leave. Are we to be forever hounded, never able to relax in our own home?"

"What would you suggest?" Clarissa asked tightly.

"Draw them out," Mr. Baxter said. "This so-called assassin seems to be a bumbling sort of fellow. None of his attempts have worked thus far. The risk is surely not so great, and with you on the case, Miss Weatherby"—he said this with a mocking sort of deference—"I am sure their identity will soon be discovered."

Lady Helmsley went to sit beside her niece. "I don't like it. That rock almost struck Rosalind! If you want to parade about in hopes that they will make a mistake, that is your prerogative. But I will brook no threat to my niece."

Clarissa knelt so she was at eye level with Mrs. Baxter. "What would you prefer?"

She met Clarissa's eyes as hesitantly as a startled fawn. "I think it is a good suggestion. To feign illness. I would prefer that we both do it. But if Oliver is not willing to keep to our rooms, I will do so myself."

"Very well." Clarissa rose to her feet. "I will continue to investigate. And I know that my contact at the Home Office is sending additional officers to assist in your protection, sir. One of his very best agents is already en route."

Mr. Baxter brightened visibly. "That is good news! Let us see if this new agent can effect any developments in the investigation."

Clarissa had half a mind to throw the little porcelain sculpture of a shepherdess adorning the end table at his head. As if she had not proven her mettle that very morning by saving his worthless hide!

Lord Helmsley cleared his throat. "One of the other guests saw the stone fall. Mr. Rupert Dupree happened to be looking out the window at the gardens. He was very concerned and even followed Miss Weatherby onto the roof."

Clarissa nodded. Gossip about the falling stone would no doubt spread through the house party guests like wildfire. "We will, therefore, need an explanation for the other guests. I think we should maintain the story we discussed on the roof—that the mason was doing some repairs and left a stone stacked precariously close to the edge."

Lord Helmsley nodded. "Rupert did seem to buy that explanation."

Mr. Baxter snorted. "Rupert Dupree would buy *any* explanation. Fairies. Unicorns. A tiny earthquake that affected only the roof."

Clarissa frowned. While Mr. Baxter was not wrong that Rupert wasn't what you would call an intellectual, she disliked hearing him mocked in this manner. Even Clarissa, who had good reason to hate him, had to admit that Rupert Dupree had a number of fine qualities.

Meanwhile, for all that Oliver Baxter was an ardent supporter of some of Clarissa's most cherished political causes, she found him condescending and short-tempered, especially toward his wife. She couldn't believe she was thinking this, but she quite preferred Rupert.

But it wouldn't do to insult the person she was charged with protecting. "We have our plan." Clarissa curtseyed to Lady Helmsley. "If you will excuse me, there is much to be done."

As she made her way downstairs, Clarissa found herself hoping that the outstanding agent Sir Henry had dispatched would arrive soon. She was no longer wondering if she was in over her head; she knew she was, without question.

CHAPTER 12

*C*larissa did her best to plaster a smile on her face as she entered the breakfast room. Her stomach might be churning with anxiety about the fact that the murderer had followed Oliver Baxter from London. But as far as the world needed to know, her only concern was finding a soft-boiled egg and a strong cup of tea.

She stepped up to the overflowing sideboard, where Rosalind Baxter's cousin, Miss Phyllis Cuthbert, was filling a plate. Clarissa couldn't help but notice her slate-grey dress. It was loose-fitting with an unfashionably high neckline, buttoning all the way up the hollow of her throat, and Miss Cuthbert had tucked a fichu around her neck for good measure.

Clarissa felt a pang of envy. It wasn't brown, but grey was the next best thing. If only she could have somehow contrived to borrow gowns from Miss Cuthbert until her trunks arrived! Instead, she was stuck wearing a fashionable white muslin morning dress topped with a jade-green spencer, these being the least conspicuous items Lady Emily had left for her.

Miss Cuthbert gave Clarissa a little smile. "I hope you will forgive me for being overly bold, but could we sit together at breakfast? I have been looking forward to meeting the famous Clarissa Weatherby."

Clarissa gave a startled laugh. "I don't know that famous is the word that applies."

"Oh, but it is! You are the most famous wallflower in all of Britain."

The words were said enthusiastically, but Miss Cuthbert's face immediately fell. "Oh, dear—that didn't come out right. I did not mean for it to sound like an insult!"

"Please," Clarissa said, helping herself to a slice of toast, "do not distress yourself. I wear that title as a badge of honor. All my sisters do, in fact. We call ourselves the Weatherby Wallflowers with pride."

Miss Cuthbert smiled. "I knew you would understand! You see, I am a wallflower, too. And as soon as I heard you were also a guest of Lord and Lady Helmsley, I knew at once that we were going to be great friends."

Clarissa thought that a bit forward, but she was careful not to let her discomfiture show on her face. These past few years, she had grown accustomed to going through life with her guard up. But everyone at Lord and Lady Helmsley's house party had been tremendously kind to her thus far— save perhaps for the man she was there to protect.

She needed to learn to lower her defenses a trifle rather than assume that every person she met had ulterior motives.

An ironic statement, considering she was on the hunt for a would-be murderer!

But Clarissa forced herself to smile blandly at her self-proclaimed friend. "How lovely. Shall we sit?"

As they settled into a pair of chairs at the far end of the table, Miss Cuthbert said, "We are going to be two peas in a pod, Miss Weatherby. I just know we are! Because you know how it feels to be a wallflower, to have the world look right past you."

Clarissa studied Miss Cuthbert's beaming face. In spite of her dowdy gown and the severe bun she had pulled her dark hair into, she was remarkably pretty, with balanced features, a beautiful complexion, and fine blue eyes.

"What is it?" Miss Cuthbert asked, causing Clarissa to realize she had been staring.

"I'm sorry, I'm just having trouble imagining anyone looking past you. You are a remarkably beautiful woman."

Miss Cuthbert shrugged. "The same could be said about you. But, as I'm sure you know, if a woman is not in possession of a good fortune, looks alone are not sufficient to secure her an admirer." She laughed darkly. "At least, not one who wishes for a respectable alliance."

Clarissa did understand that all too well. She hadn't attracted many beaux back when she'd had no dowry and a threadbare wardrobe. Only Rupert Dupree, who had promptly jilted her.

At least… she thought he had. Clarissa glanced at the far end of the table, where Rupert was chatting away with their hosts' son, Lawrence. By all appearances, it was a jovial conversation. And it had been gallant of him to accompany her onto the roof, even if he had only been in the way.

In truth, Clarissa wasn't sure what to think about Rupert Dupree anymore.

Clarissa offered Miss Cuthbert a sympathetic smile. "I remember all too well what that was like."

Teacup halfway to her mouth, Miss Cuthbert gave her a curious look. "Remember? What do you mean, remember?"

Clarissa began buttering her toast. "Oh, I'm sorry. I thought it was common knowledge. My elder sister, Eleanor, married the Duke of Norwood two months ago. This brought about a sea change in our financial fortunes."

Miss Cuthbert gestured to Clarissa's gown. "You clearly got a new wardrobe."

"This gown is actually borrowed from Lady Emily." Clarissa nodded at her host's daughter, who beamed at her from a few seats down. "My trunk has gone astray, and she was kind enough to lend me these lovely things. But you are correct—the duke was generous enough to purchase new clothes for me and my sisters." Having finished spreading the butter, Clarissa took up the pot of marmalade. "But he did more than that—he has insisted upon dowering the three of us."

Clarissa's dining companion from last night, Lady Ashington, looked up from her tea. "Did I hear that correctly? Norwood has dowered you, my dear?"

"He has," Clarissa confirmed.

"How much?" the marchioness asked, getting straight to the point.

Clarissa swallowed, conscious that the room had fallen silent as everyone strained to hear the latest *on dit*. "We each have twenty thousand pounds—"

"Twenty thousand!" Lady Ashington exclaimed. "That is a very respectable portion. Very respectable indeed."

"I am extremely grateful for His Grace's generosity," Clarissa began.

Lady Ashington did not seem to be attending. "With your looks and your new connections, there is no reason you should not make a splendid match. No reason in the world."

"Oh!" Clarissa shifted in her seat. "I honestly haven't thought much about marrying."

"Well, you're going to think about it now," Lady Ashington said. "I am going to take you under my wing. Let's see, who is looking to marry next year?"

"What about the Earl of Feltham?" Lady Emily asked.

"Lord Feltham is an excellent suggestion," Lady Ashington said. "He is young, rich, handsome…"

Clarissa could not believe this was happening. She had never considered herself as the potential bride to an earl, not once in her life!

She attempted to infuse her voice with good humor. "If Lord Feltham is such a good match, perhaps you should set your cap for him, Lady Emily."

Lady Emily screwed up her pretty face. "Oh, no—Stuart is practically a brother to me. I could never see him that way."

"There is also Viscount Burlton," Lady Ashington noted. "Not quite as handsome as Feltham, but he has all his teeth. And he's bookish. I fancy you would prefer a husband who is a bit bookish, would you not, Miss Weatherby?"

"I… I honestly haven't given it a moment's thought," Clarissa admitted. "I had assumed I would never marry, after…" She cleared her throat, conscious that Rupert Dupree, like everyone else at the table, was listening. "You know."

"Of course, dear. Of course," Lady Ashington said. "That is why you need me to guide you. Let's see, Lord Feltham, Lord Burlton… I should really get some paper and write these down."

"That is an excellent suggestion!" Lady Emily exclaimed. "Have you finished your breakfast, my lady? Perhaps we could repair to the morning room to make a proper list."

"As much as I appreciate the kind gesture," Clarissa protested, "it is truly not necessary."

Giving no sign that they were listening, Lady Ashington and Lady Emily rose from their seats. "Do you recall the name of that young diplomat?" Lady Ashington asked. "The extremely handsome one who recently returned from Denmark."

Lady Emily brightened. "Do you mean Mr. Anthony

Bainbridge? That is an excellent suggestion. I can picture Miss Weatherby as the wife of a diplomat."

"As can I," Lady Ashington murmured. "Do you speak any languages, child?"

"A few. I know French, Spanish, High German, Russian—"

"Russian!" Lady Emily cried, clasping her hands.

The marchioness's expression was smug. "I knew she had the making of a diplomat's wife." She placed her hand on Lady Emily's shoulder, guiding her toward the door. "We shall put Mr. Bainbridge's name at the top of the list."

"Please," Clarissa called, "don't get carried"—she watched as they strode through the door, heads bent together, not heeding a word she said—"away."

Attempting a self-deprecating laugh, Clarissa turned to Miss Cuthbert. "Oh, dear. I suppose that ship has already sailed."

She found Miss Cuthbert's pretty face creased into a scowl.

"Is anything the matter?" Clarissa asked, puzzled.

Miss Cuthbert's voice was snide. "How nice for you, Miss Weatherby, to have so materially improved your station in life." She snatched the pot of marmalade and began smearing it on her toast, using enough force that she tore a hole in the bread. "Perhaps we do not understand each other as well as I had hoped."

Clarissa bit back a sharp retort. Just what she needed— the sort of "friend" who resented you your good fortune.

Still, she was working on turning over a new leaf. Her new job for the Home Office required her to blend in, which meant being agreeable.

Clarissa, therefore, answered in a gentle tone. "I remember very well what it felt like to be the most ridiculed woman in all of Britain. Although my fortunes have changed for the better, I hope you do not think me unsympathetic."

"Oh." Miss Cuthbert glanced up, her eyes rueful. "My apologies, Miss Weatherby. I must own that I am jealous. I had a suitor once, but he could not afford to marry a woman without a dowry. I fancy that if I had been in possession of a respectable portion, my life might look very different from what it is today."

"Perhaps your beau might be able to earn his fortune and marry you someday."

Miss Cuthbert looked down at her plate. "Alas, that will never happen. He needed the capital a well-dowered wife would bring in order to make a start in his career. So, he married someone else."

"Oh. I am so sorry."

Miss Cuthbert glanced up, giving Clarissa a smile that did not reach her eyes. "As am I, Miss Weatherby. As am I."

The conversation moved on. By the end of breakfast, Clarissa still did not know quite what to make of her new acquaintance.

CHAPTER 13

$\mathcal{R}$upert spent the next four days doing his best imitation of Oliver Baxter's shadow.

Rupert wasn't much for stalking, but Baxter was, so Rupert borrowed one of Lord Helmsley's guns and put on a cheerful face as he wandered through the snow pretending to look for deer.

The good news was that there were no additional attempts on Baxter's life. It was enough to make Rupert wonder if he hadn't dreamed the whole thing up.

But the bad news was, Rupert couldn't seem to find so much as a minute to confer with Clarissa Weatherby. He needed to let her know that they were partners, but he needed to do it in private, and private conversations with Clarissa were suddenly hard to come by. Now that word was out that she was something of an heiress, the party guests who were of the single male persuasion were buzzing around her like flies.

Richard Garroway was particularly persistent. He was on the list of suspects Sir Henry had discussed with Rupert, so he assumed Clarissa was also aware of him. Rupert had noticed him flirting with her during their first dinner at Helmsley Castle, the one where Clarissa had worn that stunner of a red dress. But now that he knew she was plump in the pocket, he seemed to be pursuing her seriously.

Rupert wanted to protest that *he* had wanted to marry Clarissa Weatherby long before she was wealthy and well-dressed. But it didn't matter. She hadn't wanted to marry him then and she gave no sign of wanting anything to do with him now.

He was here to do a job, and he meant to do it well. His work for the Home Office had given him direction at the lowest moment of his life.

At the time he had been recruited by Sir Henry, his Aunt Imogen had been dead for two months, and Clarissa had just rejected their proposed union. He'd been on the road back to London and had stopped at an inn in Olney for the night. He had been alone, adrift, and feeling rather lousy about himself.

He had been sitting at one of the long tables in the common room of the Bull Hotel, attempting to drown his sorrows in a dozen or so pints, when a familiar face strode into the room. It was Godfrey Marsden, who'd been a couple of years ahead of him at school.

Rupert would normally have stood and offered a greeting, even though Godfrey wasn't what you would call an old chum. He hadn't been friends with Rupert's brother, but he seemed to share Francis's opinion that Rupert was worthless. Still, as a general rule, Rupert tried to do the right thing and observe the social niceties. But on that particular night, he was feeling so low that he couldn't bear the prospect of a conversation with a man who would more than likely sneer at him.

And so, Rupert did something he'd never done before—he gave an exaggerated yawn, stretched out across the table, and pretended to fall asleep.

It was a good thing Rupert had feigned sleep because Godfrey sat right next to him! After a few minutes, he felt someone prod him in the shoulder.

He responded with a snore.

He must've done a convincing job of it because Godfrey spoke to the man who'd been sitting diagonally across from Rupert for most of the night. "I have information for you."

He said it in a low voice, but as Rupert was sitting right next to him, he heard it all easily enough.

The man across the table responded in a working man's accent. "Is it worth my time?"

Godfrey chuckled. "It certainly is. But before we proceed, I want a fifty percent cut."

"Fifty?" The man sounded outraged. "I ain't paying more than five."

A round of haggling ensued, at the conclusion of which the two men agreed to a twenty percent cut to Godfrey of... whatever it was they were discussing.

"Go on then," Godfrey's companion said once negotiations had concluded. "What've ye got?"

"Lord Olney's house party concludes tomorrow," Godfrey said. "These are the carriages that will be of the most interest to you. Lady Hastings brought the Hastings emeralds with her. She and her husband will be traveling in a burgundy carriage picked out in gold. Their crest has a pair of bulls, and their servants will be dressed in dark blue livery. They'll be on the road south toward London. They're both late risers, so don't expect to see them before noon..."

Godfrey proceeded to detail every guest attending Lord and Lady Olney's house party, whether they were worth robbing or not, how to identify them, and which direction they would be headed.

Rupert knew he wasn't what you would call a clever fellow. But unless he was very much mistaken, the man who'd been sitting across from him for the better part of the night was a highwayman, and Godfrey was conspiring to help him rob a large number of people.

The prospect made him feel far queasier than the eleven pints of ale he'd consumed. Bad enough that this fellow was looking to part innocent people from their possessions. But things had a way of going wrong during a robbery. What if someone got hurt, or even killed?

Rupert could never live with himself if he just let it happen.

After they'd discussed seventeen different guests, Rupert heard the scrape of Godfrey's chair beside him. "Twenty percent. I expect it in cash."

"Yes, well, let's see if your information is any good," the highwayman countered. "Then you'll get your cash."

There was no more conversation after that. Rupert's heart was thundering like a stampede of young bucks charging toward the dance card of an heiress. Crikey! He knew he had to do something. He couldn't just stand around and let all those people get robbed! The trick was figuring out what, exactly, he should do.

He started by pretending to sleep for another hour or so. Only when he heard the scrape of the highwayman's chair, followed by a long stretch of silence, did he dare to yawn and pretend to awaken.

Rupert did the only thing he could think of. He sidled up to the bar and asked the barmaid for the name and direction of the local magistrate. She gave him a strange look but told him where to go.

That was how Rupert found himself banging on the door of Mr. Cyrus Johnson at three in the morning. Mr. Johnson was about as pleased to see him as you'd expect, but when Rupert explained the urgency of the situation, he ushered him into a parlor.

Rupert proceeded to list out the seventeen carriages that would be departing Lord and Lady Olney's residence tomorrow, which ones were going to be robbed, where, and at what time. Mr. Johnson looked baldly skeptical. "You really expect me to believe that you remembered all that? With all due respect, Mr. Dupree, you smell like you've had quite a few pints. Are you certain this conversation you overheard wasn't a dream?"

"Sorry," Rupert said, because he probably did smell like a brewery. "But yes, I'm sure. Absolutely sure." Because that was the way Rupert's brain worked. He couldn't read or write worth a darn.

But if you told him something, it stuck.

"Oh, please, Mr. Johnson," Rupert continued, "I couldn't bear it if anyone was to get hurt. The first target will be on the road north bright and early. Send a party of men out to intercept these highwaymen, and you'll see I'm telling the truth."

Mr. Johnson sighed, looking exceptionally put out.

But he sent word to the Olney estate about the possible danger. The next morning, the departing carriages were full not of rich jewels but the magistrate's hand-picked men. And more men were stationed in position to surround the highwaymen.

In the end, it happened just as Rupert had said it was going to happen. Three bands of highwaymen were arrested, as was Godfrey Marsden.

And when Rupert returned to speak with Mr. Johnson the following day, the magistrate regarded him with something resembling respect. "I would like to apologize, Mr. Dupree, for my earlier insinuation that you were making this whole thing up. Your information turned out to be accurate. Remarkably accurate." He peered at Rupert. "May I ask how you remembered all of those details?"

"I can't explain it." Rupert gave a self-deprecating smile as he tapped his temple. "The old noggin's always been this way. I guess it came in handy today."

Mr. Johnson studied Rupert for a beat. "It certainly did." He pulled out a piece of paper and began writing something down. "When you get to London, I would like for you to speak with a colleague of mine. If you are interested, I believe he may have use for your unusual talents."

Mr. Johnson slid the sheet across the desk. It looked about the right length for an address, although deuced if Rupert could read it. He'd been wound up in knots ever since he overheard Godfrey Marsden plotting highway robbery.

He made a show of patting his pockets. "Dash my wig, I seem to have forgotten my spectacles. Any chance you could read it to me?"

That was how he had come to make Sir Henry's acquaintance. As Mr. Johnson predicted, Sir Henry had use for him. He'd gone through a month of training, and then it was off to the Continent.

Working for the Home Office made Rupert feel useful. Which didn't sound like much, but prior to that, Rupert had never felt useful, not once in his life! It was heady stuff for a fellow like him.

The point was, he was here at Helmsley Castle to do a job. He wasn't looking to bother Clarissa Weatherby, even if she was everything Lady Milthorpe had promised him and more.

Whenever he finally got to speak with her, he was going to be professional.

He was already enough of a fool without making an idiot of himself over Clarissa.

~

The three days following the assassination attempt were amongst the strangest of Clarissa's life.

She was *popular*. She, Clarissa Weatherby, the most notorious wallflower in all of England, had *suitors*! A good half-dozen of them, and they hovered around her from the moment she came down to breakfast until she locked the door to her room each night. Frankly, it was inconvenient. She had a murderer to track down. She didn't have time to humor every second son in the North Riding.

Even more perplexing, most of her newfound suitors seemed convinced that the path to her heart could be forged through flowery compliments and romantic gestures. She couldn't turn around without someone presenting her with a posy of flowers collected from the hothouse or plying her with eggnog. When one man declared that he would *die* if Clarissa did not save a dance for him at the upcoming Christmas ball, she snorted out loud and only barely managed to convince him that she had something caught in her throat.

Had those men known her at all, they would have realized that they would have fared far better by making acerbic remarks or pointing out an interesting article in the newspaper. It was jarring to realize how closely her treatment was tied to her appearance. She had been thought dowdy in her dirt-colored dresses, and men had mostly ignored her. But those men who did bother to speak with her had quickly recognized her keen intelligence, which was usually not seen as a mark in her favor.

But put her in a pretty dress, and most men seemed to assume she didn't have a thought in her head beyond fashion and fripperies. It apparently did not matter what words emerged from her mouth. The same sardonic retort that before would have marked her as the worst sort of bluestocking was now glossed over with a chuckle, and the conversation would promptly revert to the same set of banal topics that were apparently of interest to most young, unmarried women.

Only Richard Garroway seemed to appreciate that Clarissa was anything other than a pretty shell. If she had thought the young M.P. was flirting with her during her first dinner at Helmsley Castle, he was really pouring on the charm now. But she did not form the impression that his heart was in any way engaged. It seemed to be more a matter of, *I have to marry someone, and you're pretty enough and come with twenty thousand pounds, so why not?*

The same applied to Clarissa's other suitors. From what she could tell, they could find uses enough for her dowry, and they certainly wouldn't mind having her in their beds. But they didn't even *see* the real her, much less love her.

Clarissa did find one advantage to her newfound appearance, and that was amongst the women. She could no longer hide on the room's fringes, but she didn't need to. She was accepted readily by the other ladies.

And so it was one afternoon, when the women had gathered in an upstairs parlor to sew and gossip, that Clarissa casually took a seat on the sofa next to Arabella Anstruther, the Dowager Duchess of Kimbolton, whom Lady Winnifred had identified as a potential suspect.

Clarissa introduced herself and pulled out the unembellished handkerchief Lady Emily had provided her. It was convenient that her trunks had been lost, so she had an excuse for not having brought any needlework. In truth, Clarissa had little patience for embroidery and possessed only a basic competence with a needle and thread.

She tried to make neat stitches for once in her life as she considered how to initiate a conversation with the duchess, but there was no need. Clarissa was the juiciest *on dit* at the house party, and the duchess was eager to have some firsthand gossip to spread when she returned to London.

"You've become quite popular, haven't you, Miss Weatherby?"

Clarissa attempted a self-deprecating smile. "I'm not sure about *quite* popular. But even having one man interested in speaking with me is more popularity than I've ever enjoyed before."

The duchess cackled. "Oh, you're popular, all right. And you'll have even more suitors come spring, should you go to London."

Clarissa shook her head. "It's all so new to me. I've never mixed in such high society." She dropped her voice low. "If it's not too forward of me, could I ask Your Grace to advise me?"

If the gleam in her eye was any indication, this request was not too forward at all. In fact, Arabella Anstruther probably would have offered her opinion whether Clarissa had requested it or not. "Don't even think of accepting any of the men sniffing around you now. Believe me, you'll be able to attract better options." She laughed. "I'm tempted to throw one of my sons across your path. Goodness knows they need sensible wives, and with your dowry and connections, they couldn't do much better. Although I suspect *you* could."

This was the opening Clarissa had been looking for. Lady Winnifred had written that the duchess's possible motive stemmed from her sons, who were reportedly having difficulty finding lucrative church livings and sinecures, thanks to Oliver Baxter's campaign that these positions should be granted based on merit rather than connections.

Clarissa tried to look interested as she made a crooked stitch. "Do you have many sons, Your Grace?"

"Eleven of them, if you can countenance it."

"Eleven!" Clarissa feigned a startled laugh, as if she had

not read this very piece of information in Lady Winnifred's note. "Are they all unmarried, then?"

"Not all of them. Joseph is married, and Charles. And William will have no trouble—he is the duke, you see. But the other eight…"

She launched into a lament about how difficult it was to see her eleven sons respectably settled. If she was hoping to convince Clarissa to take one of them on as husband, she had a curious way of showing it, for she described a variety of indecorous behaviors and spendthrift tendencies that did not render Clarissa eager to request an introduction. But Clarissa was starting to suspect that the duchess tended to be indiscreet in her conversation.

"I had been certain my cousin, Lord Draper, would award the bishopry to my third-eldest son, Cropley." The duchess shook her head. "But then, he went and granted it to some nobody, just because he had been made a Doctor of Divinity by Cambridge!"

Clarissa clucked sympathetically, but privately, she found the duchess's assumption that Lord Cropley would receive a bishopry astonishing. Had she not just complained that he had recently spent the night in gaol, having been arrested along with his friends after a drunken evening spent tipping night watchmen over in their boxes? And, gracious, if he was the third-oldest son, he must be at least thirty, meaning that this vile behavior could not be written off as a youthful folly.

He did not sound like an attractive candidate to be either a bishop or Clarissa's future husband.

But she bit her tart tongue for once in her life and said, "I had not realized it was so difficult for men of good family to find a decent living these days."

The duchess shook her head. "It didn't used to be this way. But in the past few years, there has been this furor that appointments should be made based on *merit*"—she said this last word in the same tone one might use for the word *depravity*—"and family connections are no longer worth so much as a farthing."

Clarissa very much doubted that was the case, but again, she made sympathetic sounds. "I do believe I read something about the movement you're describing. Did it not originate in political circles?"

"It did," the duchess confirmed. "It all started with Lord Liverpool, if you can countenance it. But several young whippersnappers in the House of Commons have turned it into an initiative, and now only three of my sons have any sort of living at all—and one of those 'livings' is a rectory with an income of just five hundred a year—*not* enough to live on in anything resembling a decent style. It will be even worse in five years when the last three are out of school." The duchess shook her head woefully. "It is quite a drain on the ducal estate to have to support them all."

Clarissa leaned in, dropping her voice low. "I might be misremembering, but isn't one of those young whippersnappers to whom you referred a guest at this very house party?"

She watched the duchess carefully, looking for any sign that the question made her uncomfortable.

Her expression was one of wounded dignity, but she did not hesitate to reply. "He is. Mr. Oliver Baxter. He is perhaps the most dreadful one of all. I would be quite put out with Lady Helmsley for having invited him, except I know he is married to her niece, and obviously, I cannot expect her to do without Rosalind at Christmastime." She retrieved her handkerchief and dabbed theatrically at her forehead. "Oh, but I can scarcely bear the sight of that dreadful man! Do you know what I did?"

"What?" Clarissa asked eagerly, although surely the

duchess was not about to disclose that she tried to kill him by pushing a stone off the roof.

"I heard him mention that mincemeat pies were his absolute favorite. I happened to be seated near him yesterday at teatime, and the servants came around to our table last. There were three mince pies on the platter. I asked the footman if there were any more, and he said this was the last of them." The duchess lifted her chin, eyes gleaming. "I looked him square in the face as I took all three! That showed him, don't you think?"

"It certainly did!" Clarissa cried.

The duchess prattled on for the rest of the afternoon, sharing her opinions, asked for or not, on topics ranging from the latest fashions to parliamentary reform.

Clarissa didn't *think* she seemed like a murderess. If she had designs on Oliver Baxter's life, wouldn't she have taken more pains to conceal her disdain for the man?

Unless she was lying. Clarissa didn't think she was, but it was so hard to be sure! She was still so new at this. How she wished Lady Winnifred was here, or the additional agent Sir Henry had promised was en route. She could use an experienced agent to confer with.

She had been turning the matter over in her mind, trying to determine if her fellow agent might already be in residence. It seemed likely that Sir Henry would have told them to look for Lady Winnifred, rather than herself. That would explain why no one had approached her.

The only possibility she had been able to come up with was almost too absurd to contemplate. But it seemed a bit odd that Rupert Dupree had insisted on accompanying her onto the roof when she went in search of the assassin. She could not help but observe that, while he was usually everything that was accommodating, in that instance, he had been mulishly determined to go with her.

It was a ridiculous notion. Really, Rupert Dupree!

And yet, Sir Henry had said that the man he would send had been on a lengthy assignment on the Continent. And Rupert Dupree had just returned from Switzerland. Sir Henry had also said that he would have this agent on the first carriage north. Had Rupert not told her that he had come straight through from London?

Sir Henry's words from their solitary face-to-face meeting echoed in her head. *The ideal spy is the last person anyone would ever suspect.*

Clarissa had to own that by this standard, Rupert might be the best spy in the world.

In a strange way, it fit. Still, she was unsure, and it seemed too risky to come straight out and ask him. For now, Clarissa would just have to wonder.

After another hour, the gathering concluded, and Clarissa headed up to her room, head aswirl with contradictory thoughts, feeling no closer to solving this case than she had on the day she'd begun.

CHAPTER 14

The following morning, after selecting two pieces of toast and a soft-boiled egg, Clarissa found a seat at the breakfast table, opened the *Leeds Intelligencer*, and was startled to see her own name on the front page.

RUPERT DUPREE THREATENS LEGAL ACTION, read the headline. The subheading continued, *CLAIMS HE IS NOT AUTHOR OF LETTER ABOUT CLARISSA WEATHERBY.*

Her breakfast forgotten, Clarissa lifted the paper with trembling fingers.

The Leeds Intelligencer received a letter from Mr. Rupert Dupree via his solicitor, Mr. Lawrence de Roos, claiming that he was not the author of the letter published in this paper two years ago, outlining his reasons for rejecting a proposed union between himself and Miss Clarissa Weatherby. Mr. Dupree stated that he was entirely unaware of this letter's existence until a few days ago, as he has been traveling on the Continent. He has demanded to know how this letter came to be published in the Intelligencer and other prominent newspapers under his name and has threatened to sue for defamation.

The Intelligencer is cooperating with Mr. Dupree's request for information and is reviewing the circumstances under which the letter came to be published.

"The most disturbing aspect," Mr. de Roos writes on Mr. Dupree's behalf, "is the damage done to Miss Weatherby's reputation as a result of the Intelligencer's despicable dearth of journalistic standards. Mr. Dupree holds Clarissa Weatherby and all of her sisters in the highest regard, and he is disgusted that such slanderous remarks have been attributed to his name. He will not rest until those responsible have been brought to justice."

It is our understanding that a similar letter has been sent to every paper that printed the letter attributed to Mr. Dupree. This is an ongoing case, and the Intelligencer will continue to provide updates as our investigation unfolds.

Clarissa stared at the paper, her thoughts aswirl. The article was entirely consistent with what Rupert had told her in the carriage, that he had known nothing about that letter. *I am going to make this right*, he had said.

He had certainly backed up his words with actions. The original letter had been printed in dozens of papers across the country.

Had Rupert truly threatened to sue them all?

A silver tray appeared beside her. She glanced up to see a footman. On the fringes of her vision, she saw a dozen heads hastily swivel back to face forward. Once again, she was providing the juiciest gossip to Lord and Lady Helmsley's guests.

The footman held out his tray. "A letter for you, Miss Weatherby."

She recognized the sturdy handwriting of her brother-in-law, Jasper St. James:

Dear Clarissa,

I received Rupert Dupree's letter. I am pleased to learn that the two of you have met and managed to work out your differences. I knew he couldn't have had anything to do with that nasty business in the papers. As I told Eleanor, it would have been entirely out of character.

You may tell Dupree that I will gladly join him in his suits against those miserable rags. I have a very aggressive solicitor in London and would be happy to take the lead. By the time I'm done, they will rue the day they wasted their ink printing the words 'Weatherby Wallflowers.'

Do send your sisters a letter when you get a chance. They're eager to know how you're getting on with Lady Winnifred and a bit sad about the prospect of spending Christmas without you. A word from you will cheer them immensely, and we would make both you and your mistress feel very welcome at Askwith Hall should she be willing to undertake the journey.

. . .

Warmest wishes, &c, &c,

Jasper

Clarissa blinked, realizing that her eyes had grown moist. Because that was the moment she knew her reputation would be restored. Pitiable was the fool who tried to stand between Jasper St. James and his stated goal. Jasper would stop at nothing to clear his wife's name and that of his new sisters-in-law.

No one would dare to laugh at Clarissa after this. After two years of being society's favorite object of ridicule, she couldn't quite wrap her head around it.

Just then, Rupert Dupree strolled into the breakfast room, whistling a tune.

Clarissa shot to her feet so quickly her chair scraped against the hardwood floor. It would have tipped over and fallen had a footman not surged forward to catch it. Rupert turned to stare, seeming to notice in an instant that every eye in the room was on the two of them.

"Mr. Dupree," she said, brandishing the paper, "might I have a word?"

He sketched a courteous half-bow. "Of course, Miss Weatherby. Lead the way."

She hurried down the hall and opened the first door she came to. She found a parlor with Wedgewood-blue walls. Happily, the room was deserted.

Rupert's brows rose when she shut the door behind him, but he said nothing.

Clarissa held out the morning paper. "I suppose you were expecting this."

He took the paper from her, turning it to face him. His eyes widened as he noticed his name at the top of the front page, but then he squinted.

After a moment, he glanced up. "I didn't bring my glasses downstairs. Would you mind reading it to me?"

Clarissa took the paper back and began to read. Rupert listened in silence until she reached the part about the damage that had been done to her reputation as a result of the letter.

"*Despicable dearth of journalistic standards!*" He clapped his hands. "That's capital. Absolutely capital. Good old Laurie—of course, he would know just how to phrase it." He cleared his throat. "Sorry. Please, go on."

Clarissa felt her cheeks flush as she read the next section, about how Rupert held her in the highest regard. Keeping her eyes fixed on the paper, she finished the last section, then looked up. "Did you truly threaten to sue every paper that printed the letter?"

"Well, of course. That's the only way to stamp it out. It's a good start to get the papers in London and York to print a retraction. But I'm given to understand that it ran all over. We can't have the good people of Upton Snodsbury or Barton in the Beans continuing to disparage your name, now can we?"

Clarissa peered at him, wondering if these were real towns, or if he had made them up. "I cannot say I have devoted much thought to the regard in which I am held in Barton in the Beans."

Rupert pointed a finger. "Well, we're going to leave no stone unturned and all that."

She shook herself. "This also arrived this morning," she said, holding out Jasper's letter. Recalling that he could not properly see it, she said, "Of course, you do not have your spectacles. But it is a letter from my brother-in-law, the Duke of Norwood, the gist of which is that he is ready and willing to join you in your legal pursuits."

Rupert clenched his hands into fists. "That's the best news, really the best. I'm ready and willing to sue. Of course, I am. But they'll have taken my measure financially and know that I probably can't afford to keep up three dozen lawsuits at once. But having Norwood join the case—that'll really put them back on their heels."

Clarissa grinned. "Jasper does have a talent for inspiring a hasty retreat."

"Right you are, Miss Weatherby. Right you are, and he's a good fellow to have in our corner. This is capital. Absolutely capital." He was bouncing on the balls of his feet, invigorated in spite of the fact that he was yet to have so much as a cup of coffee. "If you want to know the truth, I've felt sick ever since you told me what they printed in the papers. I know this won't undo everything you've been through, but it's such a relief to know you'll get some measure of justice."

Clarissa felt her throat constrict. She could scarcely countenance it, but Rotten Rupert, whom she had spent the past two years hating with a burning passion, had turned out to be a rather fine fellow.

"Thank you, Mr. Dupree," she said, her voice shaking. "I truly appreciate everything you are doing to clear my name."

He smiled, a genial expression that settled naturally over his face. "That's all right. The least I can do, and all that. Does this mean you believe me when I say I didn't have anything to do with that letter?"

"I do. But I am curious—you said something about another letter, one you sent to my house, and about someone sabotaging you. What really happened?"

He rubbed the back of his head. "Now, that is a long story. Not that I'm unwilling to tell it. Not at all." He glanced at the door for a beat, then turned back to her, his eyes filled with urgency. "But first, there's something we need to discuss—"

There was a sharp rap at the door. It swung open, and Lady Helmsley poked her head in. "There you two are!" The countess's expression was stern as she strode into the room. "I know you must be eager to confer, given the exciting news in the papers this morning. But it really isn't proper for you to be alone, especially with the door shut."

Clarissa chuckled. "I appreciate your care, my lady. But I am five and twenty. Firmly on the shelf."

"You are going to be one of the biggest catches in London next year," Lady Helmsley countered. "And I would never risk your sister's displeasure by allowing your reputation to be tarnished under my roof." She waved a hand. "Go on, continue your conversation. I will sit in the corner, and that will take care of the proprieties. You'll never even know I'm here."

Rupert gave Clarissa a look filled with a rueful sort of humor, and she took it that whatever he had been about to tell her, he would not care to say it in front of Lady Helmsley. "I fear Miss Weatherby was not able to finish her toast. Why do we not all head to the breakfast room so she can remedy the situation?"

Clarissa gave Rupert a significant look, one that she hoped conveyed that they would talk later. He responded with a wink.

In the breakfast room, she allowed Rupert to hand her into her chair. As the servants bustled about, furnishing her with a fresh cup of tea and two warm slices of toast, she could not help but wonder what was going on. Were she and Rupert... friends? The notion seemed absurd, and yet, she fancied that was just what they were.

And perhaps they were more than that. Perhaps he was the additional agent Sir Henry had mentioned. Perhaps he was her... partner.

The most alarming thing of all was how little that notion disturbed her.

Clarissa cracked open her egg, feeling more confused than ever.

CHAPTER 15

Rupert smiled as he stepped out the front door of the castle. The sky was a bright, cheerful blue that made for a beautiful contrast with the fresh, white drifts of snow. Lord and Lady Helmsley had announced that they had a special surprise for their guests, who had donned their cloaks and hats and were assembling out front.

It wasn't hard to spot the surprise. A cherry-red sleigh drawn by a pair of dappled greys stood waiting on the circular drive. Ropes of holly had been hung all around the rim, and little sprigs of it were even plaited into the horses' manes. Rupert could not imagine a more cheerful Christmas sight.

Lady Helmsley clapped her hands. "I thought, given the fine weather, that it would be a nice day to gather some greenery with which to decorate the castle."

Lord Helmsley stepped forward to stand beside his wife. "Meanwhile, given that we have such a good amount of snow on the ground, I thought it a fine opportunity to bring out the sleigh."

"So, we decided to do both," Lady Helmsley said, smiling

fondly up at her husband. "There's plenty of greenery in the little grove of trees just over that rise."

"And if anyone would like to take a jaunt about the park," Lord Helmsley added, "the sleigh is at your disposal."

The assembled guests murmured with pleasure. Rupert found himself grinning. What a charming way to spend the morning! He warranted that Lord and Lady Helmsley would have a hot toddy and a roaring fire ready and waiting for their guests once they went inside.

He was keeping an eye on Oliver Baxter, as always, and he'd been surprised to see that Rosalind Baxter was also out and about today. He still didn't know if she'd really been ill or if that had been a precaution. If it had been a safety measure, he could understand why she had abandoned it. There had been no signs of danger for four days. The poor lady couldn't stay in her room forever.

Indeed, Mrs. Baxter looked glad to be out of doors. She was the first guest to stride toward the sleigh. She stroked the neck of one of the greys. "What a handsome fellow!"

Rupert smiled as the horse nuzzled her. Mrs. Baxter had the reputation of being quite the horsewoman.

She turned to her husband, face glowing in spite of their recent scare. "I've always wanted to go for a sleigh ride. Shall we try it?"

Oliver Baxter responded by rolling his eyes. "Must we?"

Rosalind's face fell. "It will be good fun. I daresay we could both use a little holiday cheer."

"It is a waste of time," Oliver said tightly.

Rosalind lifted her head. Her chin was quivering, but she held herself with quiet dignity. "That's all right. You go on and do whatever you like. I'm sure I can find a few people to accompany me."

"It's too late now," he muttered. "If I don't go, everyone

will harp on me for abandoning my wife." He gestured brusquely to the sleigh. "Go on. Get in."

Rosalind climbed into the sleigh—with no assistance from her husband, Rupert noted—no longer looking very enthusiastic about the prospect. This, of course, was Rupert's signal. If the Baxters were going for a drive, Rupert needed to go with them to watch out for any funny business.

Clarissa Weatherby appeared to have had the same thought, bolstering his conviction that she was in cahoots with Sir Henry. She was already climbing into the back seat of the sleigh, saying, "You don't mind if I join you, do you, Mrs. Baxter?"

The problem was, this instigated a stampede as the half-dozen fellows who'd been dangling after Clarissa ever since she revealed she came with twenty thousand pounds all surged forward. The men began arguing about which one of them should accompany her.

Ignoring them, Rupert shouldered his way through the throng. "'Scuse me—coming through—sorry, old boy, was that your foot? I do beg your pardon."

That was right around the time Percival Ponsonby noticed that Rupert was stealthily climbing up into the sleigh next to Clarissa. "Hey there! Who says you get to ride with Miss Weatherby, Dupree?"

"Perhaps we should let Miss Weatherby choose her traveling companion," Rupert improvised. Which, in retrospect, seemed like one of his lousier ideas, which was really saying something. Clarissa famously hated him. Why on earth would she choose him over these other strapping fellows?

But Clarissa surprised him. "I would quite like for Mr. Dupree to accompany me. But please, do not distress yourselves, gentlemen. We'll just go once around the park. Rest assured, everyone will receive a turn."

Rupert knew full well that the primary attraction was Clarissa herself, not the sleigh. She had on a cloak and matching bonnet in a lovely shade of magenta, and she looked as pretty as a primrose against the clear blue sky. But her suitors accepted her pronouncement without too much ill grace, and before you could say Jack Robinson, they were off.

Rupert had never ridden in a sleigh before. It was every bit as delightful as he would have imagined. Whereas a carriage jostled you about even on the best roads, the sleigh runners slid smoothly across the blanket of snow. The sun was shining, the slight crunch of the snow beneath the runners mixed delightfully with the sound of the sleighbells, and the wind in his hair was invigorating.

Invigorating, but also cold. He glanced at Clarissa, who had a dreamy smile on her face. The expression suited her tremendously. For a moment, his heart squeezed. *Clarissa Dupree.* He couldn't help but wish things had turned out differently two years ago, that he was on this sleigh ride not as part of his duties for the Crown, but with his beloved wife. He felt certain he had never known that degree of happiness.

Clarissa shivered, and Rupert recalled the reason he had glanced at her. That pretty purply-pink cloak she had on was one of those modish things they made for women that were more for looks than actually keeping a body warm. The morning was brisk, and the sleigh really did create an astonishing amount of wind.

She was probably freezing.

He felt beneath the seat, looking for a carriage blanket. Not finding one, he pulled his fur-lined cloak—the same one they had shared in the mail coach—from around his shoulders.

"Here," he said, spreading it across her lap as well as his, then pulling it up and tucking it beneath his arms.

She started. "Oh, no. I couldn't possibly." In spite of her protestations, he couldn't help but notice the way she snuggled into the cloak.

"It's all right. I'm not any less warm this way."

"It's not proper," she murmured.

He pitched his voice low so the Baxters would not overhear. "True, but there's no one out here to see, and we'll restore ourselves to rights before we come up to the house. Besides, how often do we have the chance to go on a real sleigh ride? It's important that nothing mar your enjoyment."

She gave him a crooked smile. If Rupert hadn't known full well that she hated him, he would have said the expression was fond. "All right, you've convinced me. Thank you."

"You're most welcome," he said, ignoring the little squeeze his heart gave when she looked at him like that. *Buck up, Dupree*, he reminded himself. Clarissa didn't want anything to do with him.

Just because she was everything he'd ever wanted in a wife was neither here nor there.

"Have you ever ridden in a sleigh before?" he asked.

"I haven't." He could hear the excitement in her voice.

"I haven't, either. Isn't it marvelous?"

"It really is." She chuckled, glancing at the snow-frosted vista that surrounded them. "I consider myself to be somewhat jaded. But who could find themselves anything less than enchanted with a sleigh ride?"

At that moment, Oliver Baxter unintentionally answered her question. "What a miserable experience. My face is frozen. And these blasted horses won't stop fighting me."

"I think you might be holding the reins a bit too tightly," his wife offered quietly. "The horses know their job. If you will but give them the freedom to do it—"

"Why must you always do this?" he snapped. "To hear you

tell it, you would think I didn't even know how to drive. Is it too much to ask that you try not to publicly humiliate me for once in your life?"

He caught Clarissa scowling. Rupert gave her a commiserating look. At least this was one failing he didn't have. Of course, it wasn't the best feeling when you learned that you weren't any good at something, but the truth had a way of coming out. Far less embarrassing all around to admit it wasn't your forte, have a laugh about it, and move on. By all accounts, Rosalind Baxter was an excellent whip. Why hadn't her husband handed her the reins in the first place?

Rosalind responded to her husband's tirade by ducking her chin in silence. One of the horses chose that moment to toss his head, tugging against his short lead. Baxter responded by drawing the reins in even tighter. The horse snorted and laid its ears back.

"Oh, fine," Baxter said. "If you think you're so clever, let's see you do it. Unless you'd like to try your hand at it, Mr. Dupree?"

"Oh, no," Rupert said cheerfully. "I've heard what a marvelous whip Mrs. Baxter is. I'm sure she'll do far better with the ribbons than I ever could."

"*Fine.*" Baxter thrust the reins at his wife—not the safest maneuver, with the horses going at a steady trot—then slumped against the door of the sled, crossing his arms.

Fortunately, Rosalind managed to get hold of the ribbons. Sliding her hands a good six inches back from where her husband's had been, she called to the greys in a soothing tone. They immediately pricked their ears and fell neatly into step.

Oliver Baxter scowled out over the countryside.

Well, just because he was a miserable sort of fellow didn't mean that Rupert wasn't going to make the best of a delightful morning excursion.

He nudged Clarissa with his elbow and pointed to a snug, snow-dusted cottage peeking out between a few trees. "That's the hunting cabin. Closed up right now as Lord H. is between gamekeepers at the moment. And over there is the chapel."

Clarissa leaned forward, peering across Rupert toward the small stone building, and her shoulder pressed against his. Not that he minded. Quite the opposite, in fact. But he was surprised she didn't flinch at the contact and jerk away from him.

"I thought the parish church was in town," she said.

"It is," Rupert said, trying to sound like his usual carefree self and not as if his heart was tripping over itself. "It's a private family chapel. Only used for special occasions and whatnot."

"It's lovely," Clarissa said softly.

It was true. The small stone building was frosted in fresh-fallen snow, and someone had draped ropes of holly beneath the arched windows. "It really is, isn't it?"

Was it his imagination, or had Clarissa scooted closer to him in the sleigh? He could feel the warmth of her thigh pressed against his.

He wanted to put his arm around her. It felt like the most natural thing in the world. Of course, he couldn't do that, so he gripped a fistful of his cloak to make sure his arms didn't go getting any ideas.

All too soon, they had completed their circuit, and Helmsley Castle came back into view. Rupert smiled as he helped Clarissa, then Rosalind, from the sleigh. "Shall we gather some greenery, then?"

"I would like that," Rosalind said. "It's nice to be out of doors after having been cooped up for so many days."

Her husband groaned. "Haven't we wasted enough time with this nonsense?"

Clarissa looped her arm through Rosalind's. Her smile looked forced, and when she spoke, her voice had a cheerful yet brittle quality. "Do not trouble yourself, sir. I would like nothing better than to gather some greenery with your wife."

Baxter cast his eyes heavenward. "No, no. If she goes, I have to go, too. Otherwise, everyone will think me the worst sort of curmudgeon."

He trudged off toward the woods, stamping his feet.

Rupert handed his cloak to a footman, as the day had grown sunny enough that it was too warm for such a heavy garment without the wind created by the sleigh. He then grabbed a pair of baskets from the stack Lord and Lady Helmsley had set out and a couple of pairs of shears and handed them to the ladies. He offered one arm to Clarissa, and the other to Rosalind.

As they set out three abreast, he whispered, "The worst sort of curmudgeon. How would anyone form that impression?"

The ladies were both tittering as they headed toward the grove.

CHAPTER 16

There was a certain irony, Clarissa mused, in the fact that she had been tasked with protecting Oliver Baxter's life.

Because here she was, tempted to strangle him herself.

She knew that not all marriages were happy. Of course, she knew that.

But dear God—in Oliver Baxter's eyes, his wife could do nothing right. Why on earth had he married the woman if he was only going to berate her at every turn?

She had honestly thought that watching over Mr. Baxter would be a privilege. He was widely respected for his intelligence, and he was a champion of a number of political causes that meant a great deal to her. He had sounded like just the sort of man she admired.

But after seeing how he treated his wife, Clarissa found that she no longer cared whether he was a steadfast champion of parliamentary reform. He wasn't a good person, full stop.

And who was a good person? Again, Clarissa could not *believe* she was thinking this, but Rupert Dupree! Clarissa had to own that she had been wrong about him. Not that this was through any fault of her own. She couldn't have known that he wasn't the author of that horrible letter.

But now that she had met him, she knew Rupert to be kind, thoughtful, and good-humored. The unassuming way he had declined to drive himself and the easiness with which he had admitted Rosalind was a superior whip stood in stark contrast to her husband's petulant behavior.

Just listen to him now, peppering Rosalind with questions about her favorite childhood Christmas traditions. He was obviously trying to cheer her, and it seemed to be working.

A fortnight ago, Clarissa would have sworn that intelligence was the most important trait she wanted in a husband, if she were ever to marry.

It seemed she had been mistaken. Kindness was far more important than intelligence.

Not that she was thinking about marrying Rupert Dupree!

She sneaked a glance at him. The easy grin on his face was both natural and appealing. In fact, with such an expression on his face, he looked remarkably handsome.

She forced her eyes straight ahead. Dear God, what was wrong with her? First, she was thinking that Rupert would make a good husband, and now she was finding him handsome! What was next? Daydreaming about kissing him like a lovestruck girl?

Out of the corner of her eye, she peered at his lips. They looked... soft.

Would he taste the same way he smelled? Like almond biscuits? She had noticed his sweet scent again when he sat next to her in the sleigh.

And he was rumored to be outstanding in the marriage bed. Surely, that would extend to kissing...

Just then, Rosalind fumbled her shears with her gloved hands and dropped them in the snow. She launched into an anxious apology that was entirely disproportionate to the 'offense,' if one could even call it that—a habit, Clarissa had no doubt, she had developed as a result of her husband's excessive criticism.

Begging her not to think a thing of it, Rupert promptly bent over to collect the shears. He had to turn his back toward Clarissa to accomplish this maneuver, and as he leaned forward, she found herself confronted with the rather splendid prospect of his derriere.

Was it as firm as it looked? She felt a sudden, overwhelming desire to squeeze it so she could find out…

"Spiced cider, Miss Weatherby?" Lord Helmsley said, stealing up beside her and causing her to jerk guiltily to attention. "You look as if your mouth has gone dry."

"Yes!" Clarissa squeaked, accepting the mug the earl offered. "Thank you! I'm t-terribly parched."

Lord Helmsley smiled benignly, not seeming to have noticed the way she was leering at Rupert's rear end. He took another pair of mugs off a footman's tray, offering them to Rupert and Rosalind.

Good Lord—what midwinter madness was this? It must be the result of too much holiday cheer.

She resolved to limit herself to one glass of eggnog per day for the remainder of the house party.

Lord Helmsley moved on. Clarissa, Rupert, and Rosalind finished their drinks, placed their mugs on the footman's tray, and returned to searching the grove for greenery.

"What do you think?" Rupert asked. "Does this look like a likely spot?"

"Delightful," Clarissa murmured, trying to sound natural.

Rosalind wandered over to a fir tree and began trimming off a few boughs. Oliver Baxter plodded over to stand near his wife but made no move to assist her. Instead, he stood with his arms crossed, glaring into the distance.

Clarissa found some holly a few paces deeper in the copse and went to work with the shears. She tried to focus on her work and not steal a glance at Rupert, a task that should not have been difficult, but was.

She was able to hold out for a couple of minutes, but eventually gave in. Glancing back toward the house, she found him standing near Oliver Baxter, attempting to make genial conversation. That Mr. Baxter was primarily responding with grunts and scowls did not seem to bother Rupert a whit.

Suddenly, a glint of light shone directly in her eye, causing Clarissa to mishandle her shears. She snipped right through one of the fingers of her kidskin gloves—fortunately her own pair, and not one borrowed from Lady Emily—grazing the skin beneath.

She tugged her glove off to assess the damage. It was little more than a scratch, red but not bleeding.

She was starting to pull her glove back on when she heard an unmistakable metallic click.

Having spent the past month practicing with the little Queen Anne pistol Lady Winnifred had given her, Clarissa recognized that sound. It was a firearm being cocked.

She froze. *A firearm being cocked.* A metallic glint in the middle of the forest!

And Oliver Baxter standing in the open, unprotected.

She dropped her basket, shears, and glove and frantically scanned the trees, but she could not spot the assassin. Glancing back, she saw that Rupert was doing the same.

Suddenly, his eyes went wide. The expression on his face was not that of a seasoned spy, but a man in the throes of panic. An *Oh, crikey!* sort of expression.

Clarissa followed the direction of his gaze and spotted it —the brass-tipped muzzle of a gun, peeking from around a tree.

Oh God, oh God, oh God! She was too far away! She couldn't get there in time. Indeed, she couldn't seem to move her feet or even cry out a warning. She was frozen in place, and Oliver Baxter was going to *die*.

I'm a failure. The worst agent in the world.

Just when Clarissa was convinced that all hope was lost, Rupert sprang into action. "I say!" he exclaimed, his voice emerging a half-octave higher than it was usually pitched. "Are those some pinecones? Wouldn't those look lovely on the mantelpiece?"

He took two steps toward Oliver Baxter then made a great show of tripping over a gnarled root. Grabbing the M.P.'s shoulders, Rupert tackled him to the ground just as the crack of the gun rang out.

All the guests began screaming and panicking, because the shot had clearly come from nearby. Lord Helmsley came sprinting up. Clutching her heart, Rosalind pointed to the bullet, still smoking, embedded in a tree mere inches from where she and her husband had been standing moments before.

Clarissa scanned the forest for the shooter but could see no sign of them amongst the trees. She hurried over and helped the earl pull Rupert and Oliver to their feet. "Get the other guests back to the house," she told Lord Helmsley. "Say you've been having trouble with poachers."

Lord Helmsley nodded. "Poachers. Yes, that's good."

Oliver Baxter was already running toward the house without an apparent thought for his wife's safety, leaving Lord Helmsley to wrap an arm around Rosalind's shoulders. "Come, Mrs. Baxter. We must get you inside."

Rupert made no move to leave, which surprised Clarissa not at all. After watching him throw himself on Oliver Baxter, there wasn't a doubt in her mind that he was the other agent Sir Henry had sent.

He confirmed it immediately. "You're working for Sir Henry, too."

"I am." Some mad impulse made her grin. "I knew it was you!"

He grinned back, withdrawing a pistol from the back of his coat. It occurred to Clarissa that she should do the same. She reached into her pocket and pulled out the little Queen Anne pistol Lady Winnifred had insisted she carry.

She felt completely ridiculous. She'd practiced with the thing for all of five weeks, and besides, she was Clarissa Weatherby, bluestocking extraordinaire. She spent her days curled up in the library with an esoteric book, not stalking through the woods with a gun, hunting for assassins!

And yet, as unqualified as she felt, she knew that if Rupert had given her a pitying look, had suggested that she head back to the house because she would only be in his way, she would have kicked him in the shins.

But Rupert did no such thing. Nodding at her pistol, he jerked his head to the side. "You go right. I'll go left. We'll meet in the middle."

Even though she was terrified, she nodded. "The copse is freestanding, so we should check the perimeter. They won't be able to flee without leaving footprints in the snow."

His eyes brightened. "Brilliant, that's absolutely brilliant. That's just what we'll do." He gave her a firm nod. "All right. Take care of yourself. I'll see you in a few minutes."

Then, Clarissa found herself tiptoeing around the perimeter of the stand of trees, her miniature pistol clutched to her chest, searching for an armed assassin. She could not *believe* she was doing this, but if there was one thing she knew about herself, it was that she was far too stubborn to admit when she was in over her head. And if that meant she had to creep through the snow doing her best imitation of the Rifle Brigade, so be it.

She had found nothing of note when she spied Rupert coming around the bend five minutes later. "Did you see anything?" she asked, breathing hard.

"Nothing. No footprints, no gunman."

"Me neither." Clarissa pressed a hand against her heart.

"Let's sweep through the trees again," Rupert suggested. "Make sure they're not hiding somewhere inside."

Clarissa nodded, and they made a slow, thorough search of the stand of trees. They spread out, but knowing that Rupert was within shouting distance, even if she couldn't see him, was a great comfort.

They retraced their steps through the trees, then decided to check the perimeter one more time, just to make sure they hadn't missed anything. There was still no solitary set of footprints leading off across the snow, at least on the side that Clarissa checked.

But the assassin did leave one trace behind. While she was waiting for Rupert at the front of the grove, Clarissa spotted something brass glinting from beneath a log. She pulled it out, revealing a hunting rifle. "Look what I found!" she called as Rupert came jogging up.

"Well done, you." He tilted the barrel this way and that, inspecting it. "It certainly looks like the gun I saw."

"I think so, too." Clarissa ran her thumb, still bare from having removed her torn glove, over the firing mechanism. "It's cold, but that's probably to be expected, as it's been lying in the snow." She glanced up at Rupert. "Did you see any footprints?"

"None. You?"

"None." She swallowed as she glanced at the snow leading from the little copse of trees back to the castle. In stark contrast to the pristine fields they had just inspected, it was well-trodden with the footprints of the house party guests. "You know what that means."

Rupert nodded, a grim expression replacing his usual affable smile. "Whoever fired that shot is inside the castle right now."

"Exactly." Clarissa shuddered. She had strongly suspected that the would-be assassin was lurking in her midst.

But it was unsettling to know it for certain.

Rupert apparently mistook her shudder for a shiver. "You must be freezing. Let's get you inside."

"We might as well. There's nothing more to be learned out here. Would you hold this a second?" Clarissa asked, handing him the rifle. She pulled her damaged glove from her pocket. "I might as well put this back on."

"You're hurt!" he exclaimed, seizing her hand and stroking his gloved thumb across her finger. "What happened?"

"It's just a scratch. I was clumsy with the shears, and…" Clarissa trailed off. The cut on her finger was tiny, only about a quarter of an inch long, and as thin as a red thread.

She peered up at his face, confused. "I thought you couldn't see well without your glasses."

CHAPTER 17

$\mathcal{R}$upert jerked back, releasing Clarissa's hand as if he'd been burned. The expression on his face was the same panicked look he had worn when they'd spotted the muzzle of the gun. *Oh, crikey!*

Clarissa stared at him in fraught silence. Why would Rupert have lied about needing glasses?

The crunch of footsteps on the snow recalled her to her surroundings. She turned and saw Lord Helmsley jogging up from the castle.

"Everyone's inside," he panted. "Did you find any... Rupert!" he exclaimed, noticing Rupert, who had been partially obscured by a tree. "What are you doing out here, my boy?"

A cheerful, vacant expression settled over Rupert's face. "You won't countenance it, but Miss Weatherby was determined to look for the poachers herself! I could hardly let her go after them all alone, now could I?"

"I... I suppose not," Lord Helmsley said, turning to Clarissa. The second the earl's attention was fixed on her, Rupert gave her a pointed look accompanied by a subtle shake of his head. The earl glanced back at Rupert, frowning. Immediately, Rupert plastered the empty smile back across his features.

So, Rupert had not advised Lord and Lady Helmsley that he was working for Sir Henry. A thousand questions rattled around inside Clarissa's head. Why hadn't he been forthcoming with his friends about what he was really doing at the castle? Why had he pretended to need glasses?

What was going on?

But Rupert was her partner, and she had come to trust him enough to follow his lead. She gave the earl a cringing sort of smile and said, "Wasn't that gallant of Mr. Dupree?"

"Ah," the earl said. "Yes, well, Rupert is a very good fellow."

"He is indeed," Clarissa confirmed. She held out the rifle. "This was the only thing we found of note."

"This is the weapon, then?" Lord Helmsley took the rifle, then pulled back in surprise. "But this is one of my rifles!"

This was unsurprising, considering the assassin was someone inside the castle, but they were supposed to maintain the illusion of poachers for the sake of Rupert's cover. Clarissa asked in a pointed tone, "Did you not tell me it had gone missing recently, my lord?"

"No." The earl's eyes widened as Clarissa jerked her head toward Rupert. "I mean… yes. That's right. It went missing a week ago. I guess, uh… now we know why."

"Well, it's a lucky thing they missed, isn't it?" Rupert asked, looking unconcerned. "Say, it's awfully cold out here for Miss Weatherby. Shall we head back inside?"

"Let's," the earl said tightly.

They trudged back to the house three abreast. Once inside, Lord Helmsley peered at Rupert, no doubt wondering how to get rid of him.

Rupert made it easy for him. "After all that, I fancy a hot drink. Would anyone like to join me?"

"Thank you," Clarissa said, "but I think I'll go up to my room and change out of these wet boots."

"Ah. Jolly good." Rupert bowed over her hand. As he straightened, he whispered, "Meet me in the orangery."

Clarissa gave the tiniest nod, then turned to follow the earl up the stairs. On the landing, they encountered Lady Emily, who seemed either unaware or unconcerned that someone had attempted to kill a member of their party. "Look what I found, Miss Weatherby—mistletoe!" She gave a bright laugh. "You'd best keep your wits about you, for your many suitors will be contriving to catch you beneath one of my kissing boughs."

Clarissa smiled weakly in return. As if she had time to worry about suitors right now, with a murderer on the loose!

Although... She glanced over her shoulder. Rupert had finished passing his hat and gloves off to a footman. Catching her eye, he nodded once before heading off to find the hot drink he had mentioned.

It was the strangest thing, but "You go right. I'll go left" suddenly seemed like the most romantic words in the English language. Rupert hadn't dismissed her. He hadn't treated her like some silly girl.

He had treated her like his *partner*.

Suddenly, that seemed more important than the fact that he apparently could not read.

The earl led her to the Baxters' suite, where Lady Helmsley was also waiting. Clarissa informed everyone of what she had found in the woods. She made no mention of Rupert, and if Oliver Baxter found it a strange coincidence that Rupert had tackled him just before the shot was fired, he said nothing about it.

"At this point," Clarissa concluded, "the evidence overwhelmingly suggests that the would-be assassin is residing within the castle."

Rosalind Baxter made a bleak sound.

Lady Helmsley pressed her niece's hand. "I think you should both keep to your rooms until the threat has been eliminated."

From his vantage point standing next to the window, Oliver Baxter narrowed his eyes. "Whatever became of this experienced agent the Home Office was sending?"

It was on the tip of Clarissa's tongue to say, *He saved your life not half an hour ago.*

But, for whatever reason, Rupert preferred to remain incognito. Although she still didn't understand why, he was her partner, and she was not about to betray him.

"I do not know," Clarissa replied. "It would appear that they have been detained."

Oliver snorted. "Perfect. If we had a more competent protector, I would suggest we venture forth and try to draw the villain out. But, as we are left to the dubious protection of England's most renowned wallflower—"

"We both owe our lives to Miss Weatherby!" Rosalind snapped.

Oliver glowered at his wife. "I would seem to owe my life to dumb luck." He laughed. "Unless you're suggesting that Rupert Dupree is a highly trained government agent."

Rosalind was having none of it. "We would have already been dead. That rock would have crushed us were it not for Miss Weatherby's quick thinking. You know nothing of her career and experience. It is unfair of you to disparage her simply because she is a woman."

"I appreciate that, Mrs. Baxter," Clarissa said. "As for Mr. Dupree, he insisted on searching the woods with me while everyone else took shelter inside the castle. I thought it the act of a true gentleman."

Oliver Baxter's nostrils flared. No doubt he did not care for the implicit comparison—that Rupert had stayed to help while he fled inside, not even pausing to ensure the safety of his wife.

But before he could speak, Lord Helmsley said, "Yes, Rupert has always been a fine young man, and I will not hear anyone speak against him underneath my roof."

A sulky frown settled over Oliver's face, but he wasn't about to gainsay the earl. Instead, he glared at his wife. "Easy enough for you to be grateful. You're not going to be confined to this room, waiting for Miss Weatherby to sort this out."

Rosalind looked bewildered. "I will certainly be confined to this room. I intend to practice the utmost caution."

Her husband rolled his eyes. "You might as well go out. It's not as if anyone cares whether you live or die."

Lady Helmsley surged to her feet. "I have had enough of these dismissive comments toward my niece! I, for one, care very much whether she lives or dies, and as her husband, you should too."

"Indeed," the earl said darkly. "You will probably say it is none of my affair. But this is not the way a gentleman speaks to his wife."

Oliver Baxter was clever enough to recognize defeat when he saw it. "I apologize, my lord. The stress of today's events has put me in an ill humor." He sketched a brief bow, then headed for the connecting door to the bedchamber. "If you will excuse me, I will take some time to consider how I wish to proceed."

After that, Lady Helmsley announced that she would sit with Rosalind for a time. Maintaining the guise of poachers being their primary suspects, they determined that Lord Helmsley would question the servants to see if anyone knew how the rifle had gone missing.

And Clarissa headed out toward the orangery to confer with Rupert.

CHAPTER 18

Rupert's heart was still pounding when he heard the orangery door open. Maybe he was still worked up over the near miss in the woods. Rupert wasn't really the feats-of-derring-do sort of agent. He was more of a pretend-to-be-drunk-and-make-good-use-of-your-ears sort of agent. Then, he wrote everything up and sent it to the Home Office.

Or rather, his partner wrote it up and sent it to the Home Office. Which was the other possible explanation for his racing heart—that Clarissa had figured out that his excuse about forgetting his spectacles was just that.

An excuse.

Well, it was time to take his lumps. He hurried to the front of the orangery, where he found Clarissa shutting the door.

"Are we alone?" she asked.

"We are," he confirmed. "What happened?"

She filled him in on her conversation in the Baxters' sitting room. "He is torn between hiding in his rooms for the remainder of the house party and coming outside, trying to draw the assassin out so he can bring matters to a head." She peered up at him. "You have more experience than I do as an agent. I would be curious to hear your opinion on the matter."

"Do I?" Rupert asked. "I've only been at it a couple of years."

Clarissa gave a startled laugh. "I've been at it less than that." Her eyes grew guarded. "This is my second mission."

"Truly?" Rupert asked, genuinely surprised. "I never would've known."

Clarissa's lips tightened as if she was unsure whether she believed him. "You don't have to say that to make me feel better."

"No, really. You were fantastic. You saved them from that falling rock, for one. But when we had to search the woods, you were so confident! You looked just like an old hand."

"Do you mean that?" she asked, her guard abruptly falling away. "Oliver Baxter has been treating me like I'm worthless."

Rupert waved a hand. "I wouldn't put too much stock in anything Baxter says. You've seen the way he treats his wife."

"Yes!" Clarissa stepped forward, her eyes bright with annoyance. "The thought flashed through my mind that, had I not been tasked with protecting him, I'd be tempted to strangle him myself."

Rupert laughed. "He seems like a miserable sort of fellow, to say nothing of a self-righteous prick."

"I agree wholeheartedly." Clarissa snorted. "I was so excited about this assignment, because I admire many of his political positions. But suffice it to say, meeting him in the flesh has been quite the disappointment."

"Did he suspect anything with the way I tackled him just before the gun went off?"

Clarissa shook her head. "He did not. Speaking of a job well done, thank God you had the wherewithal to pretend to trip." Her eyes grew rueful. "I was frozen with fear. Had you not acted, I would have stood there and watched him get shot."

That was nice. That was very nice of her, considering what a slapdash effort it had been. "It wasn't much. Tripping was all I could come up with in the moment."

"Considering Oliver Baxter isn't dead, I would say you couldn't have done any better," Clarissa said firmly.

Rupert rubbed the back of his head. "Aww, that's kind of you. Really kind."

She laughed. "I am not known for being kind. I have a reputation for being too plainspoken by half." She poked him in the arm. "But it happens to be true."

Rupert was fairly certain he was blushing. "Oh, gosh. Oh, golly."

He wasn't sure how much of this unfamiliar praise a fellow like him could take, so it was fortunate that she moved right along. "I also could not help but notice that Lord and Lady Helmsley do not seem to be aware that you are working for Sir Henry. Or are they merely skilled in putting on an act?"

"No, they think I'm here on a social call. I know it's the usual practice to make certain parties aware of our activities. But I learned a long time ago that doesn't work for me. That it's better if I just go about my business with nobody the wiser."

Clarissa tilted her head, studying him. "Why is that?"

"Look, Claire." *Claire*? Why had he called her Claire? She'd specifically asked him not to use her first name, much less a nickname, but it had just... come out.

Felt quite natural if you wanted to know the truth about it.

She didn't protest, so he soldiered on. "I'm not what you would call a clever fellow. I'm sure you know that Sir Henry likes to pick agents nobody would suspect. But apparently believing that I could be of any use to the Home Office is a bridge too far for just about everyone."

Claire was frowning—apparently, he was now thinking of her as Claire and everything. But not in an angry-at-Rupert sort of way. It was definitely more of an irate-on-his-behalf kind of expression. "What did they say to you?"

"They would accuse me of having made the whole thing up. The phrase 'delusions of grandeur' was used on more than one occasion." Rupert shrugged. "I had a letter from Sir Henry and everything. I guess they thought I'd forged it." He laughed blackly. "Now, there's a task I wouldn't be any good at."

Well done, Dupree. Go ahead—bring the topic you least want to discuss right to the forefront. You're doing a bang-up job.

Sure as eggs are eggs, Claire's gaze sharpened. She was making that twisted-lips sort of face she seemed to assume whenever she was overthinking something.

But when she spoke, her voice was gentle. "I did want to ask you about that. You made an excuse about having forgotten your spectacles a couple of times and asked me to read something to you. But you seem to see perfectly well. I hope this doesn't come out the wrong way, but… can you read, Rupert?"

He appreciated that she'd asked him straight out and also that she hadn't done it in a judgey sort of way. "I can," he confirmed. "I'm deuced slow at it. I've met seven-year-olds who read more fluently than me. The thing is, though, when I get nervous, I'm ten times worse. That's why I asked you to read those things to me. I'd have stood there forever, struggling to pick my way through them."

"Ah. I see." Claire looked… thoughtful. He searched her face for any trace of disdain or mockery, but he couldn't detect any.

Deciding she might as well know the worst of it, he continued, "And my handwriting… that's the real disaster. It's the reason I almost always work with a partner, so I don't have to write up my own dispatches to Sir Henry. Believe me, nobody would be able to read them."

Claire gasped. "That's what happened, isn't it?"

Rupert didn't follow, not that this was all that unusual. "That's how what happened?"

"The letter that appeared in the papers two years ago! You said you'd been sabotaged. You asked if I'd received your *real* letter." She took a step forward. "You asked someone to take down your dictation, and they changed your words. That's how it all went wrong. Isn't it?"

Rupert inclined his head. "It is, indeed. Once I learned you weren't as keen on the engagement as Lady Milthorpe had led me to believe, I determined I would release you from it. *Privately*, mind you. I never meant for any whisper of it to wind up in the papers. But there was only person around whom I could ask—a friend of my brother's named William Ellison." Rupert shook his head. "That was my mistake, all right."

Claire frowned. "You mean to tell me that your brother's friend is the one who falsified the letter? I wonder that he would risk your brother's wrath."

Rupert sighed. "I understand why you might assume my brother would be mad about it. I get the impression that you and your sisters all get along."

Claire blinked at him, looking bewildered. "Of course. I would do anything for my sisters."

Rupert gave one of those humorless laughs. "Not my brother. How can I explain? Of course, you're acquainted with the Duke of Norwood and his younger brother, Felix."

"Yes, I met both Jasper and Felix at a house party hosted

by Lady Milthorpe. Although I would not say their relationship is always an easy one."

"To be sure, Norwood can be deuced bossy. Goes with being a duke, I suppose. But let me tell you about your brother-in-law—if anyone so much as looked at Felix sideways, Norwood would beat them into next Tuesday." Rupert's shoulders sagged. "My brother was something of the opposite in that the one he was beating was *me*."

Claire's nostrils flared, and he half expected smoke to start coming out of her ears. "That's despicable! Your own brother!"

Rupert shrugged. "You know how it is. You were telling me about your father, and how he sold your house out from under you."

She inclined her head. "That's true. So, you believe it was this William Ellison who fabricated that letter." She tapped her lip, her expression thoughtful. "You know, it's a common enough name, but I happen to know a William Ellison. His aunt and uncle have an estate just outside of Boroughbridge, so he would come and visit sometimes. He's awful. When we were younger, he would make fun of my sisters and me for our threadbare dresses." She froze. "Come to think of it, he was there visiting his aunt and uncle the summer the letter appeared in the papers."

Rupert swallowed. "That would be the same William Ellison."

"But if he was in Boroughbridge that summer…" Claire trailed off. She was studying him in a way he didn't much care for. "You said you somehow learned that I wasn't keen on the betrothal."

Her brown eyes were intense as she asked, "How, exactly, did you know that?"

CHAPTER 19

Clarissa studied Rupert in the dappled light of the orangery. Everything was starting to make sense, except for one thing.

What had made Rupert believe she didn't want to marry him?

Her heart was racing. Because it was true—she hadn't been thrilled about her proposed union with the man everyone said was an idiot.

But now that she'd met Rupert, she saw that she had been overly hasty.

There was more to Rupert Dupree than met the eye.

He'd looked nervous for much of their conversation, but his eyes turned tremendously kind as he prepared to answer her. "I arrived in Boroughbridge to meet you a couple of days ahead of schedule. I was sitting in the Crown Hotel, eating a chop, when a young lady came in to collect her family's post."

Clarissa's heart dropped to the level of her stomach. Because she had always been the one most eager for new letters, and, therefore, she had usually been the one to collect the family's mail.

She had obviously said *something*, but what was it? She honestly couldn't remember.

"It was me?" she asked in a tiny voice.

Rupert inclined his head. "The barmaid, Becky, was teasing you about your impending nuptials."

This Clarissa could imagine easily enough. *Everyone* had been teasing her about her betrothal. Something about the combination of the bluestocking and the dunce, the innocent spinster and the legendary Lothario, had made people feel compelled to comment.

Rupert cleared his throat. "Let's just say you made it clear that you didn't want there to be any nuptials."

She could almost remember it. "What, exactly, did I say?"

He shook his head. "Look, I don't want you to feel bad—"

"*Tell me.*"

He sighed. "She'd made a comment about how you were scowling now, but from what she'd heard, your future husband knew how to put a smile on your face. You said I wasn't your future husband, not if you had any say in the matter, and that you wished Lady Milthorpe hadn't involved you in her 'ridiculous scheme.' And then…"

He trailed off. Clarissa's cheeks were aflame, but she was determined to hear the worst of it. "What did I say next? Please, do not sugarcoat it. Tell me as exactly as you can remember."

He kept his eyes fixed on the floor as he added, "Your exact words were, 'He's supposed to be a blithering idiot, from everything I hear. What could Lady Milthorpe have been thinking? I would never consider such a man for my husband, not if he were the last man on earth.'"

A pregnant silence descended over the orangery. Clarissa remembered it now. Becky had always had a saucy sense of humor, and working at an inn, she'd been as worldly as Clarissa was sheltered.

She remembered how humiliating it had been, feeling as if everyone was laughing at her behind her back. And even worse, the topic of the teasing had been one she was entirely unequipped to discuss—her wedding night. Her wedding night with a *stranger*, who was apparently some sort of libertine.

As if that wasn't bad enough, Becky had brought it up in the middle of a crowded tavern. She remembered feeling like every eye in the room must've been fixed on her, that everyone would be whispering about what she would be doing in the most private moment of her life.

But it was still no excuse for her to have insulted Rupert.

Something about the words niggled around in her mind. She couldn't quite put her finger on it, but she had a distinct sense that there was something else about those words that she was failing to grasp...

She shook herself. This was no time to worry about that. Right now, the important thing was making amends.

Clarissa lifted her chin but couldn't quite bring herself to look at him. "I would like to apologize."

"That's not necessary."

"It is," she insisted, keeping her eyes fixed on the orangery's wall of windows. "I was embarrassed by Becky's remarks, especially as they regarded such an intimate topic. I was extremely innocent. I had never even been kissed..."

Clarissa trailed off, wishing she hadn't phrased it that way. She *still* hadn't been kissed, but it was too humiliating to admit as much at the age of five and twenty, so all she could do was soldier on. "What I really wanted was for Becky to stop discussing a very private matter in a very public setting. My true aim was to shut her up, but I went about it in the wrong way. I should have taken her to task for her inappropriate remarks and left you out of it, and I am sincerely sorry that I disparaged you."

"It's all right, Claire."

Claire. Her sisters were the only ones who ever called her by that nickname. Yet, for some reason, it felt right coming from Rupert's lips.

"It's not all right," she countered. "I am horrified that I said it. It's no excuse, but I remember feeling shocked that Lady Milthorpe had arranged the match for me in the first place. My reputation is for being shrewish and strident, and I had assumed I would never marry. I'm sure you weren't any more enthusiastic about our proposed union than I was."

He said nothing. After a moment, Clarissa summoned the courage to meet his eyes.

The overwhelmingly kind expression was still in place. "Honestly? I was looking forward to meeting you. Lady Milthorpe had told me how clever you were, and..." He looked away, his eyes sorrowful. "You're just the kind of woman I want to marry." He jerked upright, seeming to realize himself. "I mean, wanted! I mean..." His shoulders sagged. "Want," he admitted.

Clarissa felt horrified. She had somehow blundered into the one and only man in all of England who regarded being the world's biggest bluestocking not as a disqualification to matrimony but as an attribute greatly to be desired, and she had managed to ruin things before they'd even shaken hands.

One of them was an idiot, all right. And it wasn't Rupert Dupree.

And yet... he had said *want,* present tense. Did that mean... was it still possible that he... that he...

She summoned her courage. "Rupert, I—"

She was cut off by the faint creak of the glass door opening. She froze, her eyes flying to Rupert's.

The door clicked shut, and a woman's voice filled the orangery.

· · ·

"As I rode out one May morning across yon fields so early,
  I spied a maid, a most beautiful maid as sweet as—"

A housemaid came around a cluster of orange trees. The song died on her lips as she saw Clarissa and Rupert standing guiltily together.

She glanced back and forth between them once... twice, then dropped a hasty curtsey. "I'm sorry, miss, sir. Cook sent me to fetch some lemons for tonight's dinner. I didn't mean to... to..."

"Quite all right," Rupert said easily. "I just arrived myself and was surprised to find that the orangery was already occupied." He gestured to Clarissa. "How I would hate for anyone to form the impression that there was anything irregular going on. It's fortuitous that you arrived in time to play chaperone."

The maid brightened. "Oh, well, in that case." She gestured to a cluster of trees in the corner. "You don't mind if I pick a few lemons before we head back to the castle, do you?"

"Not at all," Rupert replied. "In fact, may I be of assistance?"

Clarissa joined in, too, giving Rupert a meaningful glance while she tugged a branch laden with lemons low for the maid to do her work. Rupert responded by waggling his eyebrows.

"There!" the maid exclaimed once she had a dozen lemons cradled in her apron.

Once the lemons were picked, they had little choice but to return to the castle with their new chaperone. Once inside, they parted ways with the maid and Rupert escorted Clarissa up the stairs. Bending his lips toward her ear, he murmured, "We forgot to discuss the mission."

She frowned. "The mission?" Her thoughts were still swirling with what she'd learned about the real reasons behind their broken engagement. She stiffened as she recalled the reason they'd gone there in the first place. "The mission!"

"Meet me in the library at midnight," he whispered.

Clarissa nodded. "The library. Very—"

"Look where you're standing!" a singsong voice called from the top of the stairs.

Clarissa glanced up to find a delighted Lady Emily skipping down the steps. She pointed to a spot above their heads. "You two are the first to get caught under my mistletoe!"

Sure enough, a jaunty sprig of the white-berried plant hung suspended over the landing by a bright red ribbon.

Time seemed to slow down. Clarissa was conscious of Lady Helmsley lingering near the bottom of the stairs. Lady Ashington and the Duchess of Kimbolton, who happened to be strolling through the foyer, paused their progress to see if they were actually going to do it. This would be the juiciest *on dit* of all, that Rupert Dupree and Clarissa Weatherby had not merely made up their spat but had kissed under the mistletoe.

Clarissa's heart was thundering. Rupert's words echoed in her head. *You're just the kind of woman I want to marry.*

And she still wasn't sure, but she was starting to think that maybe, just *maybe*, he was the kind of man she wanted to marry, too.

He was looking at her, his usual jovial expression gone, his blue eyes intense. Lady Emily's voice sounded far away. "It's just a silly tradition. You don't mind, do you?"

Rupert moved slowly, giving her a chance to protest, a chance to say no.

Clarissa did not say no. She found she was giddy to have an excuse to kiss Rupert Dupree.

And maybe it was the fact that it was her first kiss. Maybe it was the way he stroked his thumb across her forehead as he brought his hands up to frame her face, as if he treasured the experience of touching her. Maybe it was the way he was looking at her, with a mixture of longing and sorrow. Maybe it was the way his breath hitched in the moment before his lips brushed hers.

But his kiss *ruined* her.

It was the sort of closed-mouth, proper-to-a-fault kiss that one exchanged beneath the mistletoe, knowing that a half-dozen gossipy matrons were watching the whole while. And still, Clarissa was shaking like a leaf by the time Rupert lifted his soft, warm lips from hers.

He didn't seem to be in much better shape, for his breath hitched again. They stood frozen for a moment, inches apart. His lips brushed her forehead, reverently. Almost involuntarily. She felt his breath, shaky against her temple. Then he stepped back, taking her hands.

Clarissa clung to his hands because the room was reeling.

He bowed a little unsteadily. "Miss Weatherby," he murmured, then released her, heading up the stairs toward his room.

It was fortunate that Lady Emily scurried over and seized her arm, because Clarissa was not entirely certain she could stand on her own. "Oh, my *gracious!*" Lady Emily hissed. "When he kissed your forehead, I almost swooned. I think Rupert must like you! Do you like him, too?"

"I… I…" Clarissa swallowed. "I need to lie down."

"I'll take that as a *yes*." Lady Emily hooked her arm through Clarissa's and led her up the stairs.

Lady Emily somehow guided a shaky-legged Clarissa to

her bedchamber. She encouraged Clarissa to kick off her slippers and helped her climb onto the bed.

Sitting on the mattress beside her, Lady Emily smiled. "Don't you worry. I'm going to take care of *everything*."

"Take care of… wait." Clarissa struggled to push herself up. "What are you going to do?"

Lady Emily was already halfway out the door. "Leave everything to me!"

Clarissa groaned as she flopped back down on the pillow. If she left Lady Emily to her own devices, she would find herself betrothed to Rupert by sunset.

Strangely, the prospect didn't feel all that alarming.

She lay on her back, staring at the bed's yellow canopy. Her thoughts were still a swirling mess. This did not bode well, considering she had an M.P. to protect and a would-be murderer to identify.

For some reason, the words rattling around inside her head were her own, the ones Rupert had quoted back at her in the orangery. *He's supposed to be a blithering idiot, from everything I hear. What could Lady Milthorpe have been thinking? I would never consider such a man for my husband, not if he were the last man on earth.*

She couldn't quite put her finger on it, but there was something about those words, something she felt sure she was missing…

She sat up upon the bed as it came to her. The reason those words seemed strange was because they were not a general summary of what she had said about Rupert Dupree two years ago.

Those were the *exact* words she had said to Becky. She was almost certain of it.

She rubbed her temple. How had Rupert Dupree, the man everyone dismissed as an idiot, who had just admitted to her that he could barely read, parroted back to her a precise quote two years after the fact?

There was more to that man than met the eye, and they would have a long list of things to discuss at midnight in the library.

CHAPTER 20

Oliver Baxter had apparently decided that there was no point in hiding in his rooms, because Clarissa was seated next to him at dinner that night. Rosalind Baxter looked pale and drawn, but she appeared at the table as well and was seated next to Lord Helmsley.

Clarissa gave Oliver a tight smile. She wasn't much looking forward to being his dining partner, but she was determined to be cordial. "The lobster bisque is excellent," she observed. "Would you like some?"

"I would not. I have an unpleasant reaction to shellfish."

"Do you?" Clarissa asked, taking a sip of her wine. "I have not heard of that before. What does it entail?"

His expression was bored. "My lips swell, my throat constricts, and my skin becomes itchy. I never touch the stuff."

Clarissa made a sympathetic noise. "I can understand why. Shall I ask a footman if there is another soup?"

She never received an answer because Oliver had already given her his back. Clarissa found him odious, and it appeared the sentiment was mutual, because that was the last sentence he spoke to her. He spent the rest of the dinner ignoring her in favor of speaking with Lawrence de Roos, who was seated to his right.

But that was all right because Clarissa's other dining companion, Lady Ashington, quite monopolized her conversation.

It seemed that after witnessing her kiss with Rupert beneath the mistletoe, Lady Ashington and the Duchess of Kimbolton had formed the same idea as Lady Emily—that the two of them should marry. "I still think you could snare an earl if you were to go to London," Lady Ashington murmured. "But Mr. Dupree has a respectable income, and *other attractions* that make up for his lack of title, if you take my meaning."

Clarissa knew her cheeks had gone pink, but she was not quite so horrified by this remark at the age of five and twenty as when Becky had made a similar implication two years ago.

Clarissa took a sip of her wine. "I would ask if you speak from experience, but I am terrified to learn your answer."

The marchioness smirked. "I do not. More's the pity, as it seems that Mr. Dupree will soon be off the market."

The Duchess of Kimbolton, who was seated on Lady Ashington's other side, leaned forward. "Trust me, child, such *qualities* are not to be taken for granted. My husband the duke, God rest his soul, could not have found the seat of a woman's pleasure with both hands and a map from the Royal Engineers."

Clarissa choked, almost spewing wine across the table. Lady Ashington patted her on the back. "Come, child. You're not some sixteen-year-old debutante. You know of which we speak."

"I am not quite so worldly as you assume," Clarissa muttered.

"Yes, well, who better to remedy that than Mr. Dupree?" the marchioness countered. She turned to the duchess. "If your duke was using his *hands*, that is half the problem right there. And I'm not sure that a map from the Royal Engineers would help. I am thinking of a particular lover I took back in 1796. He was a strapping young cadet at the Royal Military Academy. A bright young man and very fit, but I had to teach him *everything…*"

Clarissa allowed her attention to wander as the two dowagers began reminiscing about topics that were probably not appropriate for her ears. At the other end of the table, Rupert was seated next to Lady Emily, and Clarissa could guess well enough how that conversation was going. If Lady Emily was indeed haranguing him about marrying Clarissa, he appeared to be bearing it with his typical good humor.

Well, no matter what was going on with Rupert in her personal life, their meeting tonight needed to be strictly business. Clarissa still couldn't believe they had spent a half-hour together in the orangery and hadn't managed to discuss the possible suspects!

Tonight, she vowed, they would discuss the case in detail.

There was just one thing she needed to explain to him first.

CHAPTER 21

*A*t five minutes to midnight, Rupert was pacing the library, waiting for Claire to arrive.

He wasn't nervous about their meeting, precisely. But it was deuced awkward that they'd been caught together beneath the mistletoe. Not awkward for him, of course. He had no problem kissing Clarissa Weatherby whether it was beneath the mistletoe or at the front of the church, after the vicar said, *I now pronounce you man and wife.*

But Claire had made it clear that he wasn't the one for her, and so Rupert hadn't been planning on bothering her.

But mistletoe… now that was a tricky business. Because if you said you didn't want to impose yourself on the lady, everyone assumed that was an insult, akin to saying she was hideous and unkissable. Rupert had figured the only thing worse than kissing Claire would be refusing to kiss her. It all made sense in his mind, but he wasn't exactly a master of deduction, now was he?

He'd tried to do it the way a mistletoe kiss before a half-dozen of the most gossipy dowagers the *ton* had to offer was meant to be done. Very priggish and prim, prudish and proper.

But all of that had gone straight out the window as soon as he touched her. Because he was kissing *Claire*, and all the P-R words in the world couldn't distract him from the fact that it was kind of a dream come true.

He thought he'd acquitted himself fairly well right up until the very end. He shouldn't have kissed her on the forehead, but deuce take it all, this was the only chance he was ever going to get to hold her in his arms! He hadn't meant to do it, but he'd been swept up in the moment, and his body had just… reacted.

Well, if she was furious with him, that would be his cross to bear, and nobody to blame but himself and all that. But tonight, he would be professional. He would stick to the suspects. To the investigation.

And there would be absolutely no kissing.

He heard the click of the knob. Rather than swing open smoothly, the door stuck. It had done the same thing when Rupert arrived. He was hurrying over to give it a firm yank when there was a *thunk* that probably involved Claire putting her shoulder to it, and then she was slipping into the room.

It was the most agonizing quarter of a second of Rupert's life, waiting for her to turn around so he could see if she wanted to throttle him.

But when she turned, her eyes were bright. She looked excited to see him, although surely that wasn't right. She was carrying a little book and a stack of letters.

She was also wearing a dressing gown in a celery green sort of color. He could see a hint of creamy white lace at her wrists and another peeking out above the neckline, and Rupert's mouth went dry because he wanted to touch her badly enough as it was, and here she was, looking all soft and huggable. There was also the fact that he rather badly wanted to see what she looked like beneath all those layers, and her current attire looked like it might be devoid of pesky things like stays and petticoats that would prevent him from simply rucking up her skirts and touching her all over.

He shook himself. This line of thought was not the thing. "Thank you for coming. You weren't spotted on your way down?"

"No." She crossed the room and smiled up at him, actually smiled! His heart skipped a beat or three. "I was worried, given that Lady Emily is partial to bright colors that aren't particularly conducive to skulking in the shadows. But I'm fairly certain I was not seen."

"Good. That's grand." Rupert gestured to the sofa. "So, turning to the list of suspects—"

"Wait." She grabbed his hand. Neither of them had gloves on, and he couldn't help but notice how buttery-soft her skin was. "I'm sorry, I know we need to discuss the investigation. But something occurred to me this afternoon."

"Oh?" Nothing was occurring to Rupert at the moment, other than how much he wanted to slide his hand up her wrist and keep going.

She released his hand, more's the pity. She also bit her lip the way she was wont to do when she was really concentrating on something, and it had to be the most adorable thing he'd ever seen.

"In the orangery, when you told me what you overheard me say to Becky, I'm fairly certain those were my exact words."

They probably were. That was how Rupert's brain worked, after all. "That's right. You asked me to tell you as exactly as I remembered it. So, I did."

She stared at him for a beat. "And you remembered my exact words, even after two years."

Rupert saw what she was getting at. "Oh, that. So, you remember the bit about how I can't read very well?"

She was regarding him with an affectionate sort of smile. "Mm-hmm."

"And I can't write so well, either?"

"Yes?"

"Well, you see, old Rupert's a bit dicked in the nob. As cracked as an eggshell. As jingle-brained as Lord Helmsley's sleigh. As—"

"Rupert!" She laughed. "What are you trying to tell me?"

"Seeing as I can scarcely read and can't write much of anything down, I suppose the old noodle had to compensate somehow. There was nothing for it—I just had to start remembering everything people said."

She peered up at him. "You can truly remember *everything* people say?"

"Just about. I mean, if there's three or four people talking at once, things get a bit skimble-skamble."

She bit her lip again. "Could I see?"

"Sure. I mean, if you like."

She thought a moment. "Have you ever seen Shakespeare's *Twelfth Night?*"

He shook his head. "Nope. Can't say I've had the pleasure."

"I happened to act out a scene from it at a house party a few months back. I still have parts of it memorized."

She proceeded to recite a little speech from the play. Once she was done, she nodded. "Go on."

He said it back to her:

"She never told her love,
   But let concealment, like a worm i' th' bud,
   Feed on her damask cheek. She pined in thought,

And with a green and yellow melancholy
She sat like Patience on a monument,
Smiling at grief. Was not this love indeed?"

Blimey, that was hard to get out. Because wasn't that just how he felt about Claire?

He didn't have too much time to stew about it because as soon as he finished, she grabbed his hand again. "Rupert! You've truly never seen that play before?"

"What?" He couldn't attend with her soft skin upon his. "Uh, nope."

"And you just recited an entire soliloquy after hearing it once!"

He didn't see where she was going. "I... suppose so?"

She pulled at his hand, leading him over to the rose silk sofa, where she settled facing him with one leg tucked up underneath her. They were facing the fire he'd built while waiting for Claire to arrive. It was nice. Cozy.

Claire shook her head. "You don't seem to appreciate how remarkable that is! I've never met anyone with such a good memory."

He shrugged. "Sir Henry said it was unusual. That's why he wanted me. That and because I'm about the last person anyone would suspect of working for the Home Office."

She gave him a wry grin. "That's why he wanted me, too. No one even notices a wallflower, much less suspects them. Although Lady Emily has ruined my guise with her pretty dresses."

"She certainly has," Rupert said, his voice coming out rich and appreciative. "I can't imagine anyone not noticing you."

He clamped his mouth shut, because he hadn't meant to say something like that. The investigation. He needed to stick to the investigation!

He tried to get back on track. "I doubt I'll ever have that problem. After all, who would ever suspect me? I'm the stupidest fellow in all of England."

A mulish set came over Claire's jaw. "That's not true."

"Claire," he said, voice thick with disbelief, "how can you say that? As I mentioned earlier, I can barely *read*."

The mulish expression had not budged an inch. "I will acknowledge that your mind functions somewhat differently from most people's. But you have gifts—impressive ones— along with your challenges. And, although you do have a somewhat casual manner of speaking that people might interpret as being less than serious, I have never found your underlying logic to be lacking."

"Oh, that." Rupert waved a hand. "That was Sir Henry's suggestion. You see, the stupider I sound, the less people will suspect anything. I've always enjoyed using a bit of cant, and he encouraged me to lay it on as thick as I could."

"Ha!" Claire cried, pointing a finger. "I knew it! And, speaking of Sir Henry, would you care to know what *he* had to say about you?"

Rupert chuckled nervously. "I don't know, would I?"

Claire's eyes were fierce. "He described you as one of his best men."

That took the wind right out of him. Really, who could blame him? *He*, one of Sir Henry's best men?

It was absurd. And yet… Claire wasn't the type to lie.

After a moment, he managed to whisper, "Did he really say that?"

She lifted her chin. "He most certainly did." She unfolded a letter from that stack of hers and handed it to him. "Here, see for yourself."

As if that wasn't going to prove his point—it was two pages of Sir Henry's swirly, tightly-packed handwriting. As antsy as he was at the suggestion—the *ridiculous* suggestion, might he add!—that he was anything other than the village idiot, it would be Twelfth Night before he managed to pick his way through all of that.

Claire scooted over, so she was sitting right next to him. She pointed to a paragraph near the bottom of the first page. "It's right here."

She waited patiently while Rupert squinted at the paper, mouthing the words as he slowly read.

Given the urgency of the situation, I will send as many additional assets to the Helmsley estate as can be made available. In particular, one of my best men will return any day from a lengthy assignment on the Continent. I will have him on the first carriage north.

He gasped audibly when he reached the words *best men* and covered his mouth with his hand. Because… that was *him*. It had to be. He'd just returned from two years on the Continent, and Sir Henry had plucked him from the ship, briefed him on the assignment, and stuffed him in a mail coach bound for York that very afternoon.

He sat in silence, too stunned to say anything.

Claire finally nudged him with her elbow. When she spoke, her voice was full of humor. "You look *scandalized*. You look the way most people would if they'd read something horrible about themselves. Not that they're *good at their job*."

Good at his job? Rupert had never been good at anything in his life. "But I'm not," he protested.

Claire was having none of it. "You saved Oliver Baxter from his would-be assassin and made the whole thing look like an accident. You are *demonstrably* good at your job."

Not that he had a mirror handy, but Rupert would have

bet he looked more scandalized than ever. He gave a nervous laugh. "Be careful, now. If you keep that up, I'm liable to go getting a big head."

"Normally, that would be a potent threat. But not in your case. It happens that I think you deserve to have a significantly higher opinion of yourself in general."

Rupert was fairly certain he was blushing. He cleared his throat. *The investigation.* He needed to stick to the investigation. "I suppose I should at least try to live up to your faith in me. Which brings us to the suspects. I was able to speak with Ulysses F. Humphrey."

Claire leaned forward. "I haven't been able to speak with him yet. What did you think?"

Rupert explained why he didn't think it was Humphrey. "Don't get me wrong, he's a terrible excuse for a person. Chap owns a big sugar plantation in Antigua and is every bit as awful as you would expect a slaveowner to be. But he wasn't worried about Baxter passing an abolitionist agenda in the slightest. Said it would never happen."

"Do you think he could've been saying that to throw you off?" Claire asked.

Rupert inclined his head. "While it's always possible, I don't believe so. He was drunk as a wheelbarrow when we had this conversation. Most men can't prevaricate in that condition."

"I had a similar thought about the Duchess of Kimbolton," Claire said.

"The duchess? You don't say?" Rupert screwed up his face, thinking. "Sir Henry didn't mention the duchess when he briefed me."

"My partner, Lady Winnifred, added her to my list. She has eleven sons, many of whom have been cut out of livings by Mr. Baxter's push to grant them based on merit rather than nepotism. She's irked at Mr. Baxter, all right, but she was very open about her resentment." Her eyes sparkled, and Rupert might've forgotten how to breathe. "She told me how she exacted her revenge—by eating the last of the mince pies. They're apparently his favorites."

Rupert chuckled. "Well, remind me not to cross the duchess."

Claire gave him a wry grin. "To be sure, she is a fearsome foe. But, as you alluded with Mr. Humphrey, I do not think she would have been so open about her disdain for Mr. Baxter if she realized someone was trying to murder him. She was not what you would call circumspect."

"That leaves Richard Garroway." Rupert tried to keep his tone neutral and not sound like a jealous lunatic as he said, "I believe you've had the opportunity to speak with him, yes?"

"I did, on the first night and on several occasions since. Honestly, he's not as intolerable as I expected."

As compliments went, it was on the milquetoast side. And, as many times as Rupert reminded his heart that this in no way meant that Claire thought fondly of *him*, it insisted upon swelling to three times its original size.

The fact that she had insisted that he wasn't an idiot—a ridiculous proposition, he knew—didn't help either. But worst of all was the way she was treating him, which was like a partner. She genuinely wanted to know his opinion, to analyze potential suspects with him.

For the fellow widely regarded as the biggest idiot in England, it was heady stuff.

Claire was describing her conversations with Garroway, explaining that he actually agreed with Baxter on most of the issues, including parliamentary reform. "Of course," she concluded, "he might have been lying. But I don't think he was. He seemed sincere." She peered at him across the sofa. "What do you think?"

"You have good instincts, and, going over your

conversations, I agree with your conclusions. We won't strike them entirely from our list. As you note, they could be putting on a front. But I think we should concentrate our energies on more promising suspects."

Claire made a bleak sound. "But we're fresh out of suspects."

"Then we need to come up with a few." He rubbed his jaw, which had grown raspy in the hours since his last shave. "Let's see… I don't think it would be Lord or Lady Helmsley, or Lawrence and Emily. Of course, that could be bias on my part, considering they're some of my favorite people on the face of this earth."

"I agree," Claire chimed in. "As you note, it's possible that we could be wrong. But there isn't a scrap of evidence, at least from what I can see, that suggests that any member of the de Roos family is involved. And I think your suggestion that we should focus our attention on our most promising leads is a wise one."

Rupert rose from the sofa, full of excited energy, and started pacing around the room. He couldn't believe that Claire actually wanted to hear his thoughts. It was downright invigorating to have his suggestions taken seriously. "Let's see… who could have it in for Baxter? There's Percival Ponsonby. We were all at school together, Baxter, Ponsonby, and I. Baxter and his chums stuck him with a nickname—Priggish Percival. Well, obviously, Ponsonby didn't much care for him after that. I've noticed him avoiding Baxter all week."

Claire tapped her lip, considering. "I don't blame him. Still, that was what, fifteen years ago?"

"Just about."

"I'm not sure it's an inducement to murder, especially after all this time."

"I'm inclined to agree, so let's see…" Rupert resumed his

pacing. "There's also Granville Smith-Nugent-Smith. He lost a bet to Baxter back in 1818. They wagered two hundred pounds that Smith-Nugent-Smith couldn't ride a kangaroo—"

"He couldn't *what?*"

"You know, a kangaroo." Rupert bent both arms at the elbows, holding his hands up by his shoulders, and gave a couple of hops. "Bouncy sort of creature. Comes from New South Wales."

Clarissa shook herself. "Yes, I am familiar with *what* a kangaroo is. What I am failing to grasp is why Mr. Smith-Nugent-Smith would believe he could catch one, much less ride it."

Rupert shrugged, dropping his arms. "That, I can't tell you. But Smith-Nugent-Smith sneaked over to Queen Charlotte's menagerie at Kew and gave it a go." He shook his head. "I wasn't there, but I saw him the next day. Wasn't moving too well. Seems he had a deuced bad time of it. But it was in the betting book at White's and everything, so he had to pay up. He was quite put out about it."

Claire shook her head. "Still, as irritating as it doubtlessly was, it's over and done with. I don't see that murdering Oliver Baxter would solve anything."

"I suspect you're right. Let's see, there's also…"

Rupert proceeded to relate every scandal he knew involving the house party guests. Which was quite a few, as members of the *ton* were rather talented when it came to scandal, and his brain was talented at remembering these things. There was Francis Ditherington, a young blood just out of university. Baxter had once made a withering remark about his brand-new fuchsia satin waistcoat. Then there was Lady Dewdney, whose daughter Baxter had declined to dance with back before he'd married Rosalind. He hadn't bothered to expend much tact, from what Rupert had heard.

"Nicholas Higginbotham used to hold Baxter's seat in Parliament," Rupert offered. "But then, four years ago, Baxter defeated him in the election. And then there's Phyllis Cuthbert—the gossips all thought *she* would be the one to marry Baxter, but then her brother went and lost her dowry at the gaming tables, so he wound up marrying her cousin instead."

"Rupert!" Claire laughed. "Go back! Do you mean to tell me that the man Oliver Baxter ousted from his seat in Parliament is in attendance at this very house party? That's quite the coincidence."

Rupert paused his pacing. "You know, it does seem like a better reason to hold a grudge than a man having insulted your waistcoat."

Claire started to reply but was cut off by a familiar *click*, distinct in the nighttime silence of the castle. He recognized that sound.

He and Claire turned toward the door in horror.

Someone had turned the knob, but, as it had done before, the door stuck, buying them scant seconds.

Not that Rupert was doing anything with those seconds. Oh, no—he was standing in the middle of the room, gaping at the door like one of those big-eyed stuffed monkeys they had over at the British Museum.

Suddenly, Claire reached out, grabbed him by the front of his shirt, and hauled him over the back of the sofa.

He landed on top of her, and his whole body jolted.

The sofa faced the fire, which meant its back was toward the door, so they had a bit of concealment, but not much.

Rupert tried to think, but deuce take it all, he wasn't so good at thinking in the best of times, and having a soft, squirming Claire beneath him on the sofa was not enhancing what few cognitive abilities he had.

He could hear whoever was out in the hall struggling to

open the door. "Claire," he hissed, "what are we going to do? What possible excuse could we have for being alone together in the library at midnight?"

Claire's only answer was to wrap her arms around his neck and press her lips firmly against his.

In Clarissa's defense, what choice did she have?

The only plausible excuse for her and Rupert to be alone in the library at midnight was that they were having a romantic rendezvous.

Kissing him *made sense*. She was doing it *for the mission*.

And, oh, all right—she did want to kiss him! As incomprehensible as it would have seemed two weeks ago, she quite liked Rupert Dupree. She liked him, and she had certainly liked the way he kissed her under the mistletoe. If she was being honest, she had been hoping she might have the chance to do it again.

So, when the opportunity presented itself, of course, she had seized it with both hands.

Considering her first kiss had occurred just that afternoon and had been a chaste affair at that, Clarissa was excruciatingly self-conscious about whether she was doing this right. Her sister, Eleanor, and her brother-in-law, Jasper, seemed to spend an unusual amount of time kissing, and Clarissa had walked in on them enough times that she knew she was supposed to use her tongue. Tentatively, she opened her mouth and ran her tongue across Rupert's bottom lip.

He groaned against her mouth, threading his hands into her hair. He certainly didn't *seem* to mind her clumsy efforts, so Clarissa tried again, this time stroking her tongue across his top lip. His whole body started shaking, which seemed like a good sign.

She was summoning her courage to do it again when she heard the door give way, followed by the soft sound of footsteps on the library's plush carpet.

They were about to be discovered, and here she was, worrying about whether Rupert thought she was good at kissing! Although… they needed to make it look convincing, and Rupert had gone stiff as a board. So, she ran her hands down his back, all the way to the area she had been covertly admiring for the last two weeks.

She filled her palms with the glorious curves of his buttocks. And then, she *squeezed*.

He was everything Clarissa had dreamed he would be. Taut. Warm. Neither too plump nor too scrawny. Perfect beneath her hands.

Speaking of things that were taut, a rather prominent bulge in the front of Rupert's trousers was pressing against her hip. She felt inordinately pleased that he was just as affected by her as she was by him.

Rupert was gasping for breath. "*Claire*! Dear *God*, I—"

She grabbed his head with both hands and pulled his lips down to hers. He made a strangled sound, but it wasn't of protest.

Clarissa listened with half an ear as the footsteps on the carpet paused, then slowly retreated toward the door. At least, she thought they were retreating toward the door. It was hard to concentrate as Rupert was now kissing her in earnest.

He sucked her bottom lip into his mouth, then took advantage of her gasp, swooping his tongue inside her mouth. Clarissa understood in an instant why women were so desperate to lure this man into their beds. If he could make her head swim and her pulse throb with just a kiss, she trembled to think how much he could make her feel with *more* than a kiss. It was a good thing she was already lying down because otherwise, she would have melted into a puddle right there on the carpet.

There was a muffled thump as the uninvited visitor pulled the sticky door shut behind them.

Breathing hard, Rupert lifted his head and scanned the room. "It's all right. Whoever that was, they're gone." He gave a nervous laugh. "I see what you did there. That was clever. Very clever." He raked a shaking hand through his golden hair. "I'm sure you'll be wanting me to get off—"

He grunted in surprise as Clarissa pulled him back down on top of her.

He landed with his face in the couch cushions, meaning all Clarissa had access to was his ear. Some mad impulse had her wrapping her lips around its lobe and gently biting down. She was rewarded with a shudder that went through his entire body where it rested atop hers. She had never been in anything resembling an intimate embrace with a man before. She would've thought his weight would be too much, but it felt *delicious* having Rupert on top of her.

He groaned. "Claire, what are you doing? You hate me, remember?"

She flicked her tongue over a spot below his ear and was rewarded with another shudder. "I don't hate you."

He lifted his head, and his expression was adorably befuddled. "I'm fairly certain that you do."

She brushed a kiss across his lips. "I was mistaken. You, Rupert Dupree, are not at all what I was expecting."

He went still, with one hand coming up to frame her face. There was a poignant quality to his expression that made her chest feel tight. "And you, Clarissa Weatherby, are *exactly* what I was expecting."

Clarissa didn't have much time to parse that, because Rupert began kissing her again. They were the sort of hot, open-mouthed kisses that made her head loll back and her thighs fall open. He settled between them eagerly, the bulge tenting the falls of his trousers perfectly aligned with her core. Clarissa wasn't sure why, but it made her want to squirm.

He started pressing hot kisses down her neck. His hands were a heady combination of eager and reverent as he traced the outline of her body through her dressing gown. Clarissa gasped in his mouth as he brushed her nipple, and when his hands went to the ties of her wrapper, she didn't even think of stopping him.

Her own trembling fingers were struggling with the buttons of his coat, opening it up and peeling it off his shoulders, all while never breaking contact with his mouth. As soon as his arms sprang free, she hurled the coat over the back of the sofa and began yanking at his cravat.

Rupert already had Clarissa out of her dressing gown. He leaned back and made an appreciative sound at the sight of her in her snow-white night rail. It was flannel, not translucent linen, in a nod to the chilly December weather. But judging by the way Rupert was looking at her, you would've thought it was a seductive scrap of silk.

Clarissa pushed up on one elbow, pulling his waistcoat off and sending it to join his jacket in a heap on the floor. Still, he stared at her in silence. "What?" she asked.

His voice was rich with feeling as he said, "Let me pleasure you, Claire. Just this once. Oh, please, say you'll let me!"

She couldn't hold in her smile as she gave a magnanimous wave of her hand. "If you insist."

Rupert didn't seem to notice her irony. Leaning forward, he kissed her tenderly this time. For a woman who had never felt treasured, who had spent the last two years specifically feeling like the biggest laughingstock in all of England, it was heady stuff. When his fingers went to the ribbon tie at the neck of her nightgown, she didn't feel the slightest trepidation, much to her surprise. Sharing this intimacy with Rupert felt like the most natural thing in the world.

The ribbon gave way, and Rupert pushed the nightgown open to Clarissa's waist. She had been dressed for bed and wore nothing beneath it. He froze, his eyes transfixed on the newly revealed expanse of bare skin.

Clarissa knew she had a bosom that could be described as middling. But judging by Rupert's expression, he did not regard it as the humdrum sort of affair it truly was. You would've been forgiven for assuming she was some sort of curvaceous courtesan.

"Claire," he whispered, cupping a breast, his voice as reverent as his touch.

She shuddered at the feel of his warm hands, a delicious contrast in the cold room. Or maybe it was his thumb, swirling over her nipple, that had her shaking like a leaf. She must've touched herself there a million times to wash and get dressed, yet it felt entirely different when it was *Rupert's* hand caressing her there…

He began trailing kisses down her neck, pausing to linger over her collarbone. Clarissa's breath was coming fast now. As his lips pressed against the upper swell of her breast, Clarissa threaded her fingers into Rupert's hair, hoping he would kiss her on the nipple that was peaked in the cold night air.

He did not disappoint her, and her body jolted when his

tongue swirled around her. He tormented her right breast in the best possible way, then switched to the left side. Clarissa found that her hands had wandered down his torso of their own accord, pulling his shirt from the waistband of his trousers and slipping inside to discover the warm skin of his abdomen.

Rupert sat up, tugging the shirt off. Clarissa stared at him, curious. He wasn't heavily built, but his arms and stomach were beautifully sculpted with muscles. Feeling shy, she reached out to touch one of the circles on his stomach. He groaned, then tugged her into his arms.

Her brain ceased functioning the instant her skin came into contact with his. It felt *so good*. She wanted to stay in his arms forever. She was vaguely aware of him pushing her nightgown down over her hips and then off entirely, but she was too far gone to feel self-conscious about being naked before a man for the first time.

"*Claire*," he breathed, his voice worshipful. He stroked a hand down the length of her body. He sat her up on the sofa atop her crumpled nightgown, his eyes drinking her in, and Clarissa had never felt so beautiful.

Suddenly, he was pressing soft kisses against her stomach. "I'm going to make this so good for you."

Clarissa certainly liked the sound of that. She let her head loll back, luxuriating in Rupert's hands and lips roving over her body.

Being not only innocent but somewhat ignorant when it came to the finer points of lovemaking, Clarissa didn't know precisely what Rupert was going to do to make this good for her, as he put it.

But the one thing she had *not* been expecting him to do was to kiss her *down there*.

His warm breath against her inner thigh pierced her haze of pleasure. She looked down to see that Rupert had moved to the floor, where he was kneeling between her legs. He made a sound of pleasure as he pressed a kiss to the inside of her thigh.

"Rupert?" she asked, alarmed. "What are you—"

"Shh," he said, pushing her thighs open. "Don't worry, Claire. You're going to like this."

She was unconvinced. "Are you sure you should be... *Oh!*"

Rupert was right. Or maybe he was wrong because *like* was far too tepid a word to describe her feelings regarding... whatever he was doing with his tongue.

She attempted to tell him. That she was, in fact, enjoying it. That she wished for him to continue.

"Ru... Ru... Rup..." She felt her eyes cross.

"Mm-hmm?" he murmured from between her thighs.

"Guh... Guh..." That seemed to be as much as she could manage. Giving up, she squeezed her eyes shut.

"Mmm," Rupert hummed soothingly.

Clarissa felt like a bottle of champagne, except it was pleasure bubbling up inside her, floating toward the surface. She had never experienced anything like this before, and it was a little bit frightening how good Rupert was making her feel. She became conscious that her knees were starting to tremble and her fingers had knotted in Rupert's hair. The pleasure in that little spot between her legs built and built until it was as potent as cognac. A whimpering sound emerged from her lips. She had never *imagined* that something could feel this good. The trembling grew more violent, the pleasure almost *too* much...

She gasped as the tension suddenly burst. Now, her legs were shaking violently, and she could feel the place between her legs squeezing in rhythmic pulses. Rupert slowed the pace of his tongue, then as even that was starting to become too much, he withdrew, looking up at her with a soft smile.

He rose from kneeling on the floor and scooped her up in

his arms, cradling her in his lap. She curled eagerly against his warm chest.

He pressed a kiss against her temple. "Thank you for letting me do that."

It was all Clarissa could do not to laugh hysterically. Thank *her*? He was the one who deserved gratitude for showing her the most marvelous pleasure.

It took her a minute to recover sufficiently to tell him as much. "Thank *you*, Rupert. That was *wonderful*."

He squeezed her but didn't move from his position holding her with his head buried in her hair.

After drawing in a couple more shaky breaths, Clarissa brushed a kiss across his lips. "Your turn."

He peered at her, his brow creased in confusion. "My turn? What do you...?" His eyes went wide, his expression shifting to one of shock. "Oh, you don't have to do anything for me!"

That firm bulge beneath the falls of his trousers was still pressing into her thigh. "Wouldn't you like me to?"

Was it her imagination, or had his cheeks turned pink? "Well, er... Don't worry about it."

She brought her hand down, experimentally stroking him through the woolen fabric of his trousers. "It seems like you would."

His breath was coming fast. "I mean, I *would*, but I don't expect you to... to..."

Encouraged, Clarissa started unbuttoning his falls. "You'll have to help me."

"H-help you?" he gasped as she reached inside his trousers and wrapped a hand around his length.

"Seeing as I don't know what to do." She pressed a kiss against his neck. He filled her hand perfectly.

He gave a shaky laugh. "You seem to be a natural."

Clarissa pressed the falls of his trousers open and pulled

him out. She stared at his member in fascination. Having grown up in the countryside, she knew theoretically how copulation worked and that this was the part that would go inside of her. It was hard to imagine it fitting.

She glanced up at Rupert and saw that his eyes had gone unfocused with pleasure. She quite liked that look on him. "Show me what to do," she whispered.

He covered her hand with his own and showed her how to slide it up and down his length. A drop of liquid formed at the top of his member, and it soon rendered him smooth and slippery.

Once she had picked up the rhythm, Rupert removed his hand. He let his head loll to the side so his forehead pressed against hers. "Oh, Claire," he sighed. "That feels so good."

She could tell by his face that it did, but she couldn't help but wonder if she could make it even better. "Should I use my mouth on you the way you did on me?"

His body jerked. "Oh! You don't have to do that."

"I know I don't have to, but if it would make you feel good, then I would like to." He said nothing, so she poked him in the ribs. "Would it feel good?"

His breath was coming in pants. "I mean… it would, but I don't expect you to… to… Claire?"

She moved to kneel between his legs. Tentatively, she pressed a kiss against the tip of his member. His whole body shuddered. "What do I do?"

"Keep going with your hand," he said, his voice tight. "Use your mouth along with it, up and down… *yes*, just like that."

She kept up the motion. Rupert brought his hands up to frame her face, but not so he could control her pace. No, his touch was gentle, reverent, and when she chanced a glance at his face, he regarded her with wonder, as if he couldn't believe she was doing this for him.

Clarissa couldn't help but wonder if anyone had bothered

to be kind to this man, who was so very kind to everyone he encountered.

Although she had no idea what she was doing, she must've been doing something right, because after a few minutes, she felt Rupert's thighs harden to iron. "Claire!" he gasped. "I'm about to… You're going to make me…" He laughed nervously. "I'm not sure if you know what's about to happen, but you might not want this in your mouth, and… Oh, my God—Claire. *Claire. Claire!*"

It happened that she did know what was going to happen, at least, in a general sense, and so it wasn't a great surprise when she felt a pulse of liquid fill her mouth. She swallowed it down before she had a chance to consider whether that was a good idea. Above her on the sofa, Rupert was making sounds of pleasure, and she fancied she would never forget the wonder on his face.

After the pulses stopped, he caressed her face. Withdrawing from her mouth, he pulled her up on the sofa and kissed her deeply. "Thank you," he said earnestly. "You have no idea how much it means to me that you were willing to do that."

Clarissa snuggled next to him on the sofa. "I was happy to do it." Spotting her discarded wrapper draped over the armrest, she grabbed it and spread it over them like a blanket. Considering she'd had her first kiss that afternoon, it was startling how natural it felt to sit here with her head on Rupert's shoulder, her completely naked and him with his trousers shoved halfway down his legs. For his part, Rupert seemed content to sit quietly with his arms wrapped around her and his face buried in her hair.

Clarissa yawned, feeling content. Rupert squeezed her. "None of that, now. We can't fall asleep here."

She responded by yawning again. "I don't know why I'm feeling so tired. I was full of energy a moment ago."

He pulled her more snugly against him. "It's normal to feel sleepy after a climax."

"Is it? I wouldn't know. I hadn't even kissed a man before today," she admitted.

Rupert looked up, a gentle smile on his face. "Truly?" At her nod, he laughed. "What a lucky fellow I am. But that's even more reason not to risk any damage to your reputation."

Much to Clarissa's disappointment, he scooped her night rail off the floor and helped her back into it. While she fastened her wrapper, he retrieved his shirt and did up his trousers. "Go," he said, pressing a kiss against her forehead. "We'll talk more tomorrow."

Nodding sleepily, she slipped from the room.

CHAPTER 23

*A*s he made his way down to breakfast the following morning, Rupert wondered if things would be awkward with Claire in light of what they'd done in the dark of the night. He had a bit of experience where these things were concerned and knew that just because a woman was keen to have him in her bed didn't mean she was interested in anything of the lasting kind. Normally, that wasn't a problem.

But Clarissa Weatherby wasn't your average kettle of fish. There was something about her that made his heart feel as bruisable as a ripe peach. Ever since he first heard about her, she'd sounded like exactly what he wanted, and nothing he'd seen since meeting her in the flesh had disabused him of that notion. He was heading in the exact direction he'd always suspected he was going to go, falling head over heels in love with Claire.

It probably hadn't been wise, what they did last night, at least, beyond what was necessary to make whoever had come to the library door think it'd been nothing more than a midnight tryst. Which was a bit ironical, when you thought about it, that making it seem like they were doing something that could bring about Claire's ruination was their *best* option.

The point was, he probably should have stopped kissing her the second the coast was clear, but he'd wanted to keep going, wanted to have that moment with Claire *so badly*, that longing had beaten out what little good sense he had.

He'd probably come to regret it when she went skipping off on her next assignment, and he was left heaving sighs into his cups. Or maybe he would cherish that memory with Claire and manage to see the bright side of things. After all, what did he know?

One thing he was sure about was that he shouldn't form any expectations. Plenty of women wanted him to warm their beds. It was one of the few things he was good for.

This did not mean that Claire wanted him in the same way he wanted her, which was for keeps. When he saw her, he needed to be professional, not start acting like a peanut and mooning all over her.

Rupert sighed. Acting normal wasn't exactly his specialty. But he was determined to give it a go, just this once.

As she made her way down to breakfast, Clarissa had to remind herself to walk rather than skip.

Yesterday had been her first… everything. First kiss, first romantic interlude with a man.

First time experiencing pleasure.

She was coming to accept that she had been completely wrong about Rupert. She should have known that Lady Milthorpe wouldn't have tried to match her with someone awful. And while Rupert Dupree might not be a conventional husband, honestly, a conventional husband was the last thing Clarissa needed. She was outspoken to a fault, a quality ninety-nine percent of men would consider a disqualification to marriage. But not Rupert. He actually wanted a clever wife!

And physical relations between them had proven more than satisfactory. Clarissa felt her toes curl in her slippers, remembering the sensations Rupert had conjured up within her body last night. And to think, they hadn't even done everything yet!

She couldn't wait to see what else he could show her.

That part—throwing herself at him physically—was the easy bit. What was more difficult was confessing that her feelings had changed. Two years ago, after Rupert had overheard her railing against their proposed union, they had become disengaged.

Now, she needed to explain to him that she wanted to get... un-disengaged. Which was not a word. No word existed for this ridiculous situation because nobody had ever managed to make such a muddle of things before.

She tried to picture herself broaching the subject. *Say, Rupert, how would you like to get married after all?* The mere thought had her breaking out in hives. Wasn't the man supposed to do the proposing? That was the problem all right—she wasn't supposed to be the one doing the asking, but what choice did she have, considering she had already rejected him?

She was pondering this predicament when Phyllis Cuthbert stepped into her path. "Miss Weatherby," she said, giving Clarissa a pinched, disapproving look. "Might I have a word?"

Clarissa would rather not, but she forced herself to smile. "Of course."

Phyllis led her to the Wedgewood-blue parlor just down the hall from the breakfast room, shutting the door behind them. Seeking to cut the tension that was thick in the air, Clarissa gestured to the windows. "Do you think we'll have more snow, or—"

"I saw you," Phyllis said, cutting Clarissa off.

Clarissa froze. "Saw me?"

"Last night. With Rupert Dupree." Phyllis crossed the room in three quick strides. "In the library."

"Ah." Well, at least she now knew the identity of the person who had interrupted them. Clarissa cleared her throat. "I hope I can rely upon your discretion in—"

"He won't marry you, you know," Phyllis said, her voice hot with anger.

Clarissa recoiled. "I—I'm sorry?"

Phyllis's eyes were fierce. "He won't marry you. Believe me, I know how men are. They talk a pretty game and convince you to surrender your favors. But there is only one thing they want, and after they've had that, they will move on and leave you alone to face the wreckage."

It was on the tip of Clarissa's tongue to tell Phyllis she was wrong. That Rupert wasn't like that. To watch and see because he was going to be her future husband.

But it occurred to her that, even if her hopes came to fruition and it turned out to be true, this probably wasn't her best strategy.

So, instead, Clarissa waved a hand. "Oh, I know all that. As one of England's most notorious wallflowers, I've long accepted that I'll never marry. The opportunity presented itself to exchange a few kisses with Mr. Dupree, and I will admit to being curious. I had never been kissed before, you see," she confessed. "But I know that nothing will come of it."

Phyllis shook her head so vigorously that her tightly drawn bun trembled. "You do not seem to appreciate what dangerous ground you are treading. How quickly a few kisses can lead to other things."

It happened that Clarissa did understand this. Rupert had proved more than capable of sweeping her up in the moment.

Not that she was about to admit as much to Phyllis Cuthbert.

Clarissa took Phyllis's hand and pressed it. "It is kind of you to look out for me. But truly, it was nothing more than a few kisses."

Strictly speaking, it was true.

There was no need to mention precisely *where* she and Rupert had kissed each other.

Phyllis's expression remained stony. "It takes far less than a few kisses to ruin a woman."

Clarissa pressed her hand. "I know that, but I also know that, as my friend, you would never expose me to the world's censure."

Phyllis's expression remained sulky, but she mumbled, "Of course, I wouldn't."

Eager to bring this conversation to an end, Clarissa looped her arm through Phyllis's. "I appreciate your discretion and your advice. I will certainly keep it in mind. Now come," she said, tugging Phyllis toward the door. "Let's see what Lord and Lady Helmsley have laid out for breakfast."

Inside the breakfast room, Phyllis clung to Clarissa's side. But that was all right because Rupert had taken the seat next to their new primary suspect, Nicholas Higginbotham. He was attempting, not very successfully, by the look of things, to engage him in conversation. But if anyone could draw him out, it was Rupert. Clarissa caught his eye for a brief second and an understanding passed between them. *Don't worry,* Rupert's eyes said. *I'll handle it.* Clarissa gave him a tiny nod.

Lord and Lady Helmsley were throwing the first ball of the house party that night, and the ladies were to spend the morning decorating the ballroom with festive greenery while the gentlemen went tromping around in the snow in search of the perfect Yule log. Clarissa, therefore, didn't get to speak to Rupert until luncheon.

Sidling up to him at the buffet table, she murmured, "Did Mr. Higginbotham say anything of interest?"

"Nothing. Quite the taciturn fellow," Rupert whispered.

"We'll try again tonight," Clarissa returned as Phyllis Cuthbert bore down on her, a disapproving scowl on her face as she saw Clarissa ignoring her advice and speaking to Rupert.

The ladies spent the afternoon drinking tea and embroidering, and then it was time to dress for the ball.

Having decided that red was Clarissa's color, Lady Emily sent over a cherry-red ballgown for her to wear that evening. Clarissa wasn't surprised at this point; she had quite given up on blending into the wallpaper.

But the strangest thing happened when she put the dress on. Until that point, she had recoiled slightly every time she looked in the mirror and saw herself clad in a cheerful shade of mint or apricot. But today, she recognized the woman in red staring back at her with a confident smile. Ten days of joining the party instead of skulking in the corner, of being treated as a respectable young lady instead of a despised wallflower, had transformed how she thought of herself.

She wondered if she would be able to go back to her brown gowns once the house party concluded. On the one hand, she needed them for her work for the Home Office, which she wanted to continue.

But she couldn't help but feel that those dresses belonged to someone else, a version of herself that no longer existed.

She encountered Rupert on the landing as she headed downstairs. He bowed cordially and offered her his arm.

Leaning in, Clarissa whispered, "Were you able to speak with Mr. Higginbotham again?"

"I made a go of it but didn't make any progress. I think you should give it a try to see if you have better luck."

"I doubt that I would," Clarissa murmured.

"I think you might. After all, what man can resist a beautiful woman?"

They had reached the ballroom's entrance. Clarissa stopped short just shy of the double doors. She peered up at Rupert but couldn't detect anything but sincerity in his expression.

"You really think I'm beautiful." It was a statement, not a question. Clarissa could hear a trace of surprise in her voice as she said it.

"Of course I do." Rupert's voice was husky, and his eyes… Clarissa felt a sudden conviction that if she lived to be a thousand years old, she would never forget the way Rupert was looking at her in the shadowy entryway.

Inside the ballroom, the musicians began the opening bars of a waltz. There was something vulnerable in Rupert's eyes as he asked, "Would you do me the very great honor of granting me this dance?"

"I would," Clarissa whispered.

Rupert smiled, and he led her inside.

The cream-and-gold ballroom was bright with candlelight from a dozen chandeliers. The room smelled of the fresh-cut fir boughs that adorned each arched window.

Clarissa saw it all in a haze because she could not seem to tear her eyes from Rupert's face.

He swept her into the waltz. Clarissa had always been an indifferent dancer, preferring to spend her spare minutes with her nose in a book. Rupert, on the other hand, danced elegantly, with a firm, competent lead that made her ten times better than she would otherwise have been. This felt like an apt metaphor. Did this man not bring out all her better qualities? In Rupert's company, it was so easy to be patient, kind, and quietly capable, rather than condescending. Probably because these were all things he believed her to be. With Rupert, she had nothing to prove, and the rough edges she had worn like armor these past two years melted away.

The dance passed so quickly that she felt like it had scarcely begun when the music stopped. Rupert held her a second too long before clearing his throat and taking a hasty step back. Clarissa keenly felt the absence of his warm hand on her waist.

As he led her to the refreshment table, he leaned down and murmured, "You should try to waltz with Higginbotham. That would give you the best chance to converse."

She made a bleak sound. "I don't know how I'll get him to ask me. I've scarcely made his acquaintance."

"I'll help you," Rupert whispered.

Richard Garroway claimed the next dance, and Clarissa never found herself wanting for a partner—a first for England's most notorious wallflower.

Just before the supper break, the musicians began the opening bars of another waltz. Percival Ponsonby, one of the young men who had shown a marked interest in Clarissa after learning of the dowry the Duke of Norwood had settled upon her, came hurrying over, but Rupert scooped up her arm, quick as a leopard. Percival scowled, no doubt thinking it poor form for Rupert to claim both of the evening's waltzes, but Rupert led her to the corner where Mr. Higginbotham had been standing alone for most of the ball.

Clarissa wondered what he was going to do. Mr. Higginbotham did not seem much inclined to dance, and of course, a lady could not do the asking.

"Good evening, Higginbotham," Rupert said cheerfully. "Have you met Miss Clarissa Weatherby?"

"Good evening, Dupree. Yes, I have had the pleasure." Mr. Higginbotham's words were correct, but he didn't manage to accompany them with a smile. Clarissa could not help but wonder if it was the presence of the man who had ousted him from his parliamentary seat and sent his career into disarray that had him in a less-than-festive mood.

"Do you enjoy waltzing?" Rupert asked.

Mr. Higginbotham sighed, by all appearances wishing they would go away. "I used to. But I am not much for dancing these days."

His unenthusiastic response did not put a dent in Rupert's cheerfulness. "I daresay you will recall why you used to like it so well if you could but dance with such a splendid partner as Miss Weatherby."

Mr. Higginbotham's melancholy expression did not waver, but he was not so rude as to ignore such a pointed suggestion. "Miss Weatherby, would you do me the honor?"

They found a space on the ballroom floor and began turning together. Clarissa cast about for an opening foray. "May I ask how you know Lord and Lady Helmsley?"

"Our families are friends. I was raised in Thirsk," he said, naming a town about ten miles away.

"Thirsk, really?" Curiosity showed on Mr. Higginbotham's face, so she added, "I am from Boroughbridge, you see."

"Ah. I know just where that is, of course."

Clarissa recalled that Rosalind Baxter had been raised in Thirsk. This was surely the best opening she was going to get. "I believe Lady Helmsley's sister lives in Thirsk, does she not?"

"She does. That is how I came to meet the earl and countess."

Clarissa sought to make her voice nonchalant as she said, "Then you must be well acquainted with Mrs. Rosalind Baxter."

He shrugged. "I don't know that I would say well acquainted. She is nine years younger than me, after all. By the time she was old enough to talk, I was away at school. I am good friends with her older brothers, Joseph and Gregory, though."

Clarissa's mind was scrambling, trying to figure out how to turn the conversation to Oliver Baxter without being too obvious. "I have not had the pleasure of meeting Mrs. Baxter's brothers. Do you see much of them these days?"

"I do not," Mr. Higginbotham replied, steering her around another couple. "They still reside in Thirsk, but I haven't been there in years."

"Is your business based in London, then?" Clarissa asked.

He shook his head. "York."

It was only around twenty-five miles from York to Thirsk, not even a full day's journey. It seemed significant that he would not have traversed such a short distance to visit his old friends.

She was careful to keep her voice light as she said, "Perhaps you will stop and visit after the house party. You'll have to pass through Thirsk on your way back to York, after all."

A shadow fell over his face. Over his shoulder, she saw Oliver Baxter, who had partnered with Phyllis Cuthbert, go spinning by.

His jaw worked, and he took a moment to select his words. "I will not be stopping in Thirsk," he said in a clipped voice. "There is nothing there but bad memories." The music slowed as the last few bars were played. Stepping back, Mr. Higginbotham bowed over her hand. "Thank you for the dance, Miss Weatherby."

Rupert collected Claire from the middle of the ballroom, where Higginbotham had left her standing after their waltz concluded. Which wasn't very gallant of him, but the poor fellow looked to be in something of a state.

"Learn anything?" Rupert whispered as he looped his arm through Claire's, whisking her away from three approaching suitors. This earned him another scowl from Percival Ponsonby, which Rupert returned with a bland smile.

"Possibly," Claire murmured. "Mr. Higginbotham advised me that he now resides in York and has not visited his hometown of Thirsk for several years. Thirsk, of course, being the borough that voted him out in favor of Mr. Baxter."

"Perhaps his work keeps him busy," Rupert said, snagging them each a glass of warm negus.

Claire sipped from her glass. "Perhaps, but he advised me very firmly that he would not be stopping in Thirsk on his way back to York, as there is 'nothing there but bad memories.' Additionally, a scowl settled over his face when he spied Mr. Baxter in the dance."

Rupert wasn't sure how much to read into that. Baxter made *him* want to scowl, and he wasn't the scowling sort. "I suppose there could be something there."

"It's not much," Claire agreed. "But it's better than any lead we... Wait, where is he going?"

Rupert glanced over his shoulder. As sure as death and taxes, Higginbotham was making for the ballroom's doors.

"It's probably nothing," Rupert noted. "He could be on his way to use the..." He cleared his throat. "You know."

Claire had snagged his arm and was already towing him across the ballroom. "Let's see."

Rupert couldn't resist nudging her in the ribs with his elbow. "I'll bet when you agreed to work for the Home Office that you never dreamed your job would be so glamorous. Tracking a man to the gentleman's retiring... ho, now, what do we have here?"

Higginbotham had gone not toward the necessary but the front door. Ducking into an alcove, they watched as he quietly conferred with a footman. The footman left but returned quickly bearing a cloak and hat. Higginbotham donned them and stepped out into the snowy night.

Claire dug her fingers into his forearm. "Where could he be headed?"

"At this time of night? Not a clue. It's dark out there, and deuced c-cold." Rupert stumbled, both over his feet and over his words, as Claire dragged him out of the alcove. She surprised him by heading not after Higginbotham but toward the back of the castle.

A blast of cold air hit him in the face as she opened the door leading into the gardens. Up until this point, he'd been allowing Claire to lead him around because goodness knew any suggestion she had was bound to be better than what he came up with.

But going outside in their evening kit didn't seem like the absolute best idea she'd ever had.

"Claire," he hissed, "what are you doing?"

She looked up at him, brown eyes bright with excitement, and she looked so pretty, it scrambled what few wits he had. "We have to follow him. Why would he be heading out at this time of night if not for some nefarious purpose?"

"That, I don't know. But I'm fairly certain that if we go out there, we're going to freeze to death. Especially you! At least I have a jacket on."

She pulled on his arm, undeterred. "Come on. We can't let him get away!"

Rupert shook his head, hoping to clear it. He knew this was a bad idea, but it was difficult to deny Claire anything when she sported that eager-hopeful sort of expression. "At least let me go and fetch our cloaks."

"No! If we do that, whatever servant we ask will know we went outside."

"At least let me run up to my room. I'll find something warm in my trunks we can throw on."

"There's no time for that. Please, Rupert! We have to hurry!"

Claire's lip quivered, and her eyes were full of anguish. It was the sort of thing no man wanted to see, but it was a thousand times worse when it was your girl who was making that face. Not that Claire was his girl, not really. But the point was, she held that position in his heart, even if she never would in any official sense of the word.

He sighed. How could he possibly deny her? "Fine, but only if you take my coat."

She peered up at him uncertainly as he shrugged out of the garment. "What about you?"

He waved this off. "Don't worry about old Rupert. As I

said a few days ago, I just came from Switzerland and spent the previous winter in Norway. I'm acclimated to the cold."

Claire bit her lip as he draped it around her shoulders. At least it was a sturdy, winter-weight wool. "You're quite certain you'll be warm enough?"

No. But he said, "'Course I will." He could see it was time to lay down his trump card, so he gestured across the back gardens. "We'd better hurry, or he's going to get away!"

That distracted her, just like he knew it would. She grabbed his arm, and then he was hurrying through the garden in nothing but his shirtsleeves and gold silk waistcoat. The cold penetrated his thin garments immediately, leeching away whatever body heat he'd had.

Well, at least he'd forced Claire to take his jacket.

Rupert frowned as a cloud passed in front of the moon, casting them into darkness. Unlike the garden path, the snow around the side of the castle hadn't been cleared and was shin-deep. Rupert's dancing pumps and silk stockings were already soaked through. He frowned, because Claire was also wearing flimsy dancing slippers. "I have a bad feeling about this," he muttered.

The cloud moved on, giving them a little moonlight. "Well, I have a good feeling about this," Claire countered, pointing up ahead. "There he is."

Sure enough, he could just make out Higginbotham's lonely figure, illuminated by a lantern as he plodded down the snowy road. What the devil could the man be up to? It was deuced peculiar...

"Where do you think he could be going?" Claire asked, her voice full of excitement.

"N-no idea," Rupert said through a clenched jaw, trying to hide the fact that his teeth were starting to chatter.

They walked on for around fifteen minutes, managing to make their way by moonlight. At a bend in the road, Claire ducked behind a tree, then peered around its edge. She seized Rupert's forearm. "Look!"

Higginbotham had reached the little stone chapel standing in a grove of trees. He opened the door and disappeared, taking the light of his lantern with him.

"Come on," Claire said, pulling him forward. "Let's see who he's meeting."

Reminding himself that feeling in his hands and feet was more of a luxury than anything else, Rupert stumbled through the snow after her.

The inside of the chapel was illuminated with the soft light of Higginbotham's torch, which was convenient, as another cloud had passed in front of the moon. They crept up to a window, pressing their backs against the cold stones of the chapel's wall. Squatting down, Claire crept along until she was directly beneath one of the big arched windows. Rupert tried to follow suit but lost his balance and wound up on his hands and knees in the snow.

She shot him a concerned look. He could just see her mouth form the words, "Are you all right?" in the faint flicker of light from the window. He nodded in spite of the fact that his breeches were now wet and his fingers felt like icicles.

Gripping the window's lip, Claire slowly raised her head just high enough to peer inside the chapel. Whatever she saw made her recoil.

"What is it?" Rupert whispered.

She lowered her head. "He's *praying*."

"*Praying?*" Rupert hissed. "In a *chapel?*" Although… come to think of it, that did make a certain amount of sense.

He peeked over the lip of the window to see for himself. Surely enough, there was Higginbotham in the front pew, kneeling quietly with head bowed and hands clasped.

Rupert ducked down again, glanced at Claire, and

shrugged. She still had that mulish look about her. "Let's wait a little while. See if anybody else shows up."

They waited for around a half-hour, peeking through the window every few minutes to see if anything had changed. Invariably the answer was, *it had not*. Higginbotham remained in the front pew, going about his devotions, and no mysterious miscreants appeared for a midnight rendezvous.

Right around the time when Rupert was wondering if it was possible to develop frostbite to your "stern end," the lamplight shifted behind the window. Perking up, Claire peered through the glass. "He's on the move," she whispered. "Come on!"

They crept toward the front of the chapel. The area briefly brightened as Higginbotham opened the door and strode out onto the front steps with his lantern. They watched from around the corner as he shut the door behind him, descended the steps, and started back toward the castle.

Claire leaned in. "We'd best wait here a few minutes so he won't realize he was followed."

Rupert could see her logic. The problem was, he wasn't sure his joints were going to be capable of bending if he stayed out here much longer. But protesting would have involved forming words, which he was fairly certain he couldn't do, so he stood there shivering agreeably until Claire deemed the coast clear.

But as they stood there, the other problem became clear. Higginbotham withdrawing with the lantern threw into sharp relief the fact that the moon was now completely obscured by clouds, and it was pitch black on the road.

They were going to have a deuced time making it back to the castle.

"All right," Claire said. "Let's go."

Rupert started forward and promptly tripped over his frozen foot. Claire grabbed his wrist to steady him. He couldn't really see her on account of the darkness, but he could hear the disapproval in her voice. "Rupert! Your hand is freezing!"

"S-s-sorry."

He heard her huff. "Don't be sorry. But I wish you had said something!"

"D-didn't want to b-be a b-b-bother."

She was already wrapping his coat around his shoulders, and he was too cold to even throw a fit about it. Grabbing his hand, she surprised him by pulling him away from the road. "Let's get you back to the castle. We'll cut through the woods. It's a more direct route."

Claire was correct in that going as the crow flies would cut the distance by half.

Unfortunately, it was even darker in the woods than it was on the road. Unlike the road, no attempt had been made to clear the snow.

And there were trees. *So many* trees.

Claire grunted as she tripped over yet another root. "In retrospect, perhaps we should've kept to the road."

Rupert was too cold to even attempt to answer. For the third time, he walked straight into a low-hanging limb and had to grab Claire's arm for balance.

They trudged on for a few minutes more. Claire slipped on a patch of ice and almost fell. Rupert did her one better by tripping over a fallen log and going face-first into a snowbank.

"Oh, Rupert!" Claire cried, pulling him back to his feet and dusting him off. "This is all my fault."

Rupert's tongue wasn't working so well, but he couldn't let her go thinking something like that. "S-s-s-all-r-r-right," he managed.

"It's not all right! You're freezing. I feel even worse because you've always been so considerate of me and…" Her grip on his arm tightened. "Wait, I... I think I see something!"

"'S good that o-one of us d-does," Rupert said, trying to look on the bright side of things.

Claire tugged him forward with new vigor. "Just a little bit farther. How I hope I'm not mistaken... but I'm not! We've reached the hunting cabin!"

By gum, she was right. It was a deuced welcome sight, even if the cabin was dark and cold. At least there wasn't any snow inside or any more roots to trip over.

The door proved to be locked. Fortunately, Rupert managed to overcome this obstacle by losing his balance, stumbling into the front window, and cracking a pane.

Claire brightened. "Well, since it's already broken," she said, jabbing a proper hole with her gloved fist. She reached inside and had the lock undone in a trice.

They staggered inside. "F-fireplace should be... over here," he said, tugging Claire toward the back left corner.

They promptly bumped into the sofa. "Here," Claire said, guiding him around. "You sit down. I'll take care of it."

Rupert was too cold to argue. Besides, he couldn't imagine he'd be anything but in the way, considering he couldn't move his fingers.

A metallic crash rang out from the far side of the cabin. It took a few seconds for the cacophony to die down. "Everything's fine!" Claire called from across the room. "That was nothing, nothing at all."

Rupert grunted. He found a wool blanket draped over the back of the sofa. He managed to wrap it around himself with numb fingers.

He heard a great deal of thumping and a few muttered curses as Claire banged around, searching for the tinderbox. His first indication that success was nigh was a pleased sound in the darkness. A few seconds later, she managed to light a brief spark, which looked startlingly bright after being in total darkness for so long.

On her next attempt, Claire managed to light a rush. From there, she got a couple of candles going, including the candelabra she had knocked to the floor in the dark.

Five minutes later, she sat back on her heels as the beginnings of a fire took hold in the hearth. Once she satisfied herself that it was spreading nicely and wouldn't go out, she hurried over to Rupert.

"Your shoes are soaked," she noted, pulling them off and tossing them on the floor. "As are your stockings, your breeches, your shirt…"

Rupert laid back and enjoyed the fact that she was undressing him. It reminded him of one of those bawdy novels where a couple is forced to take shelter from a storm in a deserted cottage and has no choice but to take off all their clothes and huddle together for warmth.

As if you would be so lucky, he chastised himself.

Still, like most men, Rupert only wore drawers when he was planning on spending the day outdoors in the cold, so once Claire had stripped him of his damp things, he had only the blanket to preserve not so much his modesty as his pride. His cock was as cold as a well digger's arse, as they said in Denmark, which meant that it probably wasn't what you would call an impressive sight.

Once she finished hanging his unmentionables before the fire, Claire hurried back over to him. "Can you stand? I'd like to scoot the sofa closer to the fire so we can get you warmed up."

That sounded like a capital suggestion, so Rupert wrapped up in the blanket and struggled to his feet. He even managed to lean against the sofa and help her scoot it across the plain wooden floor.

Once it was in place, he flopped back down, none too

gracefully, mind you, but this wasn't the time to be prideful about such things. The fire felt so hot on his skin that he thought it might burn him, yet he still felt chilled to the bone, a peculiar sensation.

He wondered if a cup of tea would help, but he didn't want to put Claire to any trouble fetching water and whatnot. He glanced at her to see if perhaps the same idea had occurred to her...

... only to find that she was *unbuttoning her dress.*

Rupert's four non-frozen brain cells ceased functioning. Claire caught his eye, and he shut his mouth, because, of course, his mouth was gaping open.

"My dress is wet around the hem," she explained. "My stockings and petticoats as well. I'd best get out of my wet things."

Far be it for Rupert to stop her. Turning his face toward the back of the sofa would have been the gentlemanly thing to do, but he didn't have the fortitude at the moment, and Claire didn't so much as ask him to avert his gaze.

Once she was down to a whisper-thin linen shift, she walked over to the bed in the far corner. Rupert figured she would climb beneath the blankets, but she surprised him by pulling off the quilt, then surprised him even more by bringing it back to the sofa and spreading it over him.

She crawled in with him, taking him in her arms, and he thought his frozen heart might burst with delight. "Is this all right?" she asked.

"This is wonderful," Rupert replied, burying his cold nose in her warm shoulder.

She stroked soft fingertips across his bare back. "It should help you warm more quickly if we share our body heat."

Rupert made a garbled sound that was the closest he could come to a laugh. Weariness had descended upon him, and it was suddenly difficult to keep his eyes open. "Here I thought that was my line."

"What?"

"Nothing," he muttered, pulling her closer. Claire had crawled not only beneath the quilt but inside the woolen blanket with him, meaning that a whisper of linen was the only thing separating his body from hers. It was a testament to how well and truly frozen Rupert was that he wasn't sporting a cockstand right now, with all of Claire's warm, soft curves pressed against him.

It was probably for the best. He didn't want to go ruining the moment. He would always cherish this memory of the time he got to fall asleep with her in his arms…

"Rupert?" He'd never heard Claire's voice sound so small and hesitant before.

He yawned, trying to fight off the sleep rapidly overcoming him. "Yes?"

She was silent for so long he was starting to drift off when she finally spoke. "I know now that it was my fault that you called off our betrothal two years ago."

He shook his head. "You mustn't… blame yourself. Just wasn't meant to be, I suppose."

"But what if things had happened differently?" she said in a rush. "I know I can't go back and unsay those words. That I can never fix things. But is there any chance… I mean, would you ever consider…"

Rupert felt a tingly sensation at the base of his skull. He had a feeling this was one of those important conversations, but he couldn't quite put his finger on it. "What is it, Claire?"

Her voice was little more than a whisper. "Do you think you could be happy being married to someone like me?"

Rupert sighed.

Of course, he would be happy being married to Claire. She was everything he had ever wanted.

That had never been the problem. The problem was that she didn't want the likes of him.

"I would be happier than I could possibly say, being married to you," he answered honestly. "You're"—he paused as a yawn escaped—"perfect."

Claire squeezed him tight. She was saying something, but sleep was pulling him under.

He drifted off to the soft voice of the woman he loved, snug and happy in her arms.

CHAPTER 25

*C*larissa awoke to the smell of almond biscuits.

The fire was low but still burning, and the first faint glow of morning light was showing at the windows. The hunting cabin's air was crisp against her face, but the rest of her felt wonderfully warm snuggled up with Rupert.

They would need to return to the house soon. The odds were high that their absence had already been noted, which would mean she was ruined.

She smiled against Rupert's chest. The thought of losing her good name should not have been a happy one, but she wasn't worried about it.

Not after what Rupert had said last night.

He still wanted to marry her! She hadn't spoiled everything after all. She had somehow found this wonderful man who liked her just as she was, and she would get to go through life with him by her side.

She couldn't wait to tell Lady Milthorpe that she had been right all along, that they were, indeed, perfect for one another. That, in spite of the universe... or at least, William

Ellison… conspiring to keep them apart, they had managed to find each other and promptly fell in love.

It was enough to make you believe in fate.

Beside her, Rupert was stirring. She couldn't resist pressing a kiss against the underside of his jaw. His stubble was both rough and smooth at the same time.

He made an appreciative rumble, his voice pitched low.

She trailed her lips toward his ear. "Wake up, Rupert."

"Don' wanna wake up," he mumbled, burying his nose in her hair. "Havina good dream."

Clarissa had a notion what his dream might be about. Whereas last night Rupert's body had been alarmingly chilled, there was currently something torrid going on in the general vicinity of his groin.

In fact, she could feel it poking her in the stomach.

The realization made her feel lightheaded in a good way. She eased her shift up so she could wrap a leg around his hip.

This made Rupert purr like a lion, which only fanned the flames sparking to life between Clarissa's legs. "What are you dreaming about?" she asked, her voice coming out breathless.

She could hear the smile in his voice. "Claire, of course."

"*Of course*," she echoed, pleased by his answer. She began dropping teasing kisses across his jaw. "But I think you'll find yourself just as happy when you wake up."

"Oh, no," he said, smiling with his eyes closed. "Nothing could be as good as this dre—"

He didn't get to finish his sentence because Clarissa kissed him full on the mouth. Rupert immediately kissed her back, his tongue twining with hers in a way that made her squirm against him.

She nipped at his bottom lip, and his eyes popped open. "Cl-Claire?" he said, sounding startled. "I'm sorry, I didn't realize… I thought it was a—"

She cut him off with another kiss, and he groaned in her mouth.

When she finally broke the kiss, they were both panting. "Good morning, Rupert," she said, tracing her hands down his back and squeezing his taut buttocks.

"Good morning, Claire," he said, his voice rich and appreciative.

She nipped his lip again. "We need to get back to the house soon." She brought her hands around to frame his hips, then circled her fingers there, teasing him with the prospect that she might bring them all the way to the front. "But I think we have time to do a few things before we do."

Rupert brightened. "A repeat of what we did in the library? Believe me, I would be more than happy to oblige you." He started kissing his way down her neck.

"Yes. And no." At Rupert's curious look, Clarissa added, "I want to do *everything* this time."

It wasn't possible, strictly speaking, to stumble when one was already lying down. Yet somehow, that seemed the most apt description for what Rupert's body did. He collapsed face first into the sofa's cushions.

He managed to push up on his forearms. "But Claire, if we do *everything*… I mean, people would say you're…"

"Ruined?" At his nod, she continued, "I don't think of it that way. Not at all. I'm eager to do this with you, Rupert. And I'm perfectly happy for us to have our first time right here."

He really was adorable when he was confused. "Our first time? Do you mean—"

She cut him off with a kiss. "Unless you don't want to?"

He laughed as if this was the most absurd thing she could have possibly said. "Oh, I want to, all right. I just… you're sure? Completely sure?"

She kissed his chin. "Completely sure."

His voice was rich as he said, "I'm going to make this so good for you."

She smiled. He was already kissing his way across her collarbone. "If anyone can do it, it's you." At his curious look, she added, "You have quite the reputation."

"Oh, that?" He ventured below her collarbone, dropping three more kisses. "Do you know why I think that is?"

"Why?" she asked, enjoying the way he was touching her all over her torso.

"You see," he said, pausing to kiss the swell of one breast, "most fellows don't take too kindly to being informed they're not an expert at something. And that goes double when the something in question is their performance in the bedchamber."

"Is that so?" she asked, shuddering as he flicked his tongue over her nipple through the fabric of her shift.

He lifted his head long enough to say, "It is," before returning his attentions to her nipple, which had gone hard as a pebble. "Most men throw a fit at the mere suggestion that they're not a veritable Cassanova. Not old Rupert, though," he added as he shifted to the other side.

Clarissa's eyes rolled back in her head as he sucked the opposite nipple into his mouth, using his tongue to rub the fine linen against her sensitive flesh. The only response she could manage was a weak, "Oh?"

"That's right," Rupert said, kissing his way down her stomach. "Whether a woman says, 'Stop that, Rupert,' or 'That's not even close to the right spot, Rupert,' or even, 'What on earth are you doing down there, Rupert?' I respond with good humor. I say, 'All right, then, what *would* you like?' Then, I actually do it. That's the difference between me and all those other fellows."

"Really?" she gasped.

"Really." He pushed her shift up, pressing a reverent kiss

against the inside of her thigh. "You can't imagine how much useful information I've received over the years."

Clarissa had an inkling. Because if every other man was capable of making a woman's thoughts flee and her thighs tremble like a raspberry jelly, surely they would spend every waking moment doing *this*, instead of darning their stockings and balancing the household budget and making sure their children didn't wander off and get eaten by a wolf.

Rupert's lips were wandering painfully closer to where she needed them to be, but somehow never reached that magical spot. Clarissa could hear herself making sounds that in any other circumstances she would have found humiliating. But she wasn't capable of stopping, and besides, Rupert actually seemed to be enjoying them, if she was interpreting his encouraging grunts correctly. She, therefore, decided not to care.

Finally, his lips brushed that sensitive bud, far too gently. Clarissa cried out, and Rupert chuckled.

Men. She threaded her fingers into his hair to help him understand *exactly* what she wanted. He began circling his tongue around that magical spot, and she forgave him in an instant. He chuckled again, but then got serious about his business, giving her a succession of teasing flicks, quick light strokes, and finally a deep, rhythmic rubbing with the flat of his tongue that had her thrashing on the sofa without a single care as to how ridiculous she looked.

She would have bet everything she had that it was not possible for something to feel better than this, but she would have been wrong, for at that moment, Rupert sealed his lips around that perfect nub and started to *suck*.

"Rupert!" she gasped, sitting halfway up. "Rupert, I... Oh, my *God*, you're going to make me... I... I... I'm going to—"

He glanced up at her, and she could see the smile in his eyes, but he did not pause the exquisite ministrations he was performing between her thighs. Then his face blurred as a blinding flash of white-hot pleasure washed over her. She could hear herself crying out, her thighs shaking uncontrollably, her hands fisting in Rupert's golden hair. He didn't seem to mind, for he kept pleasuring her through her storm until suddenly the beautiful sensations were too much and she cried, "You-you can stop now!"

Chuckling, he slid up the sofa and took her in his arms, pulling the blankets up to ward off the chill in the cold cabin.

As soon as the room stopped spinning, Clarissa peeled her shift up over her head and dropped it to the floor. Rupert made an appreciative sound.

She reached for the only article he still had on, the silver locket around his neck. "I don't think we want Auntie Imogen watching for the next few minutes." She placed it on the floor and covered it with her discarded shift. "We wouldn't want to shock her with our uncouth behavior."

Rupert laughed, but his expression quickly grew serious. "You're sure about this, Claire?"

She attempted to pull him on top of her. "Completely sure." After all, with the snow-covered ground, it might be a week or even more before they could make it to York to secure a bishop's license. That would be the fastest means by which they could marry.

Clarissa didn't want to wait a week. She was ready to start her forever with Rupert right away.

Rupert didn't seem quite as eager, for all that his man-part was poking her in the stomach. Try as she might, she couldn't manage to pull him on top of her.

"I know I am not as familiar with the general process as you are," she said, grunting with her fruitless efforts to tug at his shoulders. "But I believe for this to work, you need to be over here."

She could hear the smile in his voice as he said, "What's your hurry?"

She glanced up at him, biting her lip. "Do *you* not want to do this?"

He gave an appreciative huff as he stroked a hand down her side. "Oh, I want to do this, all right." He wrapped his arms around her, pulling her close, and brushed a kiss across her lips. "Trust me," he whispered.

He kissed her lazily, seeming to savor her sharp intake of breath, the way her lip quavered when he brushed his tongue across it, asking her to open, and the way she relaxed against him as he deepened the kiss. Rupert was patient, and Rupert was kind, and he kissed her as if he had all the time in the world. As if *he* had been the one to just receive a satisfying release and he now had no thought in his head beyond pleasing her.

His hands explored her body with equal nonchalance, delighting not just in the shape of her breasts or the treasure that lay between her thighs, but in the curve of her neck, the tender skin on the inside of her arm, and the full length of her spine.

By the time his warm hands found her breasts, her breath was coming fast again. She curled a leg around his hip, which had the effect of bringing the tender flesh between her legs into contact with the underside of his hardened cock. Whimpering, Clarissa couldn't help but squirm against him.

"That's it, Claire," he said encouragingly, sounding slightly breathless himself. "Do what feels good."

"Is it time to… to…"

He pressed his forehead against hers. "Soon, I promise."

Rupert's definition of *soon* differed from Clarissa's, for he continued kissing her as if he hadn't a care in the world. It took her a few minutes to find the right angle, the right rhythm, but she figured out *just* how to rub herself against his thickness.

"Ah, Claire," he gasped, burying his face in her shoulder. "You're s-so good at this." He gave a breathless laugh. "I'd best get you ready before I spill in the… I was going to say sheets, but I don't guess there are any."

"I'm ready," she insisted, trying once again to pull him on top of her.

His voice was deep as he murmured, "Let's just see, shall we?"

He reached between her legs, and she moaned because his thumb returned to that little spot where she loved to be rubbed. But this time, he also slid his middle finger inside her.

He made it about as far as his middle knuckle before she couldn't help but stiffen. "Shh, it's all right," he said, pressing kisses against her neck. "Give yourself a minute to adjust."

Just like that, he was back to his patient kisses and not-a-care-in-the-world caresses, but this time he accompanied them with little swirling strokes of his thumb upon her nubbin. It felt *so good*, and it almost came as a shock when Clarissa felt Rupert's hand come into contact with her outer petals. While he had been working on her, he had managed to slide his finger in fully, and she hadn't felt any pain, none at all.

"Hold on," he said, his voice growing tight. "Let me add one more finger."

She nodded against his throat, and he continued his gentle torture. The second finger took a little coaxing but went in far more easily than Clarissa would ever have guessed, and before she knew it, Rupert was withdrawing his hands.

Her throat seized. It was time, at last.

But instead of settling between her thighs, Rupert rolled

onto his back. His engorged cock settled on his stomach, pointing up toward his chin. "Go on, then," he said, patting his hip. "Climb aboard."

Clarissa started. "You want me to… to…"

"If you'd like. I haven't got any experience with deflowering virgins. But there are certain advantages to this position that I think will serve us well."

"All right," Clarissa said, suddenly feeling shy. She'd been naked with Rupert for the last half hour, but she hadn't felt nearly as exposed when they were snuggled up together beneath the blankets as when she was sitting up straight, straddling him. But the warm admiration and naked longing in his eyes went a long way toward reassuring her.

She had a general idea how they fit together, and, taking his member in her hand, positioned him at her slick entrance. "Should I, er…"

"Do whatever feels good for you." She started to slide down, and his eyes lolled back in his head. "God, Claire! You feel *so good*…"

She smiled. It felt… strange, having him inside of her. She felt stretched, just a little bit *too* full. She only managed to sink an inch or two down his length.

But Rupert didn't complain. Instead, he brought his hand to the juncture of her thighs and resumed teasing that little spot that was the center of all things delightful.

"Mmm," she moaned, tossing her head back. "That feels good."

"My God, if you're not the most beautiful sight I've ever seen," he said, swirling his fingers faster. "See if you can sink down another inch for me, Claire."

She complied with a whimper. It was going well until it wasn't. Without realizing it, she reached her barrier, which suddenly gave way with a sharp tear.

"Son of a *cucumber*!" she shouted, shuddering this time with pain rather than pleasure.

"Oh, sweet Claire," Rupert said, stroking her hip. "I take it we just located your maidenhead."

"That had better have been it," she muttered.

"Stay there a moment, darling. Rupert will make it good again."

He proceeded to do something extremely wicked with his thumb, which had Clarissa gasping in spite of the pain. Dear God, this man was good with his hands. Clarissa could not countenance the fact that some woman had not snapped him up already, but far be it for her to complain. Unlike whatever women had come before her, Clarissa Weatherby was no fool. She knew a good man when she saw one, and their loss was about to be her gain.

Rupert brought his fingertips together, gently grazing the tip of her bud then stroking down the sides. Clarissa groaned and began circling her hips. The pain was still there, but it was now more of a dull ache.

The ache for completion, on the other hand, was growing with every passing second. When Rupert put his thumb on that magical little spot and started shaking his wrist, the pain was all but forgotten.

She started to squirm, and Rupert gasped. Encouraged, she rose up a few inches and experimentally slid down.

Rupert made a strangled sound. "Cl-Claire! So guh… guh… guh…"

"Do you like that, Rupert?" she asked teasingly as she did it again.

"Ehrmagawd," he gasped. "Heaven. This is *heaven*."

Clarissa found she was enjoying driving him out of his mind just as much as what he was doing for her. It took her a few tries to figure out how to move, but she managed to settle into a rhythm that had Rupert's head tossing against the cushions.

He seemed to remember himself after a minute and resumed his ministrations to that spot between her legs. Clarissa's head lolled to the side. It did feel good, what he was doing, in spite of the slight soreness she still felt.

Rupert stiffened beneath her. "Claire," he gasped. "Claire, I'm getting close. You should… pregnant. You could get pregnant if you… if we…"

Clarissa attempted to quicken her pace. "I'm not worried about that." They were getting married, after all.

Rupert looked adorably confused. "You're not?"

She leaned forward, dropping a kiss on his nose. "No."

"Gosh, Claire—you really don't mind if I… if I…" His body began to tremble beneath her. "Oh, God, I'm… I'm going to…"

His eyes rolled back in his head, and he grasped her hips, pumping into her with quick, desperate strokes. Clarissa welcomed this treatment and did her best to move with him.

His left hip bucked off the sofa. His fingers dug into her hips, and suddenly, he was shaking and babbling nonsense as his body shook and his head rolled back and forth against the cushions.

Just as abruptly, he collapsed, boneless, on the sofa. Taking her hands, he tugged her down on top of him. "Sorry," he said, his breath coming fast. "Sorry. I'll see to you in a minute. Just… need to hold you."

Clarissa kissed his neck, enjoying the feeling of his warm hands tracing gentle patterns across her back in the cool room. She would enjoy the promised release, but she also loved how special it felt, and how intimate, lying here with Rupert after what they had just done.

After a few minutes, he stirred. Clarissa became

cognizant of the fact that the area between her legs was wet in a way that was not merely slick but... squelchy.

Rupert urged her to sit up and withdrew from inside her. There was a little blood on his lower abdomen—her maidenhead, no doubt—but not too much.

He helped her to stand then fetched his handkerchief and gently cleaned her before seeing to himself. Dropping the soiled cloth on the flagstones before the fireplace, he abruptly scooped her up. Clarissa shrieked, wrapping her legs around his waist as he carried her two steps back to the sofa.

He set her down and kneeled between her spread thighs. "Rupert," she gasped, "you don't have to—"

"Oh, yes, I do," he said, pressing a kiss against the inside of her thigh. "I want to see you quaking with pleasure. Touch your breasts for me, darling—there's a good girl."

He went to work flicking his tongue over that little bud between her folds. It felt so wicked, sitting here spread out before him, fingering her own nipples while he pleasured her between her legs. And Clarissa *loved* it.

As aroused as she was from what they'd been doing earlier, it only took a few minutes before the feeling of desperation swept over her. "Oh, Rupert!" she cried. "You're going to make me come again!"

He made an encouraging sound and began massaging her with the flat of his tongue. It almost felt *too* good, and Clarissa's thighs clamped around his ears. He glanced up at her, eyebrows raised.

"Don't stop," she gasped, threading her fingers into his hair. Her body had already adjusted to the intense pleasure he was giving her. "Please, don't stop! I want to... Oh... Oh, my God, I... *Rupert!*"

She shattered right there on the sofa, spread out before him so he could watch her take her pleasure. He didn't stop stroking her with his tongue, but she caught his eye and could discern the gleam of masculine satisfaction that he had just pleased her so thoroughly and so well.

When she grew too sensitive, she pulled him up for a kiss. They cuddled there on the sofa for a few minutes, foreheads pressed together, but then Clarissa sighed. "I suppose we should be getting back to the castle."

Rupert sighed. "You're right, of course. I just wish we didn't have to go. I wish we could stay here all day."

Clarissa did, too. But that was all right. This wasn't an ending, not really.

This was the first day of her future with Rupert, not her last.

A half-hour later, Clarissa was trudging through the snow with Rupert. He was wearing his jacket, and Clarissa had borrowed a blanket from the hunting cabin to wrap around herself.

"Hopefully our absence hasn't been remarked upon," Rupert said.

Clarissa thought this might be too much to hope for. Judging by the sun, it was mid-morning, but she expected most of the house party to sleep until noon after staying up late to attend the ball.

They might be able to slip back into the castle unobserved. But the fact that she and Rupert had disappeared before the supper dance was likely to have been noticed.

They made much faster progress in the daylight than they had last night. It was difficult to say if anyone spied them stealing up to the castle from one of its many windows, but they were able to slip inside the back entrance without encountering anyone. "Go on," Rupert whispered, taking the blanket from Clarissa. "You head upstairs. I'll stash this somewhere and give you a bit of a head start."

Clarissa squeezed his hand as she nodded, then hurried toward the servants' stairs. She made it up to her room without being spotted, then hurriedly removed her gown, draping it over the back of a chair.

She slipped beneath the fluffy white counterpane and spent a pleasant hour somewhere between sleep and wakefulness, hugging the spare pillow and dreaming she was snuggled up with Rupert.

Someone knocked softly at her door.

"Come in," Clarissa called.

Lady Helmsley slipped inside the room. "There you are, Miss Weatherby. I had been wondering where you disappeared to."

Clarissa sat up in bed, pulling the counterpane up to her chest. "I apologize, my lady. I retired early last night. I had a bit of a megrim."

This was, of course, a lie, and judging by Lady Helmsley's skeptical expression, not one she found convincing.

The countess cast a pointed look toward the clothes Clarissa had borrowed from Lady Emily last night. The slippers were drenched from trudging through the snow, and the bottom eight inches of the dress was similarly damp.

"Perhaps I am willing to accept that explanation," the countess said. "But I very much doubt that every guest at this house party will do the same, especially considering that Rupert absented himself from the party at exactly the same time. Servants gossip, too, and you will note that the fire in your room has already been made up this morning." She gave Clarissa a speaking look. "I had a word with the chambermaid who visited your room, which I hope will prevent any gossip. But you know how these things have a way of getting out."

Clarissa felt her cheeks warm. "I… er…"

Lady Helmsley sighed, then drew one of the chairs from the table next to the window to the side of Clarissa's bed. Sitting, she pressed Clarissa's hand. "There is one surefire way of silencing any potential talk. A wedding."

Clarissa couldn't suppress her smile. "I am pleased to reassure you, then, that these rumors will be silenced in the coming days."

The countess clapped her hands, delighted. "Good! Very good. It cannot have escaped your notice that Rupert is very, very dear to our family. It will be a relief to see him settled with someone who clearly cares for him."

"I do," Clarissa confessed. "Very much."

"I am happy for you both." Lady Helmsley gave her a firm look. "You'll need to act with some haste. Without question, you must settle things by the end of the house party to make sure my guests don't fan out across the country spreading goodness knows what sort of rumors."

"I agree, and I will speak to Rupert about it after breakfast."

The countess nodded, satisfied. "Excellent. There was one more thing I wanted to mention, my dear."

Clarissa stifled a yawn. "Oh?"

Lady Helmsley's eyes were warm. "It was kind of you to cajole Mr. Higginbotham into dancing last night. I despaired of him even attending the ball, much less dancing, given how hard this time of year is for him."

Clarissa tilted her head. "Why is this time of year hard for him?"

The countess started. "Oh, did you not know? Five Decembers ago, his wife died in childbirth. The babe did not survive, either. A little girl." She shook her head. "It was just before Christmas. In fact…" She tapped a finger on her chin. "I believe today might be the anniversary of their deaths."

"How terrible," Clarissa said, her thoughts aswirl. That would certainly explain why Mr. Higginbotham had slipped away from the party as the clock struck midnight to hold a silent vigil in the chapel.

Lady Helmsley nodded sadly. "Poor man. It was a love match, you know. I'm given to understand that he couldn't even bear the sight of his old house in Thirsk. That was the reason he gave up his seat in Parliament, you know."

Clarissa leaned forward, clutching the counterpane to her chest. "He gave up his seat? Here I thought Mr. Baxter defeated him in the election."

The countess waved a hand. "He had already filed to run for reelection at the time of his wife's death, so his name was on the ballot, it's true. But after Helen's death, he decided to move to York and return to his first profession as a solicitor." The countess dropped her voice low. "Just between you and me, Mr. Baxter would never have won that seat had Mr. Higginbotham wished to retain it. Mr. Higginbotham is a local, you see. But everyone in Thirsk knew of his wishes to leave that house where his wife and child died, and that is the only reason they voted for Mr. Baxter instead."

Clarissa's thoughts were flying. "So, there is no bad blood between Mr. Higginbotham and Mr. Baxter?"

"Gracious, no." The countess patted her hand, then stood. "In any case, I wanted to thank you for the kindness you showed to Mr. Higginbotham." She strolled over to the door, then paused, giving Clarissa a speaking look. "Resolve the other matter. Today, if possible."

Clarissa nodded. "I will arrange the announcement with Rupert."

"Good."

Once she was alone, Clarissa flopped back on her pillow. It seemed that Mr. Higginbotham was not a likely suspect after all.

Who, then, could it possibly be? Their initial trio of suspects did not seem promising, and it turned out that Mr. Higginbotham bore Oliver Baxter no ill will.

Someone wanted to kill the man, though. Clarissa tried to recall the other names Rupert had mentioned in the library. Could it truly be Percival Ponsonby, angry at having been given the nickname Priggish Percival? Or Francis Ditherington, whose fuchsia satin waistcoat Mr. Baxter had derided? Surely men did not kill over such things.

She climbed out of the bed and rang for a maid to help her dress. She paced the room as she waited. There was also Granville Smith-Nugent-Smith. Rupert had said the wager he had lost to Mr. Baxter was for two hundred pounds. It didn't *seem* worth killing over, but perhaps the loss had come at a bad time. And it certainly seemed a stronger motive than having been called an unflattering nickname...

She hadn't thought of any more likely suspects by the time she made her way down to the breakfast room. As it was just past noon, the spread included both breakfast items, for those like Clarissa, who had slept in, and traditional lunch fare for the early risers who had broken their fast hours ago.

She found Rupert standing at the buffet, almost finished filling his plate. Clarissa sidled up to him with an empty plate, striving to look casual. "I learned something from Lady Helmsley," she murmured. "We need to talk."

"Meet me at the orangery in one hour," he whispered.

She gave a subtle nod, and he turned to find a seat.

Clarissa was helping herself to a soft-boiled egg when a man loomed next to her. Startled, she fumbled the spoon, dropping the egg back onto the platter.

She glanced up and saw it was Oliver Baxter. "Mr. Baxter, good morning!" She laughed awkwardly. "How clumsy of me."

He grunted in response.

She attempted to recapture the egg, but her hands were clumsy, and she struggled to get it into the spoon. "I apologize," Clarissa said after a moment. "Am I blocking you from reaching the soup?"

His voice was put-upon. "Not the soup, but the rolls." She stepped to the side, and he took two rolls. "I believe it is crawfish soup. As I mentioned the other day, I cannot eat shellfish of any kind."

"Of course. I did not realize it was crawfish… crawfish soup."

Mr. Baxter had already moved away, leaving her talking to herself. But Clarissa's thoughts were flying. The soup that had been poisoned… that had been crawfish soup, too. She was almost certain of it.

The poison had been put in a dish Mr. Baxter never ate. Of course, if the would-be assassin was a passing acquaintance, they might have been unaware.

But now that she thought on it, the bullet had been fired into the morning room, which seemed like a more likely haunt for Mrs. Baxter than her husband.

And the wheel of the curricle had been sabotaged. For most couples, one might reasonably assume that the intended victim was the husband.

But Mr. Baxter was a terrible driver. Surely, he did not take the curricle out on a regular basis.

It was his *wife* who was the great whip.

What if… what if they had been wrong all along? What if Oliver Baxter wasn't the killer's target?

What if it was his wife, Rosalind?

Clarissa pretended to be absorbed in the paper while she picked at her breakfast. Her thoughts were so scattered that she could not possibly have kept up the thread of a conversation.

Now that she thought on it, even the attempts on Mr. Baxter's life at the house party seemed suspect. It was Rosalind Baxter who had been pacing in the garden before the stone was pushed from the battlements above. Her husband had only joined her seconds before the stone fell.

No attempts had been made on Mr. Baxter's life while his wife remained sequestered in their rooms. Then, as soon as she emerged, the shot had been fired in the woods. Clarissa had assumed that Mr. Baxter was the target, but Rosalind had been standing next to her husband...

Clarissa somehow made it through breakfast in her distracted state without spilling tea down the front of her dress. She consulted the clock on the mantelpiece. She didn't need to meet Rupert for another fifteen minutes, but she decided to head over to the orangery to gather her thoughts.

As she was exiting the breakfast room, she spied Rosalind Baxter coming down the corridor.

Deciding she had enough evidence that a warning was needed, Clarissa hurried up to her. She dropped her voice low. "Mrs. Baxter, might I have a word with you? There has been a material development in the case. One that concerns you."

Her eyes went wide. "Of course. What have you—"

"Anything that concerns my wife concerns me," a man's voice said firmly from over Clarissa's shoulder.

She turned and saw Oliver Baxter, his forehead creased into a frown.

Clarissa gestured with an open palm. "Of course, Mr. Baxter. Let us find a place where the three of us can talk."

She checked a handful of rooms, but they were all occupied. Sensing the annoyance radiating from Mr. Baxter, Clarissa gestured to the back doors. "It's cold out, but this won't take long. Let's speak in the gardens."

At least the gardens were deserted. Clarissa led them

toward the entrance to the hedge maze. She turned to Rosalind. "Something occurred to me this morning. A piece, falling into place. You, Mrs. Baxter, are in grave danger."

Rosalind gasped, but Mr. Baxter scowled. "What is this nonsense?"

Clarissa ignored him. "I fear we have been wrong. We have been wrong from the very beginning, and the killer's true target is—"

"Cease this nonsense!" Oliver Baxter shouted.

"It isn't nonsense," Clarissa insisted, keeping her eyes fixed on Rosalind. "Consider the first attempt. The poison was put in the crawfish soup. But your husband cannot eat crawfish soup. He—"

"That is hardly common knowledge," Mr. Baxter snapped. "They probably slipped the poison in whatever dish they could lay hands on."

Clarissa ignored him. "And then the shot through the window. Which one of you spends the most time in the morning room?"

"I do," Mrs. Baxter said. "I was at my writing desk, as I often am at that hour. Oliver happened to have come in to ask me a question, and—"

"You're being delusional," Oliver barked. "The idea is absurd on its face. Why would anyone want to kill you? You're not important enough to justify the effort."

Rosalind flinched, looking wounded. Clarissa glared daggers at Oliver Baxter. "That is your opinion, sir," she said in a voice as frosty as the snow-encrusted gardens. "One that does you no credit, might I add. But I intend to follow the evidence." She turned to Rosalind. "The curricle—which of you drives it more frequently?"

"I do." Rosalind gasped. "In fact, on the day of the accident, I was the one who asked for the horses to be harnessed. I was going to take a turn about the park, but

Oliver received an urgent summons from Lord Liverpool, so he wound up commandeering it!"

Clarissa seized her hand. "Surely you see the reason for my concern. That the soup was poisoned could have been an accident perpetrated by an ignorant assassin. But when you look at the three attempts altogether—"

Oliver Baxter stepped forward, snatching Rosalind's hand away from Clarissa. "I will not have you filling my wife's head with this nonsense!" he roared. "She is frightened enough as it is. It is cruel of you to prey upon the fears of a hysterical woman."

"She has never struck me as hysterical," Clarissa countered. "And I say this not to frighten her, but so that, armed with knowledge, she can take necessary precautions."

"*I* will decide what is necessary for my wife! You are not to speak to her again, Miss Weatherby. And you should know that I intend to ask Lord and Lady Helmsley to remove you from this house party." He huffed. "As soon as I return to London, I intend to speak with the Home Secretary. I am appalled that the Home Office employs such incompetent agents!"

Clarissa ignored him, locking her eyes on Rosalind's. "Go up to your room. Go up to your room and lock the door. Admit no one but myself or Lord and Lady Helmsley."

Rosalind nodded and started back toward the castle.

Oliver cast a poisonous glare at Clarissa, then turned and stalked after his wife. "Rosalind! Come back here this instant!"

Swallowing, Clarissa hurried toward the orangery. For the life of her, she could not understand Oliver Baxter's callous disregard for his wife's safety. She knew many men paid little heed to their wives' thoughts and feelings, but Mr. Baxter seemed strangely determined to override Rosalind at every turn. What did it hurt him if she wanted to stay in their room?

She opened the door to the orangery. A quick search revealed that Rupert was not yet there—which was unsurprising, as she was ten minutes early.

Peering out through one of the tall glass windows lining the front wall, she saw that Rosalind had not, in fact, retreated to her room. She and her husband were still standing in front of the hedge maze, arguing animatedly. He was standing between her and the back door to the castle, and Clarissa watched in shock as he blocked her from going back inside once... twice... three times. Finally, Rosalind threw her hands up in frustration, then spun on her heel, disappearing into the hedge maze. Oliver watched for a moment, then hurried inside the castle himself, the great hypocrite.

Trying to tamp down the dread pooling in her stomach, Clarissa hugged herself, waiting for Rupert to arrive.

CHAPTER 27

Rupert was running late for his meeting with Claire.

It was on account of Lady Helmsley, who had cornered him outside the breakfast room, requesting a word. In her personal sitting room, she fixed him with the sort of disappointed look you might give a spaniel puppy who's piddled on the floor. "If you have been telling yourself that Miss Weatherby's and your disappearance last night went unremarked upon, allow me to disabuse you of that notion."

Rupert didn't have it in him to lie to Lady H, but he attempted to prevaricate a bit. "Oh? Did Miss Weatherby leave the ball around the same time I did?"

Judging by the look Lady Helmsley gave him, she wasn't buying it. At all. "Don't play coy with me, Rupert. I am expecting an announcement. And I would prefer you make it today."

An announcement, as in, a betrothal announcement. Rupert's body sagged. There was the rub, all right. He would like nothing better than to announce that Claire was going to be his bride.

There was just the pesky detail that she would never agree to such a thing. She'd just been looking for a bit of a dalliance last night. She'd mentioned his reputation for making things good for the lady. But she'd given him no indication that she was after anything permanent.

Still, he had already resolved that he would put the question to her that morning. It was the only decent thing to do, considering he'd taken her maidenhead, not that proposing was any great chore. To be married to Claire was everything he'd ever wanted.

He knew full well she was going to say no. Hearing her say the words and seeing the pity in her eyes as she turned him down were going to rip a hole in his heart the approximate size of Siberia.

But he was determined to ask her, all the same.

Lady Helmsley was awaiting his answer. He selected a version of the truth. "If there isn't an announcement made today, it won't be on my account."

She clasped her hands. "Excellent! Now, go and find Miss Weatherby and work out the final particulars. Go on, now. Go. Go!"

Rupert allowed her to shoo him out of the room. He hurried toward the back door, his pocket watch revealing that he was five minutes late.

As he passed the hedge maze, he saw that the Baxters were having a row, but what else was new? He pretended not to notice as Rosalind gave a cry of frustration and stalked off into the hedge maze, doubtlessly as sick of her husband's company as Rupert was.

In the orangery, he found Claire in something of an anxious state. Rupert wasn't doing much better, truth be told, between the fact that he was about to make the woman he was head over heels for an offer of marriage and the fact that he was all but certain she was going to say no, but it had to be done, now didn't it?

He wiped his sweaty palms on his trousers, then took her hand. "Claire, there's been something I've been meaning to ask you." He started to lower himself down onto one knee. "Would you—"

Claire seized his hand in a surprisingly strong grip and hauled him back to his feet. "We haven't got time for that! I figured something out this morning."

Rupert was trying to deduce if this was Claire's way of stopping him from issuing a proposal she had no wish to hear. It seemed sadly likely. But what if he was wrong about that? He wanted to make sure she understood that she had options, but he didn't want to go making a bother of himself, and now he didn't know *what* to do, and—

She tapped the back of his hand. "Rupert, are you paying attention? Oliver Baxter is not the one the assassin is after. It's his wife, Rosalind!"

"*What?*" That certainly snapped him out of his muddled haze.

She proceeded to explain about the crawfish soup and the fact that the shot had been made toward Rosalind's writing desk and how the whole business with the curricle didn't make any sense on account of what a shit driver he was.

"You're right." Rupert shook his head. "Of course, you're right."

"And that means we've been asking the wrong question," Claire said, eyes wild. "We've been asking who wants to kill Oliver Baxter. But what we really need to find out is who wants to kill *Rosalind*."

For once in his life, Rupert had the answer in an instant. "That would move Phyllis Cuthbert to the top of the suspect list." Claire gave him a blank look, so he continued, "Remember? I told you in the library—*Phyllis* was the one everyone thought Oliver was going to marry. But then, her brother lost her dowry at the gaming tables, so he married Rosalind instead." Something else occurred to Rupert. "And the footprints! The ones up on the roof, after the stone was pushed. They were small. Almost certainly made by a woman or a boy."

"I agree, it's very suspicious," Claire agreed. "We should definitely keep an eye on her. Can you think of anyone else who might…"

She trailed off, striding toward one of the tall glass windows that overlooked the gardens.

"Claire?" Rupert asked, trailing after her. "What's—"

She seized his hand in another of those vice-like grips you wouldn't think she would have, on account of her being such a lissome young thing. "*Look!*"

Striding purposefully across the snow-covered grass was none other than their new primary suspect, Phyllis Cuthbert.

At the entrance to the hedge maze, she paused and looked around, as if checking to see if anyone was watching.

Beside him, Claire gasped, and Rupert's heart sank into his boots.

"I think Phyllis just made a dizzying ascent up the list of suspects," Claire whispered.

Rupert wasn't about to disagree. Because clutched in Phyllis's hand was a pistol, glinting in the crisp December sunlight.

CHAPTER 28

They ran hell-for-leather across the gardens to the entrance of the maze.

Rupert was struggling to formulate a plan—a tricky proposition for him during the best of times, and this was decidedly not the best of times, when the woman he loved was about to run headlong into a hedge maze so she could confront a crazed spinster with a gun.

At the entrance to the maze, he grabbed Claire's arm. "Did you bring your pistol?"

Her face paled. "I forgot it. I was so flustered this morning, and—"

He withdrew his own gun from the waistband of his trousers. "Take mine," he said, pressing it into her hands.

She pulled her hands back. "I couldn't possibly—"

"I insist," Rupert said, and something about his expression must've given her to know that he wouldn't be gainsaid in this, because for once in her life, Clarissa Weatherby didn't argue.

"All right," she said, her voice clipped with nerves. "Thank you."

He studied her. Her eyes had a flighty quality about them. He knew she was as scared as he was. "Are you sure you want to do this, Claire?" he asked softly.

She nodded jerkily. "I do. It's my job, and I won't have anyone saying I quit as soon as the going got tough."

Rupert sighed. "I was afraid you would say that." He cleared his throat. "Well, then. You go right, I go left?"

She nodded again. He was just about to head in when she added, "And Rupert?"

He turned, and she grabbed him by the cravat with her free hand, hauling him in. She kissed him the way Andromache must've kissed Hector before he headed off to face Achilles in single combat, the way Juliet kissed Romeo before she plunged that dagger into her heart. She kissed him like it was the most important thing she would ever do. It was a kiss that made him feel precious, made him feel like he was good enough, made him feel like maybe, just maybe, she cared about him, too.

They were both breathing hard by the time they broke apart. "Be careful!" Clarissa said fiercely.

Rupert touched her cheek, hoping his eyes would tell her everything he had in his heart. "You too, Claire."

Then they turned and ran in opposite directions into the maze.

Rupert had been inside the hedge maze at Castle Helmsley before, but not so often that he knew where he was going. He immediately got turned around and hopelessly discombobulated, but he figured that was to be expected, and the thing was to keep going.

He tried to creep silently along and not give away his approach. But time was of the essence, so he was attempting to do this at a run, and he knew he had to look a right idiot doing a ridiculous sprinting tiptoe with his arms flapping around for balance.

An opening appeared in the wall of hedges to his left, leading him deeper into the maze. He paused to peer around the corner. He didn't see anyone and couldn't hear anything but the hiss of the wind.

He guessed left but quickly ran into a solid wall of greenery. Turning around, he started back the way he'd come, and that was when he heard Rosalind's voice from a few rows over.

"Oh, my—Phyllis!" Nervous laughter floated over the top of the hedge. "You startled me."

"On edge, cousin?" Phyllis's voice held a note of poison.

There was a pregnant pause before Rosalind said, "You know I've been anxious ever since these attempts on Oliver's life began." Rupert could hear the hesitation in her voice, could sense her wondering if she could trust her own cousin.

Phyllis laughed, a bitter, ugly sound. "You expect me to believe that you care what happens to Oliver?"

"Of course I do. He is my husband, and—" Rosalind suddenly shrieked. "Phyllis! Is that a *gun*?"

Shit shit shit. Rupert started moving his feet again, because a great lot of good he was doing standing here listening to Rosalind get shot.

The two women were worked up sufficiently that Rupert could still hear them even when he wasn't standing still, straining his ears.

"You stole him!" Phyllis shouted. "Oliver and I had an understanding. He was supposed to marry *me*!"

"You know I didn't want to marry him!" Rosalind cried. "You know my father forced me to agree to the match!"

"You should have refused," Phyllis spat.

Rupert came to an opening in the hedge that took him toward the voices. He ran through, but it led nowhere, so he went right back out again.

Rosalind's voice was tremulous with feeling. "As far as I am concerned, you may have him. He can sue me for divorce. I won't contest it. Then we can see how well you like being married to a man who belittles you at every turn!"

"How dare you speak of him that way! You've never been worthy of him, never had a thought for his well-being. If you did, you wouldn't dare suggest something as ridiculous as *divorce*. The scandal would be the ruination of his political career!"

Rosalind laughed, disbelieving. "You think there won't be a scandal if his wife is found dead in a hedge maze with a bullet through her heart?"

Rupert came to a dead end and turned. The only place to go was an opening that would push him out even farther from the center of the maze. It didn't seem that he had any choice, though, so he took it, running as hard as he could.

"He will be seen as a tragic figure," Phyllis said with absolute confidence. "Freed at last from the shackles of the mad wife who took her own life."

Now Rosalind sounded angry. "What nonsense! I won't do any such thing."

Phyllis laughed. "Oh, but everyone will think you did. I'll make sure of it!"

"I offered you a place in my home after your brother was forced to sell your house!" Rosalind snapped. "And this is the thanks you show me? You will burn in hell for this!"

Phyllis's voice contained nothing but indifference. "I am merely correcting a wrong, undoing an unholy union that never should have happened. Besides, the greater sin would be to let Oliver's child be born a bastard."

"You… you…" Rosalind sputtered as Rupert sprinted around the back side of the maze. "You've been carrying on with *my* husband? Under my own roof?"

"He never wanted you," Phyllis said, voice shaking. "He always wanted me, and that never changed!"

It sounded like Rosalind was crying. "I know Oliver doesn't love me. That he never has. But he wouldn't want me to *die!*"

Phyllis's voice was full of satisfaction. "Who do you think told me you were here in the maze? Who do you think sent me out to finish the deed? You've been in our way for far too long. But that ends today!"

Rupert heard the metallic click of a firearm being cocked. Rosalind gave a piteous cry.

But then, there was another voice.

"Don't even think about it, Phyllis!" It was Claire's voice, of course. She sounded confident. Fierce.

Unlike Rupert, who felt sick with terror.

"Pull that trigger," Claire continued, "and you will be the next to die."

Rupert came to a gap in the hedge. It led to a dead end, but when he turned the other way, he found another opening that led deeper into the maze. The voices were just a row or two over. He was getting close. He knew he was.

"How *dare* you!" Phyllis shrieked. "You, the most scorned woman in all of England. You were supposed to be on my side. *You were supposed to understand!*"

Another gap opened just ahead. As he sprinted through it, Phyllis came into view. He could see the deranged anger on her face as she looked over her shoulder at someone behind her. The gun was pointed the opposite direction, at someone deeper in the maze.

But not for long. Rupert watched in horror as Phyllis wheeled around, turning the gun on Claire.

He saw the terror in Claire's eyes, watched as she fumbled to cock her own weapon.

Phyllis narrowed her eyes and pulled the trigger.

Screaming her name, Rupert leaped. Hurling his body in front of Claire, he felt the air go out of him as the bullet slammed into his chest.

<h1 style="text-align:center">CHAPTER 29</h1>

"*R*upert!" Clarissa screamed. "*Noooooooo!*"

He collapsed in the snow and lay unmoving.

Clarissa hurried to his side… which was stupid, she knew. Phyllis Cuthbert was still there, bent on murder.

But Rosalind Baxter suddenly seemed to recall that *she* was the great sportswoman in the family.

And Phyllis no longer had the advantage of a loaded gun.

Rosalind let out a bellow of rage. She came charging through the maze and tackled her cousin, and the two of them landed with a hard thump in the snow.

Rupert lay crumpled, face-down. Clarissa turned him over and pulled him into her lap. She caressed his beautiful face, which was almost as colorless as the snow beneath him.

"Rupert," she begged. "Talk to me! *Please*, tell me you're all right." His eyes refused to open. She shook him, needing him to wake up. "You can't be dead, Rupert. You just can't. I—I can't do without you!"

His head listed to the side. She pulled it up gently, stroking his brow.

A tear coursed down her cheek. This couldn't be

236

happening. They had only just found each other! This was supposed to be the start of their life together. Suddenly, a life without this wonderful man beside her loomed before her, colorless and devoid of joy. Because that was what Rupert was—joy in its purest, most unadulterated form.

"Please, Rupert," she begged, her voice breaking. "I love you."

Her eyes were blurred with tears. She, therefore, felt rather than saw him stir.

"Rupert?" she asked, framing his face.

His only answer was a groan.

"Rupert!" she cried, shaking him. "Rupert, are you alive? Please tell me you're alive!"

"I'm not," he said in a groggy voice.

She chanced a glance down at his torso, fearing the worst. His cravat had been blasted to bits, and there was a hole in his shirt just over his heart.

But there wasn't a speck of blood anywhere. *How was that possible?*

Hope flared in her heart. "Rupert, wake up! You're not allowed to die. I need you."

He tossed his head but didn't open his eyes. "I'm definitely dead."

She stroked his brow. "Does it hurt terribly, my love?"

He drew in a shuddering breath. "It doesn't hurt at all. Claire said she loves me!" He shook his head, burying his face in her lap and wrapping his arms around her waist. "I've obviously died and gone to heaven."

She let out a little sob, but she was smiling. "Ru-pert," she said, gently turning him so he was facing up again. "Open your eyes."

Frowning, he opened them just a slit as if terrified of what he would see. His face went slack when he spotted her smiling down at him. "Claire!" he cried, reaching up to cup her cheek. He glanced around, confused. "I—I'm not dead?"

She smiled through her tears. "I don't believe so, no."

"And you… you love me!"

"*So much.*" She cradled him against her. "I didn't realize it would come as such a surprise. I told you last night."

An adorable look of befuddlement stole across his face. "You did?" He ducked his chin sheepishly. "I think I might have fallen asleep."

She laughed, wiping her face with the back of her hand. "Well, that's my fault for asking you to marry me when you were falling down from exhaustion."

His eyes went wide. "Asking me to—" His voice suddenly sounded gruff. "Do you mean it? You really want to marry me?"

She pressed a kiss against his forehead. "Of course I do. I love you. I want to spend the rest of my life with you."

"Oh, Claire!" Suddenly, he was kissing her all over her face. "I love you so much. I can't believe it. I never thought that *you* would want a great dunce like *me*."

She squeezed his hands. "We'll have no more of that talk. You're the most wonderful man I've ever met, and I won't hear a word against you." She pressed her forehead against his. "Even from you."

He kissed her then, and in spite of the fact that her knees were going numb with cold and her groom-to-be was wearing half a shirt and smelled of gunpowder, it was, without question, the most perfect moment of Clarissa's life.

When he lifted his head, they were both smiling. "But how did you survive, Rupert?" she asked. "That bullet tore your cravat to shreds."

"I suppose it must've been a miracle." He started feeling around his chest. "Oh—here's the bullet, I think."

He pulled something out of the hole in his shirt.

It was his locket, the one his aunt had given him all those years ago. It was mangled beyond recognition, with a bullet embedded in the silver-colored metal.

Suddenly, Clarissa wasn't the only one crying. Rupert was blinking rapidly, and he scrubbed at his eyes with the side of his hand. "Auntie Imogen," he whispered.

Clarissa squeezed his hand. "She really is watching over you!"

He nodded, incapable of speech.

That was when the strangest thing of all occurred.

Rupert was holding up the locket, Clarissa's hand wrapped around his.

Suddenly, a delicate yellow butterfly fluttered down into the hedge maze. It circled them once, then landed on the locket.

Clarissa gave a startled laugh. "A butterfly? In December?" She smiled as the butterfly crawled down the locket and perched on her finger. "Where on earth did you come from?"

The butterfly didn't answer, of course. It flapped its wings three times, then wafted into the air. It flew around them once more, landing for a split-second on Clarissa's nose, then flitted off toward the pale blue December sky.

Rupert laughed. "Would you look at that? It almost seems like a—"

He didn't get to finish that thought, on account of Rosalind giving a high-pitched shriek.

Clarissa and Rupert swung their heads around, suddenly recalling that they had an audience.

"I'm sorry," Rosalind grunted, struggling to subdue her cousin, whom she was holding face-down in the snow. "I was…*ugh*… trying not to spoil the moment. But she *bit* me!"

Rupert was already on his feet, pulling Clarissa up behind him. "Sorry, Mrs. Baxter."

"Please," she said through gritted teeth, "call me Rosalind. If I never hear the name *Baxter* again, it will be too soon."

Clarissa hastily brushed the snow off her knees and hurried over. "More than understandable. Please, call me Clarissa."

"And you must call me Rupert." He started to grab Phyllis's arm but then paused. "Sorry, it's just... never thought I'd find myself laying hands on a woman. I know we've got to turn her in to the authorities and whatnot. But it's deuced awkward, is what it is."

"Don't fret, my love," Clarissa said, grabbing Phyllis's arm and yanking her none-too-gently to her feet. "Rosalind and I are more than capable of handling it."

Clarissa fancied that she would never forget the way Rupert smiled at her. "I know that. Without a single doubt." He bent over, scooping up Phyllis's spent firearm. "Now, who remembers the way out of this maze?"

CHAPTER 30

*R*upert wasn't the least bit surprised that the arrests of Phyllis Cuthbert and Oliver Baxter caused no small amount of gossip amongst the house party guests. There was no hiding the fact that Rupert and Claire had witnessed Phyllis's confrontation with Rosalind in the maze, but everyone assumed the newly betrothed pair had been trying to sneak a romantic moment and stumbled upon the ugly scene by accident. They chose not to disabuse their fellow guests of this notion, and thus did their status as agents for the Home Office remain a secret.

Rosalind decided to sue Oliver Baxter for divorce. It was nigh impossible for a woman to obtain a divorce, even when her husband had committed infidelity. But considering Oliver had impregnated her own cousin and encouraged that cousin to commit murder to clear the way for the two of them to wed, it seemed that this case might be the exception that proved the rule.

The snow finally cleared sufficiently that Rupert was able to jaunt down to York to secure a common license. While he was there, he posted a letter Clarissa had written to her sisters, begging them to come to Helmsley Castle for a special surprise.

One week later, on the morning of Christmas Eve, Rupert found himself happily ensconced in the blue parlor with Claire, listening to her read him selections from a letter she'd received from her former partner, Lady Winnifred FitzSimon:

As vexed as I am to be losing the most promising partner I've had in more than a decade, I cannot find it in me to hold a grudge. I had the pleasure of meeting your Mr. Dupree years ago, and he formed the most favorable impression. He struck me as an extremely nice young man and a very fine agent, and I cannot blame you for wishing to ally yourself with such an outstanding gentleman.

As to your concern that you have gained a reputation for being something of a beauty and cannot go back to skulking amongst the woodwork in your brown gowns, allow me to reassure you that there is no more effective way for a woman to conceal her intelligence than by being young and pretty. That you have a thought in your head beyond ribbons and reticules will occur to absolutely no one of the male persuasion. I fear it will be terribly dull for you, smiling vacuously while men explain things you already know using the simplest terms. But I have absolute confidence that you will adapt and be every bit as effective as you ever were in your dirt-colored dresses.

Rupert was chuckling when a footman appeared in the doorway. "Miss Weatherby," he announced, snapping to attention, "Toddington asked me to inform you that a carriage bearing the Duke of Norwood's crest is pulling up the drive."

Naturally, Claire squealed and scurried down the stairs, with Rupert following close on her heels.

They stepped outside the castle just as the carriage drew to a halt. The carriage door burst open before a footman had a chance to approach, and two babbling young ladies came scrambling out.

"Clarissa!" the blonde girl Rupert assumed to be Pippa cried.

"We missed you," the brunette, who had to be Kate, murmured, pulling her in for a hug.

They were quickly joined by a third woman, a bit older than her sisters and of decidedly regal bearing. That would be Eleanor, per Claire's description. She strode over and wrapped her arms around all three of her sisters.

The Duke of Norwood unfolded his long frame from the carriage and strolled toward the castle. "Dupree," he said easily, offering his hand, "it's nice to see you again."

"Likewise, Norwood," Rupert returned, clasping his hand. "Merry Christmas."

"Merry Christmas to you, too."

A few feet away, Pippa laughed. "I say, Clarissa—what on earth are you wearing?"

Claire had on a snow-white gown, topped with a cerulean-blue spencer trimmed in white fur. "I was separated from my trunk on the journey here. Lady Emily de Roos was kind enough to share her wardrobe with me."

Kate grinned. "I daresay you'll be relieved when you're reunited with your dirt-colored dresses."

"Actually, I've found that I quite enjoy wearing bright colors." Clarissa gave a rueful smile. "I think I wore brown gowns for so long not because I truly liked them, but because I wanted to hide myself from the world. Now that I'm no longer the biggest laughingstock in the British Isles, I don't feel the need to hide anymore."

All three sisters were gaping at her in shock, but they recovered quickly. "That's wonderful, dear," Eleanor said.

"You look beautiful in blue," Kate added.

Pippa sounded as if she might burst into tears. "Oh, Claire —I'm so happy for you!"

Another round of hugging ensued. When the sisters broke apart, they were all smiling.

"Well," Eleanor said crisply, "that was a shock. But a happy one!"

"And that's not the only surprise I have for you today," Claire hastened to say. "You're probably curious why I summoned you here so urgently."

Pippa laughed. "Do tell us. Although I doubt anything could be half as shocking as learning that you've abandoned your dirt-colored dresses!"

Claire caught Rupert's eye, her grin turning wicked. "The surprise I have in store for you is a wedding. *My* wedding. Allow me to introduce you to my future husband"—she strolled over and looped her arm through his—"Mr. Rupert Dupree."

Kate and Pippa's gasps were drowned out by Eleanor's cry of alarm. The eldest Weatherby sister surged forward, pressing the back of her wrist against Claire's forehead.

She rounded on Rupert, her eyes earnest. "When did she hit her head?"

Naturally, this made Rupert and Claire burst out laughing. Once Rupert managed to recover himself, he reassured Eleanor, "She hasn't hit her head. Believe me, I'd be fussing over her like a mother hen if she had. I'm absolutely chuffed to meet you and so pleased that you made it in time for the wedding! Claire's told me so much about you three that I feel like I know you already."

Claire's sisters were peering at him disbelievingly as if he were a monkey at the Tower menagerie who had suddenly started to speak.

"Jasper!" Eleanor hissed, waving her husband over.

The Duke of Norwood hastened to his wife's side. "Yes, my dove?"

"Is that man really Rupert Dupree?" the duchess stage-whispered.

"He is," Norwood said solemnly.

Eleanor looked Rupert up and down, skepticism bald on her face. "*That* is Rotten Rupert? The most wretched villain in all of England?"

Norwood patted his wife's hand. "He is quite possibly the least-rotten, least-villainous man I have ever met."

Rupert decided to jump in. "I know it's difficult to believe, after that whole mess in the papers. But I swear, I didn't write any of those despicable things. I didn't even know a letter had been printed in my name, on account of me spending a few years traveling around the Continent." He shook his head. "I can't tell you how awful I felt once I learned what had happened. I think I know who's responsible, though, and I'm determined to set things right. My good friend, Lawrence de Roos, is helping me. He's a solicitor and a dashed good one, too. Capital fellow. Absolutely capital. If anyone can fix this mess, it's him. I'll tell you what we've got planned, but why don't we step inside first? I'm sure you'd like a seat by the fire and a hot drink after your journey."

Pippa nudged Kate in the ribs. Her face was creased with confusion. "He isn't what I was expecting," she whispered.

"Nor I," Kate murmured.

Clarissa gave him a friendly push forward, so Rupert offered one arm to Pippa and the other to Kate. "So, Miss Philippa. Claire has told me about your new kittens. How are they settling in at Askwith Hall?"

It took him all of three minutes to win Pippa over. Eleanor and Kate were more cautious, even after Lady Helmsley, who came bustling in to greet her new guests, assured them that "Our Rupert would *never* have written such a letter!"

But after Claire told the story of what had happened in the hedge maze, including the part where he had thrown himself in front of a bullet for her—which was pretty good as far as grand gestures went, now that he thought about it—they decided he must be all right. Next thing you knew, Norwood was pressing his handkerchief into his sniffling wife's hands, and Kate was offering to paint a new eye miniature of Auntie Imogen, assuring him that she could create one based on a portrait of her that hung in the sitting room at Drayford House.

Claire snagged Lady Helmsley before she could slip from the room. "It's probably too much trouble, but as my sisters are all here, is there any chance we could have the wedding today?"

Lady H. clapped her hands. "A Christmas Eve wedding!" A faraway look came over her face. She nodded, resolute. "We simply *must* have it today. I'll send a footman to fetch the vicar at once."

The vicar was happy to oblige. And so it was that two hours later, Rupert, Claire, the Weatherby sisters, and the entire house party trooped over to the little chapel on the castle grounds. Laurence de Roos and the Duke of Norwood stood up with Rupert. In addition to her sisters, Claire had Lady Emily serve as a bridesmaid, which pleased Lady Emily to no end.

Not that Rupert could see anyone but Claire, pledging to be his for all eternity.

Clarissa Dupree. Sometimes, dreams really do come true.

After the ceremony, the wedding party hung back so Kate

could make a quick sketch of Claire and Rupert at the altar, as they'd looked when they were saying their vows. She said she would add some watercolors to it later. It was such a thoughtful wedding present, and Rupert thanked her very sincerely.

Afterward, they strolled back to the castle. Rupert was eagerly anticipating the wedding night, in which he would get to share a bed with Claire—and by a bed, he meant an actual bed, as opposed to a sofa—when a black lacquered carriage drew to a halt in front of the castle and out climbed his brother, Francis.

Honestly, Rupert wasn't particularly pleased to see his brother, as Francis had always made his disdain as clear as cut crystal. But it had been a few years. Maybe old Francis had turned over a new leaf. And besides, it was Christmas!

So, he smiled as best he could and said, "Francis! What a surprise. This is my brother, Francis, everyone. Or Viscount Riddington, as he's properly called."

On his arm, Claire had gone all stiff, and she was giving him a flared nostrils sort of look as he'd told her enough stories about Francis that she wasn't precisely excited to make his acquaintance.

But Pippa had no idea that their relationship was somewhat less than fraternal. "Oh, dear," she cried, "I'm so sorry you missed the wedding! We would have waited for you if we'd had any idea you were coming."

Francis scowled as he flicked a speck of lint off his sleeve. "Wedding? Do you mean to tell me my idiot brother has actually tricked some woman into marrying him?"

Pippa gasped and clutched her heart as if unable to believe anyone could be so horrible.

Alas, Rupert was used to it. "Merry Christmas to you, too, brother," he said dryly. "Since it seems you didn't come all this way to congratulate me on my nuptials, why don't you go ahead and tell me what you're doing here?"

Francis strode up to Rupert and dropped his voice low. "You've caused a lot of trouble for William Ellison with this nonsense about suing for defamation."

Claire's eyes were shooting sparks. "Maybe he caused himself trouble by writing down a bunch of lies!"

Francis looked her up and down. "I take it you are my brother's new bride. How he convinced the likes of *you* to marry him, I have no idea. But this doesn't concern you. It concerns Clarissa Weatherby and those wallflower sisters of hers."

Claire's eyes were shooting sparks. "I *am* Clarissa Weatherby!"

"Not anymore!" Rupert observed cheerfully.

She looked up at him, her expression abruptly turning fond, and squeezed his arm. "That's right. As of a half-hour ago, I am Clarissa Dupree."

Rupert felt a pleasurable hum go through his body to hear those words on her lips.

She rounded on Francis, poison flooding back into her eyes. "But the point is, it is very much my concern, as your friend William Ellison wrote those horrible things about *me!*"

Francis's lips were pinched. "Look, Ellison didn't mean anything by that letter. He was just having a bit of a joke."

A shadow fell over Francis's head. "So," Jasper St. James boomed from behind him, "you admit that William Ellison is the author of the letter slandering my wife."

Francis was so startled, he actually jumped. "Norwood!" he squeaked. "I didn't notice you there."

"Not sure how you managed to miss him," Rupert said, his gaze traveling the length of the duke's six-and-a-half-foot frame. "He's remarkably noticeable. And you also failed to mark my solicitor, standing just behind him. You getting all this, Laurie?"

"I most certainly am," Laurie replied.

"Look, Norwood," Francis began, a drop of perspiration beading on his temple in spite of their snowy surroundings. "I'm sure you don't want any trouble."

The duke stalked around, so he was facing Francis. "Indeed, no. My wife and my sisters-by-marriage did not want any trouble. And yet trouble came and found them." He leaned in, his voice growing menacing. "Nor did your brother deserve to have his reputation sullied, to have dishonorable words he never wrote attributed to him."

Francis made a mocking sound. "I will own that it is unfortunate that one of the women caught in the crossfire turned out to be your duchess. Wretched luck, that, although no one could have foreseen that she would have such a precipitous rise. But Rupert?" Francis snorted. "Nobody cares about *Rupert*."

The duke loomed over Francis. His voice was downright dangerous as he said, "*I* care about Rupert. Rupert is my brother now."

Francis gulped, his face taking on a green hue that would've looked nice next to the festive garlands bedecking the castle's halls. Not that he was going to be invited inside, if the way Laurie and Lady Emily were glaring at him was anything to go by.

But Rupert's heart was feeling warm and toasty, in spite of the fact that he was standing outside in the snow. *Rupert is my brother now!* He hadn't thought of anything beyond having Claire as his wife. But he'd also managed to obtain a new brother, the right kind this time, the kind who punched bullies in the face for you, instead of the kind who punched *you* in the face for absolutely no reason at all. As well as three sisters who could not be more delightful.

Ever since Auntie Imogen died, Rupert hadn't felt like he had any family left. His father and brother thought he was an embarrassment and preferred to pretend he didn't exist.

But, by marrying Claire, he had managed to get himself a family ready-made, and quite a splendid one at that! Up until that very second, he hadn't realized how much that would mean to him.

Francis seemed to have realized that his efforts to cozy up to the duke would not be successful. "Fine," he sneered, his nose in the air. "We'll see how well you enjoy being Rupert's brother." He spun on his heel, his efforts to look haughty suffering when he slipped on the snowy ground. But he managed to stay on his feet as he swept back into his carriage with an air of wounded dignity.

As they watched the horses start forward, Norwood clapped Rupert on the shoulder. "I believe I will enjoy it just fine." He inclined his head toward the castle. "Now, did Lady Helmsley not say something about a luncheon?"

They started toward the castle, but Claire held him back. "Are we really required to attend the luncheon?" she whispered. "I can think of one or two things I would *much* rather be doing."

Rupert hummed appreciatively. "I can think of several dozen things I'd rather be doing with you. But I wouldn't hurt Lady Helmsley's feelings for all the world. I know she went to a lot of trouble to put something nice together on short notice."

Claire sighed theatrically. "Very well. But let's plan on mysteriously disappearing as soon as the dessert course has been served."

Rupert smiled at his new bride. "I love the way your mind works."

She beamed up at him. "And I love everything about you."

Rupert found it difficult to formulate a reply. Those were words he'd never thought to hear.

But the one thing Rupert had learned over the years was that if you kept trying, every once in a great while, things broke in your favor.

He smiled as he entered the castle with his new partner, in every sense of the word.

Keep reading for a special preview of Book Three in The Weatherby Wallflowers quartet, *One Bed for the Bluestocking*!

Would you like to catch up with Clarissa and Rupert a few years into their marriage, to see how their happily-ever-after (and their spy work!) is going? I write a free bonus scene for each of my books, exclusively for my newsletter subscribers. If you choose to subscribe, you'll receive updates from me about twice a month with Regency fun, all my latest news, and the occasional video of me starting a fire whilst dabbling in historical cooking. You can sign up at https://courtneymccaskill.com/newsletter/

In the Revenge of the Wallflowers series, the wallflowers are getting the last laugh! Read a new story from some of your favorite authors every week from now until March 2025. You can browse the full collection here.

PREVIEW: ONE BED FOR THE BLUESTOCKING

It's the worst idea Kate Weatherby has ever had.

Back when Kate and her sisters were penniless and despised as the Weatherby Wallflowers, they made a pact to apply for whatever respectable positions they could find. Now, one of the employers who initially rejected Kate, an academic at the University of Edinburgh looking for a scientific illustrator, has written back, eager to hire her.

There's just one problem.

The holder of the position must be enrolled at the University, which does not admit women. Kate knows that donning breeches and trying to pass herself off as a young man is a terrible idea. But the sting of her father stealing credit for her illustrations has never faded. Yearning to see if she can succeed in the scientific world on her own merits, Kate accepts the position and heads north to Scotland.

One problem? Make that two.

It's hard enough passing herself off as "Kit Witherspoon." But the naturalist who hired Kate, Nathaniel Sterling, isn't the fusty old professor she imagined. Oh, no—Nathaniel is young, kind, brilliantly clever, and heart-stoppingly handsome in precisely the tweedy way Kate finds irresistible.

And, to make matters worse, an opportunity has just arisen— a trip to the Outer Hebrides, to document the flora and fauna particular to the islands. Nathaniel and Kate will be going alone.

And, academic budgets being what they are, they're expected to share a room.

One Bed for the Bluestocking will be available in 2025. Pre-order your copy today!

HISTORICAL NOTE

In writing Rupert, it was my intention to create a character who has what we would now call dyslexia. Dyslexia was first described by German physician Adolph Kussmaul in 1877, and the term took many more years to become widespread. With this story being set in 1823, it seemed likely that the majority of Rupert's peers would conclude that he simply wasn't very intelligent.

I described Rupert as having developed an amazing facility for aural memory in order to compensate for the fact that he reads slowly. This particular adaptation was inspired by David Boies, a highly successful attorney, who developed a similar ability. I encountered Mr. Boies' story in the book *David and Goliath* by Malcolm Gladwell.

I also want to say a quick word about Helmsley Castle. Residents of Yorkshire are doubtlessly protesting that Helmsley Castle does not look remotely the way I describe it in the book! My go-to technique for coming up with faux peerages for my characters is to browse an old book of maps. That is how I landed on the names Lord and Lady Helmsley. Only later, after deciding to give them a castle, did I discover that a real Helmsley Castle exists! I decided to stick with it and weave the history of the actual Helmsley Castle into that of my fake Helmsley Castle. I imagined that it remained in the hands of the de Roos family, who held it in the twelfth through fifteenth centuries, and that it underwent a significant reconstruction in the mid-eighteenth century. So please be advised that I have taken some significant liberties with the history of Helmsley Castle.

ACKNOWLEDGMENTS

I would be lost without my fabulous editor, Diana Bold, and my proofreaders Linda and Kesha. Many thanks to Dawn Brower and Amanda Mariel for kindly including me in the Revenge of the Wallflowers series. I am extremely grateful to the members of my ARC and Street Teams for all of your support and encouragement! Finally, all of my love goes to my wonderful family, especially V and J.

This book is dedicated to Diana Bold. You loved Rupert, so you can have him! I love having you as my editor. Thank you for everything!

ABOUT THE AUTHOR

After reading Black Beauty for the 1,497th time, Courtney McCaskill was inspired to write her own stories. Reviews of her early work were mixed, with her fourth grade teacher, Ms. Compton, saying, "Please stop writing all of your assignments from the point of view of a horse." But Courtney didn't give up, and today, her books have received prestigious awards including the Maggie and the HOLT Medallion.

She lives in Austin, Texas with the hero of her own story, who holds the distinction of being the world's most sarcastic pediatrician. Her son informs her that she gives THE BEST hugs, "because you're so squishy, Mommy." In 2022, Regency Fiction Writers honored her with its Lady of the Realm award in appreciation of her volunteer work, both on its Board of Directors and as the Coordinator of the Regency Academe. When she's not busy almost burning her house down while attempting to make a traditional Christmas pudding, she enjoys rock climbing, playing the piano, learning everything there is to know about Kodiak bears, and of course, curling up with a great book! Visit her online at www.courtneymccaskill.com .